I opened the screen door and pushed on the inside door to shout a hello. When the smell hit me, I froze. I knew instantly what it was. It was the smell of death.

I took a slow step inside, heart pounding from a sudden rush of adrenaline, breathing through my mouth to avoid smelling the stench. The house was quiet. The kitchen blinds were drawn, and my eyes slowly adjusted to the dimness. I didn't have to look far. A man's body was slumped over the kitchen table, and it had been there for a while. I snapped on the kitchen lights and looked at his face. The sightless eyes of Judge Stanley A. Wroblewski stared back at me.

A couple of big, black houseflies buzzed around his head, and a wave of nausea suddenly washed over me. The smell was getting to me. I pinched off my nose and took a few quick steps out to the back porch to gulp some fresh air. Smog never tasted so good.

★

A

Michael
W. Sherer

FOREVER
DEATH

WORLDWIDE®

TORONTO • NEW YORK • LONDON
AMSTERDAM • PARIS • SYDNEY • HAMBURG
STOCKHOLM • ATHENS • TOKYO • MILAN
MADRID • WARSAW • BUDAPEST • AUCKLAND

A FOREVER DEATH

A Worldwide Mystery/July 2003

First published by Five Star.

ISBN 0-373-26463-1

Printed in U.S.A.

A
FOREVER
DEATH

ONE

PUPPY DIDN'T REALLY CALL at the best of times, but his call didn't come at the most inopportune time, either.

A social gathering is a group of friends getting together after work for a couple of beers, or long-time acquaintances milling around the hors d'oeuvres table and the bar at Brandt's annual Christmas fete, or even four of us sitting around a bridge table on a weekday night munching cheese and crackers and trading news. But a social *affair* sparkles with diamonds and emeralds, glistens with Dior silks, smells of exotic perfumes, colognes, and previously uncirculated spicy rumors, tinkles with laughter and titters with chatter, shifts and swirls in eddies like the blue-gray smoke of fine cigars, slides over the palate with the double-edged bite of good cognac, leaving one just a bit breathless and giddy. It is an event to which a seemingly exclusive set of conspicuous consumers is invited—those with townhouses in Aspen and Acapulco and two or three Mercedes are the most likely candidates. But as the old saying goes, we all know how to live rich—it's simply that the rich have had more practice.

I'd been invited to this particular "affair" to provide local color, I'm sure. Some of that ilk recognized my name from my byline—Emerson W. Ward—on magazine articles, and even fewer said they'd actually read the one novel I'd published. Generally, when it's discovered that

I'm neither famous nor rich, it's assumed that either a horrible mistake has been made or that I must be "Myrna's new friend."

As it so happened, I *had* come with Myrna, but we were old friends, not new friends. Myrna Goodwin was a charming and vivacious sixty-something lady who wore the years even better than the collection of clingy designer gowns she owned for occasions such as this. With a couple of nips and tucks, a chemical peel, and a lot of hard work with a personal trainer in the privacy of her own weight room in her twenty-fourth-floor Lake Shore Drive co-op, she packed all that vibrant energy into a petite five-foot-two body that exuded the looks and sensuality of a woman twenty years younger.

She had gobs of money by virtue of the fact that she had outlived all three husbands, all of whom had been very wealthy men. She had made the mistake of latching onto the twenty-year-old son of her friend, the senator, one summer for a brief dalliance. The boy got greedy, or stupid, and stole a large portion of her jewel collection. Lord knows how he thought he was going to unload the stuff, but dear Myrna was caught between a rock and a hard place. Not wanting to call the police, she had asked Brandt Williams for advice, and he had recommended me. I had shaken the boy up some, scaring the wee out of him, and had returned the lady her jewels intact. We had since been good friends, although on occasion Myrna had hinted broadly at other favors I could do for her.

If I put my mind to it, I can play the game as well as anyone, but just then I was hard-pressed stifling yawns. The "my-fortune-is-bigger-than-your-fortune" competition was not holding my attention, and I could think of only three reasons why I was still where I was: out of deference to my host, who was a good friend; because the charity for which the affair was raising money was a good cause; and because a woman who looked like she didn't belong had attracted my attention.

I'd caught glimpses of her throughout the evening, and each time had felt a strange stirring inside more akin to curiosity than desire. She now stood on the other side of the room among a small group, nodding and smiling faintly at a little balding man who was talking oh-so-earnestly to the little knot of concerned citizens. But it seemed to me that the smile was merely polite and the nods automatic. I stood for a moment and watched, absorbed in a new game.

After a moment, she glanced around the room, and her eyes briefly met mine. They were the glass eyes of a rag-doll, reflecting emptiness, and I sensed a cold steel door behind those eyes that perfunctorily and emphatically shut out the world. The game took on a new dimension.

I drifted casually across the room, considering various opening gambits, not finding anything in my repertoire that might be suitable. With little effort, and no one taking notice, I silently became a part of her small group, using my gangly six-foot-four frame to cut her a step away from the group like a calf from the herd. She made room for me, and I discreetly divided my attention between her and the balding man. At this distance, I now judged her to be early to mid-thirties, even more attractive than I'd originally thought, and as cold as a February breeze off Lake Michigan. Three minutes of that chill was almost more than I could stand. When an opening came, I seized it almost vindictively.

"Are you always so wonderful?" I murmured, turning toward her so that we were slightly separated from the knot of rapt listeners. The things we do to relieve boredom.

"I'm sorry?" She turned to look at me, her eyes devoid of expression.

"If your friend wasn't so taken by your beauty," I said, nodding my head toward the bald man, "it would be patently obvious to him what a conceited, condescending bitch you are." My smile was disarming, and my voice was friendly, without animosity, but I was getting the expected reaction.

"Who *are* you?" Her eyes widened, but still gave nothing away.

"Nobody special."

"As if I couldn't guess."

"I'm sorry if I've insulted you. It was terribly ill-mannered of me, but I gave up making excuses for myself a long time ago. You know, standing next to you is like standing next to an air-conditioner." It was a mean game, and already I felt twinges of shame for having started it, but I'd already come this far.

There was the barest flicker of life in those amber eyes. "I don't know why I'm standing here expending energy in intensely disliking a total stranger."

"Then walk away."

She didn't move, indicating her own degree of boredom, her consent to play the game, or her determination to stand her own ground. The rest of the party vanished around us. It was just us, predator and prey, squared off. I looked her up and down, and there was a lot to look at. Even the modest and conservative dress couldn't hide the full breasts and generous swell of hips, nor could it hide the grace with which she carried all that perfection.

"Such a waste. Oh, not just the body—bodies are easy to come by, even ones as shapely as yours. It's just such a damn pitiful waste of a *person*. You never let go, do you?"

"What on earth would *you* know about it?"

"Maybe nothing." The eyes had more depth now, and suddenly I had a flash of what lay behind that steel door. I took a wild guess. "Daddy's little girl," I murmured softly, "all grown up in a body she can't even stand to look at."

She bit her lower lip, and now the eyes held fear. "You are positively nasty," she whispered in disbelief.

Before I could think of a reply, someone grabbed my arm just above the elbow.

"Here you are, you naughty man." Myrna to the rescue. "How on earth did you manage to escape my clutches?" She laughed. "I see you've met the lovely Ms. Meriwether."

"No, as a matter of fact I haven't," I said. "But I was just commenting to Ms. Meriwether that I have never seen a glacier more lovely than she."

"Oh, for God's sake, stop it!" Meriwether cried, causing a few heads to turn in our direction. For an instant, it looked as if she might burst into tears, but the amber eyes flashed with anger as she regained control and slammed the steel door shut. A quick look of disgust faded into the bland mask she'd worn before I'd traversed the room, and she spun away into the crowd.

"Come, Emerson," Myrna said, looking at me curiously. "I want you to meet some dear friends of mine."

"Yes, Myrna dear." I let her lead me away, and when we had gotten halfway across the room, she stopped me and turned to face me.

"What on earth was *that* all about?"

"I was bored."

"What did you say to the poor girl? Good lord, I thought only women were that vicious. I thank my lucky

stars I wasn't the object of your displeasure. I hope I don't
bore you. I don't bore you, do I, dear?''

"No, you don't bore me, Myrna.'' I smiled.

"Thank goodness for that.'' She sighed.

Myrna's dear friends, however, did bore me, and I soon
got fidgety again, so I excused myself to go order another
drink. I took my time getting back, surveying the crowd
on my way. There were probably well over sixty people
gathered in three rooms and the patio, all in formal evening attire, many of whom were recognizable from the
society pages and local television. Just then I did not feel
especially privileged to be part of that group. Aren't they
just folks like us?

I watched as a maid approached my friend Greg Edwards, our host, and asked him something. He looked up
and began searching the room until his gaze fell on me,
then he gestured at me and said something to the girl. She
started in my direction. Puzzled, I met her halfway.

"Mr. Ward?''

"Yes?''

"There's a phone call for you, sir. He says it's terribly
important. If you'll follow me?''

"Yes, of course.'' I followed her to the foyer to take
the call.

I bowed to modern convention some years ago and got
a cell phone, but still refuse to take it anywhere I think it
will be a nuisance. Call me old-fashioned, but I think it's
rude to talk on a cell phone in restaurants, theaters and
black-tie parties. I also don't think I'm so important that
people have to track me down day or night, so I was
surprised that someone was calling me at Greg's.

I don't know the statistics, but in my experience, phone
calls herald good news far less than fifty percent of the
time. The thought did not make me overly eager to pick

up the receiver, but the evening did need a little excitement.

"Emerson Ward here."

"I smell a party, and you didn't invite me. Some friend." A man's voice. Familiar, but...then I had it.

"I'll be damned," I said softly. "Puppy?"

"Yeah, it's me. You were maybe expecting a call from a Hollywood agent, huh?"

"Hell, I didn't even know you were still alive, you sorry son of a bitch. It's been a long time."

"Agh. You know they can't kill me. The gods look for tastier tidbits than I'd make."

"How did you find me, Puppy?"

"I called Brandt when I couldn't reach you at home. I'm surprised he's not there."

"Me, too, but he said he wasn't feeling very well."

Brandt was on the board of just about every charitable organization in the city. For him to miss the opportunity to press the flesh for a good cause meant he really was under the weather, or that a bigger priority had demanded his attention. His presence, I realized selfishly, would have made the party more bearable.

"They told me it was important, Puppy. Is it?"

"As a matter of fact, yes." His voice suddenly went serious. "I need your help, Emerson. Can you break away?"

"Where are you?" It came without hesitation. I owed Puppy more than a few favors, and a friend in need... He gave me the name and address of a bar within easy walking distance, and I told him to give me fifteen minutes. After I'd hung up, I gave Greg my apologies for running out on his party. Then I went to find Myrna.

"I hope you can manage to get home by yourself," I said when I'd explained the situation.

"Oh, dear. And I'd so hoped that you would spirit me away from all this and take me someplace cozy and intimate."

"Myrna, you are a charming and attractive woman, and I'm delighted to be your escort on occasion. But I will not bed you, now or in the foreseeable future. I much prefer being your friend to being your pet."

"My, you do have a way with words." Then she laughed. "Damn your morals, Emerson. You make me feel old and wicked. All right, run off if you have to. I'll manage by myself somehow."

"I'm sure you will—you always have. Goodnight, dear."

"Goodnight. Oh, Emerson? I wish you wouldn't try quite so hard to be a bastard. It doesn't become you."

Full moon? Some new industrial goop in the atmosphere? Male menopause? I didn't know, but as I stepped out of the old brownstone into the warm air of a July evening, I decided that Myrna was probably right. When something is awry in our own personal worlds, we tend to externalize the problems, to blame them on someone else's shortcomings. Brandt tells me it's my own inferiority complex occasionally rearing its ugly head, that I'm afraid that these people, because of their material wealth, are somehow better than me. I, in turn, get on my high horse to try to elevate my perspective. I shrugged off the feelings. By morning, I would probably forget what had made me so ornery.

Greg's house was on Astor Street on Chicago's near north side, a quiet and lovely street, only a block or so from my own. Stately and elegant brownstones and oak trees lined either side, so walking was pleasant. I crossed over to State Street, passing the more modest abode that I'd had the good fortune to buy before real estate prices went through the roof. It had been in disrepair, making the price even more attractive. Just down the street I passed the Ambassador Hotel and headed towards the glitter and hustle that make up Rush and Division Streets.

The bars and restaurants there are the domain of the singles set, the pride of the Near North—Michigan Avenue advertising folk, LaSalle Street bankers, lawyers and commodities traders, and Washington Street doctors. Yves St. Laurent, Ralph Lauren, Calvin Klein, Charles Revson, Diane Furstenburger, and Bill Blass have made fortunes on these people, and they, in turn, are making comfortable livings off the gullibility, needs, and desires of the rest of us.

I stepped into a quiet side street and up the stairs of a small saloon. The raucous sounds of the street did not intrude here. Instead of the blaring, pounding pulsation of dance music, Tony Bennett crooned softly out of a corner jukebox. The rowdiness and shouting of the singles bars gave way to muted conversations. I relaxed in that atmosphere, and didn't even feel out of place in my tuxedo.

Puppy was sitting at a small table in a corner, and even though the light was dim, he would have been hard to miss. A six-foot-bed is a few inches shy of being able to accommodate my frame, but Puppy made me look small. At six-and-a-half feet and almost three hundred pounds, he is a size that large men feel challenged and threatened by. He never asks for trouble, but he is often the subject, or victim, of someone out to prove himself. Puppy was a living Everest—men had to try to conquer him. It was how I'd met him.

I had been sitting at the corner of the bar in a small club down on Delaware that no longer exists. It was out of the way, and not very well known, but life memberships were a buck, and they'd served an excellent steak and a good bottle of wine at reasonable prices, and had a good steam room in the back. Puppy had been sitting at the middle of the bar by himself, and a couple of over-juiced hockey players had been sitting at the other end.

I'd watched unobtrusively from my corner as the hockey players muttered loudly about taking "the big man" out in the alley. Puppy ignored them, quietly sipping his drink, but every so often he glanced in my direction, and in those glances, we established a sort of nonverbal communication. Dennis, the bartender, decided to have nothing to do with whatever was going to happen, and the louder the jocks got, the more furiously he polished glasses behind the bar. The corner I was in was dark, and the jocks hadn't really noticed me. Finally, Puppy turned to them and spoke.

"Gentlemen—however much a misnomer—I would advise against contemplating violence to my person. But if you're determined to make an issue of insulting me, I will gladly take you both outside and break your legs."

"Yeah, you and who else?" one of them sneered.

"Me," I said quietly, standing up and stepping into the light. Puppy hadn't even turned around to look for support. He merely gestured with his thumb over his shoulder.

"My friend here has been known to have once bitten a man's nose off before breaking all the fingers of his left hand. He's vicious. Didn't you fellows see enough action at the Stadium tonight?"

The hockey players had reconsidered—something they wouldn't have done on the ice in the heat of a game—muttered to each other, and called us both a lot of nasty names before finally leaving. Dennis had heaved a sigh of relief, and Puppy and I had burst into laughter.

"Brady Barnes," he said, sticking out a huge paw.

"Emerson Ward," I replied, socketing my own hand deep into his to match his grip without getting my knuckles ground to dust.

"Friends call me Puppy. Can I buy you a drink?"

I'd laughed because the name fit. Once you got to know what lay behind that fierce facade—the black eyes set deep beneath the jutting shelf of eyebrow, the grizzled gray beard—he resembled a shaggy St. Bernard puppy.

"Emerson," he said now as I sat down at the table, "it's good to see you." He was in his early sixties, and I could see age beginning to creep up on him in the wrinkles around the eyes, and the looseness of the skin around the throat, and the way in which the hulking frame seemed to have shrunk, leaving his clothes a size too big. But he was still impressive.

"How are you, Puppy?"

"As good as can be expected, I guess. I'm not a young man anymore, Emerson. It's a hard thing to admit." He smiled.

"How's Kitty?" Puppy's third wife.

"The Kitten is always the same. She is the only thing that keeps me as young as I am. Otherwise, I'd feel ninety. She asks about you a lot, you know. You really should stop by more often."

"I don't know why I haven't." I paused. "Bad trouble?"

"Bad enough." He stared into space for a moment as if trying to decide how to tell it. "The whiskey account is in town," he started.

I couldn't remember which one it was—Hiram Walker, Seagram's—one of the big distilleries. Puppy was a commercial photographer, one of the best.

"They're in town for a long session this time," he continued. "Two or three weeks. It's unusual, but I don't argue with clients. They've been here just over a week now. One of the shots they want, they want done with sparklers, so we borrowed their jewel collection, which is, as you may or may not know, just a bunch of loose stones—emeralds, sapphires, diamonds. But they are as impressive as hell. We've worked with them a lot in the past.

"I set up the usual arrangements—keep them in the bank vault, with a special courier to bring them in when we need them. And, as usual, I double-checked the insurance policy to make sure we're covered in case of loss or theft. I've become a very cautious man when I'm dealing with a lot of someone else's money. I double-checked the studio alarm system and the safe in case we had to keep the stones in the studio for any reason. I took every precaution I could think of.

"But none of them were enough. Two nights ago, we were shooting late. We've had trouble all week with the damn shot. Couldn't get the lighting right, couldn't get the filtration right, the lab butchered a couple of chromes. Anyway, we worked late that night, so the stones had to go into the studio safe. I put them in myself, and checked the alarms before we left. We worked on a couple of other shots yesterday, so the jewels weren't even taken out of the safe. I checked them, but saw no reason to take the risk of transporting them back to the bank and then back to the studio again, so they stayed in the safe. This morning we went back to work on the sparkler shot. And some sorry son of a bitch, who is simply trying to make my life complicated and miserable, switched fakes for the real thing.

"I never would have known except that one of my damn fool girls—I have two new ones doing set design and things like that—managed to knock one of the smaller stones off the set. Lord knows how she did it, but when she went to pick it up, she got tangled up in a cord and knocked a studio light over on the stone. It shattered. The stone, I mean.

"I don't know where everyone else was at the time, but we were the only two people on the set. Poor Nancy nearly went into hysterics. I got to her quick, and told her that if she even breathed one word of what happened to anyone, I'd not only see that she never got another job in the city of Chicago, but that I'd give her bare hide a spanking she'd never forget. Well, she quieted down pretty quick, and helped me sweep up the shattered stone. Then I told Nick that I just couldn't concentrate on the sparkler shot and that I was locking them up for the day.

"I had a man I trust—Dave Kliewer—come over tonight after we closed up shop to look at those stones. All fakes. He said they're good. They'd slow up even the best eye. Probably cubic zirconium. Good or not, what the hell am I going to do with a couple hundred bucks worth of synthetic gems? I could claim on the insurance policy, but that makes me a bad risk, and it makes me look bad in front of the client. No, I want those stones back. More, I want the bastard who stole them. Can you help?"

"Hell, Puppy, you know I'll try." I leaned back for a minute, trying to think. "Who knows the jewels are fake?"

"Right now, I'd say you and I, and my jeweler friend. And whoever switched them. I don't think even Nancy figured out they were fake. I think she was upset because she thought she'd managed to shatter a real diamond, and they will if you hit them in the right spot."

"Okay. How about people with access to the safe?"

"Me, Nick Fratelli—you remember him; he's my chief photographer. The client, Irv Steinmetz—he's what I guess you might call the official caretaker of the collection. And Marty Hopkins, my chief assistant.''

"Whoever switched them had to be someone who knew way ahead of time that you were going to be shooting the jewels, right?''

"Not necessarily. Dave tells me you can pick up cubic zirconium in any color and just about any weight. A good faceter can cut them pretty quickly, if you put up enough money. A week, maybe.''

"How many stones in the collection?''

"About thirty.''

"That sounds like a lot to cut in a week.''

"The other problem is that it didn't have to be someone who knew the combination to the safe, either. A good thief could probably get around the alarm and into the safe. Those stones were in the safe for a day and a half. And there were a ton of people who knew we were shooting the collection. The ad agency knew, it was hyped in *Advertising Age* over a month ago—Christ, it scares me to think how many people knew.''

"But let's assume it had to be one of three people, not including you. Any ideas?''

"I agree it's more likely that someone who knew the combination was the thief, but I can't imagine it being any of those three. That's why I need your help, Emerson. I need an objective opinion of those three, because if I start suspecting any of them, I'm liable to start suspecting myself.''

"Then I guess we start there. I'll need background on all of them, and an excuse to start snooping around the studio.''

"Okay, we can start there, but I think that we ought to include everyone in the studio.''

"Why?''

"I've got a lot of faith in that alarm system, Emerson, but everyone in the studio knows the code. And I'll bet that at one time or another everyone there has been given the combination to the safe. We usually don't keep anything of much value in there, but we often lock up merchandise to ease the client's mind if it has any value at all. And if Nick, Marty, or I don't have time to go open it, we just tell someone to do it. Whether everyone there can remember the combination or not, I don't know. I've never seen anyone write it down. I put a lot of faith in the people who work for us. I run a pretty open operation, as you know. Anyone who wants to use the studio in their spare time is welcome to. All the precaution with the alarm system is to keep outsiders from stealing the equipment and props. There's a lot of money tied up in that studio, but I trust my people."

"Obviously, somebody has abused that trust." I sighed. "What about the client? Isn't it possible that they gave you a fake collection in the first place? Maybe they were worried about using the real jewels."

"Maybe. But why? Why even do the shoot if we weren't going to use the real thing? Besides, I'm not sure I want to tell Irv just yet. If the real stones *were* stolen, I don't want to give him a heart attack."

"You don't make things very easy. Okay, where *do* we start?"

Puppy sat back and thought, staring into space again. I watched him mull over the problem, and was startled by a strident voice that came from behind me.

"Hey, what you lookin' at, bud?"

It startled Puppy, too, and he looked up sharply at the speaker.

"Quit starin' at my lady friend, bud. It upsets her."

"I didn't realize I was staring," Puppy said.

The man looked like he'd had just enough liquid courage to try to tackle Everest, so I quickly stood up, putting myself between him and Puppy.

"Let's go," I told Puppy quietly. I turned to face the drunk. "No offense intended, sir. We'll leave."

I stood in front of the man with a placid expression until I saw Brady round the table heading for the door. The lady in question was gently pulling at the man's arm, murmuring at him to stop making a scene, and he finally sat down heavily in his chair. I gave them a pleasant smile and followed Brady out to the street.

"Why can't they just leave well enough alone?" Brady sighed.

I didn't have an answer. We continued in silence up Dearborn Street toward Puppy's house. All in all, so far it had been a rotten evening, and as we neared the home of Brady and Katherine Barnes, it took a sudden turn for the worse. I almost missed the flash of flame as thick as a finger that came from the bushes next to Puppy's building, but there was no mistaking the loud, sharp report of a small handgun. Puppy grunted and started to crumple to the sidewalk. I gave him a shove that sent him all the way over just as the second crack shattered the stillness. I had ended up in a crouch next to Puppy, and heard the small sigh that sounded so terribly final, had seen the spot where the bushes had spit flame, and something snapped. My peripheral vision disappeared as a burning rage caused me to do probably one of the dumbest things of my life.

Like mad Quixote, I charged the bushes with a banshee yell. I ran as I had been taught as a tight end in college, cutting and feinting, not seeing anything except those bushes, like a goal line between two buildings. The bushes spit flame a third time, and something twitched at my sleeve, but I barely heard the report over my own yell. A dark shape burst out of the bushes and scurried like a rat between the buildings toward the alley. I took a deep breath and changed course to follow him. He rounded the back of the building into the alley, disappearing, but I caught sight of him again as soon as I burst into the alley behind him.

He was fast, but I was no longer a person; I was an all-consuming rage attached to legs and lungs that couldn't feel pain, and I steadily gained. Halfway down the alley, he ducked in between a garage and a fenced-in yard. I followed without breaking stride. I burst out into the street only twenty feet behind my prey, and still I gained.

I wasn't ready for his next move, so when I saw it coming I had difficulty shifting gears. He stopped dead, and *then* I anticipated the rest of the maneuver. As he whirled to fire, I did a feint right and went left, but somehow got the feet tangled up in the move and went head over heels. He hadn't stopped to see if the shot had hit home, and by the time I got untangled, he had a fifty-foot lead.

The knee and the elbow do not hurt. Go, go! He was out in the street now, running close to the cars. His own must be nearby. There! And now he was fumbling to open the door. My feet left the sidewalk a good ten feet from the car, and I hit the roof in a belly flop that took the breath out of me, and slid over the top, hitting him chest-high. We went to the ground together, but my momentum took me rolling beyond him. Something clattered on the street next to me as I fell, glittering metallically in the streetlight. I couldn't see him, but I heard him coming and knew I had no time. I got a hand on the gun, rolled and heaved it as far as I could.

And then I saw him, aiming a heavy boot at my head. I rolled again, catching the toe on the point of my shoul-

der. My right arm went numb, but I managed to catch his
ankle with the other hand and yanked it hard. He went
down, and we raced to see who could get up faster. I won,
swarming over his back before he was half on his feet. A
frightened man is a strong man, and I had few doubts that
I'd put the fear of God into this man. Grunting, he got to
his feet with all my nearly two hundred pounds on top of
him and tottered backward, slamming me into the side of
a car. He gave me both elbows in the gut, and I lost my
grip, crumpled over, and gasped for breath. And then he
was gone. I managed to stand and look around, clutching
my belly, and spotted him pawing through the bushes in
front of a high-rise apartment building thirty feet away.
The gun!

I must have taken lessons from that mad windmill-
chasing Spaniard in another life. Never say die, say I.
With some effort, I gathered myself up for another charge,
and with a hoarse cry, I ran on slightly wobbly legs toward Puppy's assailant. He whirled to meet me, foolishly
thinking I would stop. I did not. I lowered my head like
a wounded bull and ran into him full steam. We went
crashing into the bushes, and like some strange comedy
team, did our scrambling routine again, trying to get to
our feet. He got there first this time, and I barely managed
to stop a roundhouse right with the side of my head. If I
had been an instant slower, he would have missed me.
My ears rang and the world went black. Dimly, I heard
someone shouting, and then the squeal of tires.

''What's going on here?''

My eyes cleared in time to see the car vanishing around
the corner on smoking wheels. The doorman from the
high-rise was standing a few feet away from me, looking
at me with some trepidation. I would give him cause to

tremble. I was still filled with unvented rage, and I felt at the moment like a creature from a dark corner of hell.

"Call an ambulance!" I roared. "And if it isn't here in under ninety seconds, I'll have your head on a spit!"

I must have sounded convincing because he was on the phone in three seconds. I followed him into the entrance, rubbing the bump on my head. I asked him for a flashlight, and it was produced almost magically. I took it outside, and by the time I heard the sirens coming up the street, I'd found the gun. I gingerly put it in a pocket after checking the safety, returned the flashlight, then went out into the street to meet the ambulance. It screeched to a halt, and I hopped onto the running board and grabbed the rearview mirror.

"Around the corner," I snarled through the open window. The driver didn't question me, merely nodded and stepped on the gas.

I roused Kitty, found her purse and got her into a coat and sent her out to make sure they got him to Northwestern as fast as that crate would take him. She accepted stoically, and I thanked the gods that she didn't crack on me. I was close to the edge myself. I used her phone to call Lieutenant Lanahan down at the Chicago Avenue station, and told him I'd meet him at the hospital. Then I went back outside to watch them shut the doors on two of the best human beings I've ever known, the huge, grizzled photographer, and his petite wife, both with hearts big enough to embrace the whole world. The sad howl of the siren as the ambulance pulled away sent a chill through me, reminding me that we are all mortal after all.

TWO

THE EMERGENCY ROOM at Northwestern was probably slow for a Saturday night. One of the few hospitals left in Chicago's troubled trauma network, Northwestern served a smaller geographic area than others in the system, but was perhaps only a little less inundated by the overload of accident and violent crime victims that flowed hourly into the system. Emergency room staffs at all the trauma centers were frazzled and burned out from the combination of the deluge of patients and lack of adequate facilities and personnel.

Both ambulance bays were occupied as paramedics worked to unload their cargo of human suffering. The waiting room, decorated with orange-brown carpeting and bright green and yellow vinyl furniture, was full of anxious friends and relatives sitting with the patience of the important, numbed more by the unenlightening wait than shock or concern.

The front line of the emergency room hierarchy was a well-groomed and immaculately dressed woman at a desk just inside the door to the street. She looked more like a Junior League member than a hospital employee, and sat with a clipboard on her desk, the repository of information on the fates of all those still in triage. I passed her by and strode across the room to the door just beyond the two policemen. No one stopped me, or even glanced in my direction that I could tell.

Once through the door, I found myself in the wide corridor linking the ambulance bays with the triage room. I turned left and walked into the emergency room proper, scanning the room to look for Kitty's blond head. It was even busier here than in the waiting room. At least a dozen occupied stretchers littered the room, most half-hidden by drawn curtains that served as dividers between examining stations. Blue-suited doctors, residents and nurses scurried to and fro, determining dispensation of patients depending on malady or injury. The room was filled with a loud, even babble, occasionally pierced by a groan or cry of pain.

I caught sight of Kitty on the far side of the room and headed in her direction. She sat on a low stool next to a stretcher, a grim look on her face. The body on the stretcher was concealed from this angle by a curtain. As I made my way toward her, a doctor gently grasped her shoulders from behind and pulled her to her feet and away from the stretcher to make more room for the medics milling around Puppy's body. She looked over her shoulder at her husband, biting her lower lip, then turned and saw me.

"Oh, God, Emerson," she cried softly, throwing her arms around my waist and burying her face in my side. "I don't want him to die."

I stroked her hair and held her close. "They won't let him die, Kitty. He's too strong."

She snuffled, and I could feel her pull herself together, resolve stiffening her spine, putting energy back into the slack muscles. In a moment, she pulled away and tipped her head back to look up at me.

She was a tiny woman, the top of her head barely reaching my sternum. Her large bright green eyes were red-rimmed from crying. Her blond hair was cut short and brushed back. I gently pushed a stray strand out of her eyes with my fingertips, revealing the oval face that had just a tad too much point to the nose and chin to be truly beautiful. But it was a strong and attractive face, and I felt strangely guilty that it now held so much sorrow.

"How is he?"

"A mess, from what I can tell. Nobody will give me a straight answer. They're trying to get him stabilized before they take him to surgery." She sniffed and dabbed at the tip of her nose with a dainty knuckle.

"Okay. I'll be here, for as long as it takes. You stay with him. I've got to meet Lieutenant Lanahan to file a report. I'll check with the desk to find out when he's going into surgery, and I'll meet you there."

"Thank you." The corners of her mouth turned up in a small attempt at a smile. She gave my arm a quick squeeze, then turned to step back through the curtains.

Lanahan was standing in the middle of the waiting room when I got back, looking around the room with a distasteful expression on his round, ruddy Irish face. He wore a rumpled gray suit in summer-weight wool, tie loosened at the collar of an equally wrinkled oxford button-down.

"Hello, Lieutenant," I said, walking up to him.

"Hullo, Ward." He looked me up and down. "You're a mess."

Puzzled, I glanced down at my clothes, then realized what he meant. The front of the tux was filthy from rolling in the street, and there was a bloody tear in the pants at the knee where I'd skinned it. The patent leather pumps were scuffed and scratched.

"Come on, let's go for a walk. I hate hospitals." He took my arm firmly and pulled me toward the door.

"You know, we have detectives for this sort of thing, Ward," he said when we were outside. "I was just about to go home. I don't think I've seen Marge in a week." He yawned.

"I didn't know you were married, Lieutenant." I looked at him curiously, matching his slow stride down Superior Street toward the lake. Lanahan and I had had a few amicable run-ins, and I contributed to the police charities he occasionally hit me up for. We'd established a certain level of mutual trust and more than a passing acquaintance, but I suddenly realized how little I knew about him.

"Cops have home lives, too."

"Sorry to keep you on the job. No offense, but I didn't want a detective on this one. I wanted you."

"I'm flattered, but you know I'm just going to pass this on when I get back to the station. What have you got?"

"Attempted homicide—if he makes it. The real thing if he doesn't."

"Brady Barnes, the photographer, right?"

"Right. You know him?"

"I know of him. Tell me what happened."

In short, clipped sentences, I related what had happened on the way back to Puppy's house. He listened attentively as we walked, his head cocked a little to one side, but he made no attempt to take notes.

"Tell me about the perp," he said when I was finished.

"Black. About six feet. Maybe one hundred eighty pounds. Strong," I said, remembering how he'd carried me on his back. "Black windbreaker, an expensive one, but not one of those satin team jackets. Black slacks—no, I think they were jeans. Oh, and boots. Strange in this weather, but real cowboy boots. Gray, with a pattern, like lizard skin. Expensive boots, too.''

''Anything else?''

''No. Sorry. It happened too fast, and it was hard to get a look at him rolling around on the street like that.''

Lanahan sighed. ''Okay, what about the car?''

''Older model two-door with some muscle under the hood. An Olds Four-Four-Two. I'm sure of it. Late Sixties. Hard to mistake it. Six-digit plate, three letters and three numbers. I couldn't read the letters, but the numbers were one-two-two.''

''What color?''

''Um, puce.''

''Puce.'' He stopped and turned to look at me. ''You damn writers are all alike. Like purple, you mean?''

''Well, yeah, but light purple, almost lilac,'' I said with a little embarrassment. ''Ugly color. What a thing to do to a car like that.''

''You sure?''

''It was parked right under a street light.''

''That's it?''

We'd almost reached Lake Shore Drive, and Lanahan stood still, waiting to see if there was anything else.

''That's it.''

''It's not much, Ward. Nothing special about the perp, a lilac car, and a partial plate number. Not much at all.'' He shook his head.

''Wait,'' I said, remembering the weight in my jacket pocket. ''There's this.'' I pulled out the gun.

''Hey, careful with that.'' His eyes widened.

''There won't be any prints on it but mine. He wore gloves, now that I think of it. Black gloves, too. Driving gloves. The kind with holes over the knuckles.''

Lanahan took the revolver out of my hands and turned it over under the lights of the Drive.

"Three-fifty-seven magnum. Nice piece, but not the usual weapon of choice for the type of asshole you describe. I would have expected a Saturday Night Special, or something like a nine-millimeter Beretta at best. I hope he was using standard shells, or your friend Barnes is in a world of hurt. What did it sound like?"

"When he fired? A loud, low firecracker. Kind of like a cherry bomb."

He nodded, snapping open the cylinder to look. "Magnum loads sound more like a cannon going off at close range. And hollow points would have put a big hole in Barnes. I think he'll make it."

"Thanks, Lieutenant, for the expert opinion." I couldn't keep the sarcasm out of my voice.

"Sorry." He said it matter-of-factly, then turned and started strolling back toward the hospital. I hurried to catch up.

"This could help," he said when I pulled abreast. He put the pistol in an evidence bag he pulled from his pocket. "We'll check the serial number, see what comes up. Barnes' wife, she's at the hospital?"

"Yes."

"We won't bother her tonight. We'll catch up with her tomorrow, see if she knows of anyone who might have held a grudge. It doesn't sound like attempted robbery. Which means you're right; somebody wanted Barnes dead. You could help, too, Ward. Think about enemies he might have made."

"I didn't know him *that* well. Until tonight, I hadn't seen him in a year."

"You never know what you might come up with."

We walked a ways in silence.

"Why did you say he called?" Lanahan glanced at me quickly, then looked back down at the sidewalk.

"He hadn't seen me in a while. Said he wanted to have a drink and talk a little."

"You left a black tie party to have a drink with an old friend." It wasn't asked like a question, but it was obvious he expected an explanation.

"The party was boring. Lots of hoity-toity folks with whom I don't have a lot in common. Puppy's a good man. Like I said, I haven't seen him in a while. Having a drink sounded like a good excuse to get out of there."

"Mmm." He took a few steps without speaking. "Sounds like he went to a lot of trouble to track you down."

"Look, Lieutenant, I suppose he had something on his mind, something he wanted to talk to me about. He never got around to it," I lied.

"Okay, Ward. You just seem to have a habit of getting involved in things that you have no business sticking your nose in."

"I called *you,* remember?"

"Yeah, you did. And you'll call me if you have anything else to tell me, right?"

"Sure, Lieutenant."

"You just gave me a hell of a lot of paperwork. You owe me big time, Ward."

"So, I guess it wouldn't hurt to ask another favor?"

"Naw, shoot. Might as well."

"Can you keep it quiet? They don't need reporters hovering."

"I won't release Barnes' name until the family's been notified. S.O.P.—best I can do."

"Thanks."

"I'll be in touch."

We were suddenly in front of the emergency room entrance again, and Lanahan left me there, crossing the street to his car.

It was a long night. The slug had punctured Puppy's right lung and lodged near his spine. They cracked him open like a giant walnut and went in after it, trying to repair the damage left in its wake. He was in surgery for nearly five hours, and when they finally came out, they said the prognosis was good. They wouldn't be able to tell about possible paralysis until he was conscious, but they didn't think the bullet had come close enough to cause trauma to the spinal cord.

They wheeled him into intensive care, wired to machines and dripping bottles like a mad scientist's experiment. He was breathing on his own, but they had a respirator plugged into him to help, feeding him oxygen. Tubes leaked liquid into his arms, replenishing his body with glucose, electrolytes and loading him with antibiotics to ward off infection. The wires connected him to monitors that rhythmically beeped and flashed vital signs. Everything seemed to be working fine.

And then he died.

The machines bleeped and burped irregularly, then settled into a steady tone that sent the ICU staff into a frenzy of activity. Like blue-garbed worker bees around their queen, they hovered and buzzed, thumping him, bagging him, sticking him with a long needle containing epinephrine or adrenaline, and zapped him with enough electricity to bring a movie monster to life. And after an interminable three minutes that aged us years, they jump-started his heart and got it beating regularly again. The decibel level slowly subsided as the staff drifted away to other duties until there was just a lone nurse adjusting knobs and tubes and fussing with bedclothes.

Kitty clung to me so hard during those long, awful moments that there were deep, small blue welts on my wrist from her nails. I hadn't noticed the pain, nor the fact that I'd held my breath for a good portion of the three minutes, gulping air only when the whump of the electric paddles sent an empathetic reflex jolt through my body, too. When the scare was over, Kitty sank numbly onto a chair, still clutching the sleeve of my dinner jacket. I gently pried her fingers loose, took her hand between my two and squatted down to look her in the eye until she focused on me. The grim set of her face slowly relaxed to the point where she could force a tight smile, and she finally nodded her head.

"I'm all right," she murmured, reading the question in my eyes. "Thank you."

I patted her hand and touched her cheek softly.

The clock on the wall in ICU said it was nearly 5:00 in the morning when I decided to call a hiatus to the bedside vigil. There was little point in trying to convince Kitty to go home, but I knew that I would be a lot more helpful after a few hours of intimate propinquity to a soft pillow. So, I made Kitty write down a list of things she needed and where to find them, borrowed her house key, and after extracting a promise that she would at least try to get some sleep, I left.

As I walked north up the Inner Drive, the sun popped up over the flat blue expanse of Lake Michigan, a platinum disc with a fiery yellow corona that bathed the highrises in golden light. Two gulls hovered and swooped over the calm water, their cries of hunger rising over the sound of the few rushing cars on the drive. A couple of lonely health addicts jogged the lakefront strip between the Oak Street and North Avenue beaches, locked into the solitary rhythm that would eventually produce enough endorphins to make the exertion worth it.

The thought of all that huffing and puffing just made me wearier, and as I turned up Goethe to my house, I could hear the inviting call of the big double bed. I let myself in the front door, stripped as I climbed the stairs, and fell naked between cool sheets.

The harsh rasp of the alarm jarred me out of an uneasy sleep shortly after 10:00. I didn't remember setting it. Reaching out reflexively with one hand, I swatted the clock into silence, a firm reprimand for rousing me so unfeelingly. Still groggy, I rolled out of bed and stumbled into the shower. The skinned knee had stiffened and scabbed over, and I soaped it gently, working away the grit and dried blood. When I got out of the shower, I found some antiseptic ointment in the medicine chest and daubed it on the scrape, then covered it with a large adhesive bandage to keep it supple.

After dressing in khaki pants, short-sleeved shirt and deck shoes, I went down to the kitchen to make a pot of strong coffee. The phone rang just as the last few drops were plopping into the full decanter. I picked up the kitchen extension and cradled the receiver between my ear and shoulder while I poured a steaming mug of the dark aromatic brew.

"Good morning," a nasal voice said in a soft Texas twang—Brandt.

"Good morning to you. How are you feeling?" I gulped some of the coffee.

"Better thanks. Whatever it is, I'll get over it." He sniffed into the phone. "And how are you?"

"Tired. I didn't sleep much."

"Out too late? I hear I missed a good party. Myrna

Goodwin called me this morning to ask me why I don't keep you on a leash with a choke-chain collar.''

"I was out way too late, but not because of the party. Brady was shot last night.''

"What? He phoned here looking for you, but I didn't know it was an emergency. How is he?''

"Not too good.'' I told Brandt what had happened, and he listened without interruption.

"Kitty's still at the hospital?''

"Yes. I'm going by the house as soon as I wake up a little to pick up some things for her, then I'll head back to Northwestern.''

"I'll send flowers. Give her my love, and tell her if there's anything she needs to give me a call.''

"I'll do that.''

PUPPY'S RED BRICK VICTORIAN looked almost cheerful in the light of morning. The only indication of the previous night's violence was a small, unremarkable rust-colored spot on the sidewalk in front of the house and a few broken branches dangling askew on the bushes beneath the bay window. Wooden steps with a wrought iron railing led up to a massive oak door painted cherry red and trimmed with bright brass hardware, like a Dublin door. The key turned smoothly in the lock, and the door swung open.

The interior of the house was dim and a little musty. The faint odors of lavender, dusty chintz, and pipe tobacco were reminiscent of my grandmother's house, comforting yet haunting. Inside the entryway, a wide oak staircase with a dark green oriental runner led to the upper floors. To the right was a large living room cluttered with antique furniture and bric-a-brac. Through an archway, an ornate crystal chandelier hung in the formal dining room beyond.

Pulling Kitty's list out of my pocket, I ascended the stairs. Framed photographs hung like steps on the wall up to the second floor, still-lifes that echoed the emptiness of the big house. The master bedroom was at the end of the hall. Roomy and comfortable, it was old-fashioned like the rest of the house. Centered against the far wall was a double four-poster bed with a cluttered nightstand and lamp on each side. Mismatched dressers stood on opposite sides of the room, one massive, dark oak with square corners, wide drawers and round ball feet squatting close to the floor, the other more dainty, with curved sides and front, shallow drawers, and slender legs holding it aloft.

The personal effects on top of each were further affirmation of the gender of its owner. The oak dresser was strewn with a set of keys, pocket appointment book, brass collar stays, a small open box containing cufflinks, watches and tie clips, bits and pieces of camera equipment, batteries, a couple of golf balls, two wood and brass framed pictures of handsome children, and some paperback novels. Over the dresser hung a large oil painting of a mountainscape, bold, colorful and full of majesty.

Atop the other dresser under a gilt-edged oval mirror sat a small crystal vase with fresh cut flowers, sterling hand mirror, comb and brush set, a few items of make-up, and a five-by-seven color photograph in a crystal frame of Brady and Katherine Barnes in a happy moment. Taken outdoors, the camera had caught Puppy sitting on the grass with one leg tucked up under him, arms around Kitty, who reclined against him, head against his chest. They both smiled broadly for the camera, a natural smile brought on by an inner glow evident in their faces, not some self-conscious grin.

To the left of the door was a tall, wide armoire with mirrored double doors. In the far corner was a *chaise lounge* upholstered in white. An antique brass floor lamp stood behind it, its green glass shade hanging over the back of the chaise. In the opposite corner stood a small jewelry armoire with a porcelain vase full of dried flowers on top.

To my right, in the same wall as the door to the bedroom, was a louvered door leading into a large walk-in closet. A switch just inside the door turned on track lights on the high ceiling, bathing the narrow room in light. Men's clothes hung in a row down one side, women's on the other. Above the clothes rods were open shelves holding sweaters, blankets, linens, purses, and other clothes, and cupboards with doors rose up to the ceiling above the shelves.

On the wall against the far end of the closet, a single framed photograph illuminated by a circle of light caught my eye. I moved closer to admire it. It was a black-and-white shot of a woman's foot, slender and graceful, toes pointed and extended, without blemish or callous, full of strength and soft curves at the same time. A foot is such an odd, misshapen part of the body so embarrassing at times that it was hard to think of one as sensual, but this one was. Full of light and shadow, bold lines and soft edges, the foot in the photograph beckoned the imagination, conjuring up a body just as sensual.

I smiled then, and shook off the tendrils of fantasy. Not only was Brady good, he had a sense of humor. On the floor below the photo as though part of the set piece was a worn, clunky pair of leather work boots, and poking their heels out from under the hanging clothes were pair after pair of neatly placed shoes—sneakers, loafers, pumps, flats, wingtips, espadrilles, and more.

I stepped backwards away from the picture and pushed through another louvered door into the large bathroom, intent now on filling the list Kitty had given me. I found a small overnighter in one of the cupboards in the closet and filled it with make-up and toiletries, a pair of jeans and a couple of blouses, some culottes and a long-waisted, sleeveless, cotton shift. From the dresser in the bedroom I took two pairs of filmy panties, and as I turned to place them in the bag I felt a startling flash of warmth rushing to my groin.

Flushed and embarrassed by this adolescent reaction to the silky feel of a woman's undergarments, I sat heavily on the bed, wondering what had triggered it. The photo of the foot? Remembrance from the night before of the soft, subtle smell of perfume in stark contrast to the cold, empty eyes of Miss Ice Queen, or Myrna's not-so-subtle advances? Subconscious fantasy of comforting the widow Kitten, who was not yet a widow, on the soft, downy expanse of this four-poster bed?

I had a fleeting vision of myself as a pubescent kid and smiled. With no more self-consciousness, I stood and zipped the bag closed, humming softly to myself.

Puppy and Kitty were asleep when I got back to the hospital. Both appeared uncomfortable, and both wore troubled expressions. Brady's was one of pain that reached up through layers of anesthesia and consciousness to contort his face into what was almost a grimace. He lay on his back, a giant fly caught in a tangled web of tubes and wires, his slow, labored breathing and the soft incessant bleep of an infusion pump the only signs of life. Kitty sat curled up in a chair next to the hospital bed, feet tucked up under her, chin on her chest. Her mouth turned down at the corners, and worry showed through on her face.

I set the overnight bag down quietly next to the chair and went in search of the cafeteria for coffee. The food-service staff was noisily gearing up for lunch, but the dining room was still practically deserted. Two nurses on break chatted at a table in a far corner, and a middle-aged couple stood in the center of the room carrying trays, looking bewildered, as if not sure where to sit. With time and room to browse the food counters, I amended my list, went back for a tray, and then loaded it with a couple of big bran muffins, fresh fruit, a carton of milk, and two small bottles of juice in addition to two large coffees. The cashier was surprisingly pleasant, and when she saw me start to stuff my purchases in my pockets, she grinned and told me to wait while she went back into the kitchen to find me an empty box.

I had drained one of the bottles of juice, and finished almost a third of a cup of coffee and half a muffin when Kitty stretched and opened her eyes sleepily. She started when she saw me, then rose and padded barefoot to the bed to look down at Brady.

"Get any sleep?" I asked between mouthfuls.

"This is a teaching hospital, Emerson. I'm surprised the patients can even sleep. There have been nurses and doctors in and out of here ever since you left. A big troupe came through around nine, peering and poking and prodding him like he was some kind of alien specimen.

"The police were here, too, a couple of hours ago. They didn't stay long since I couldn't tell them much. And Brady's not exactly in a talkative mood."

From the side, I could see the frown on her face. Then she turned toward me and stretched again. Up on the balls of her feet, laced fingers reaching for the ceiling lifting her breasts up and out against the thin fabric of the dress, she still was diminutive, almost girlish.

"How is he?"

"Critical, they say." She yawned. "Not much change. He came out of the anesthesia briefly early this morning, which they say is good, but he's been asleep ever since, and they're not venturing any guesses. It's maddening."

"Are you hungry?"

"In a minute. I think I want to freshen up a bit first."

She picked up the bag, slipped her feet into the shoes lying half under the chair and headed for the door. When she returned fifteen minutes later, her scrubbed clean face had only a sparing touch of makeup, and she wore jeans and a loose cotton blouse. To look at her, there was no way to tell her forty-fifth birthday had long since come and gone. Though I was gentleman enough not to ask, I was pretty sure she had just turned fifty.

"Thanks for the clothes. You chose well. I don't know what I would have done without you."

I handed her a cup of coffee. "I suppose I must have been female in another life."

There was the barest hint of a smile on her face as she sat back in her chair. "Maybe you practice at home in front of the mirror," she teased, then covered up the widening smile by lifting the coffee cup to her lips.

There was a long silence, and her expression grew more thoughtful as she sipped the hot coffee. She seemed to be staring into space, but when I followed her gaze, I could see she was loosely focused on the man in the bed.

"Seven years," she finally murmured, still looking at Brady.

"Has it been that long?"

"You know, I'll always be grateful to you for introducing us." She turned her head to look at me. "You knew me back then. I felt old and unwanted."

"You weren't old, and you just hadn't found the right guy yet."

"But there's a certain desperation that sets in when you feel your biological clock ticking down, and you're not yet 'attached.' I think you have to be a woman to know what I'm talking about. You saved me. I could see myself ending up the world's oldest flight attendant, a gray-haired old lady still waiting on jerks thirty thousand feet up. Actually, it wasn't the job that was bad, it was the sense of not belonging, of not having a family of my own.

"Anyway, I remember Brady was in the middle of a second childhood when we met. Actually, I think he'll always be a child. I figured it would never work, and though I loved you dearly for trying, I thought your matchmaking this time had reached a new height of silliness. He was so much older than me, yet he played the singles scene with more gusto than those ridiculous twenty-year-olds who constantly tried to get me to sleep with them.

"I guess it didn't take me long to see through his act. I think I fell in love on our second date. I could see the vulnerability, the kindness, and I figured that maybe it was worth taking the time to knock down a few walls and see if there was anything there. When I finally realized that he loved me as much as I loved him, I got scared. I knew that someday I would lose him. I just didn't think it would be so soon. Not this way."

Her eyes glinted with tears, and she bit her lower lip to keep them back.

"You haven't lost him yet. He'll pull through." I hitched my chair closer to hers and took her hand in mine.

She nodded, sniffed, and forced a smile. "I know, I know." She paused. "I wish we saw more of you these days. I've almost forgotten what it's like to sit around the fire with a bottle of cognac and talk until all hours of the night. I miss that.''

She looked at Brady again, but left her hand in mine.

''You know, I think the last time we really played was two years ago. Brady took me to Puerto Vallarta for a 'second honeymoon.' Two glorious weeks of nothing but sun and sand and good food. I've been there a hundred times before, I'm sure, but with Brady it was the first time it felt so romantic, so exotic. We rented a little hacienda overlooking the water, with a housekeeper and a cook, and we did absolutely nothing but eat, sleep, lie in the sun, and make love. It was paradise.''

''What happened?'' I asked softly.

''I don't know.'' She shook her head slowly, then looked at me. ''Brady's just been so serious. He tries not to show it. He tries to be light with me, but after seven years, I can figure out when something's bothering him.''

''Recently?''

''More so recently, but it's actually been a while. He'll go through moods when he's an absolute bear, and suddenly things are fine, and he's his normal, cheerful, nutty self. Now that I think about it, I noticed the moodiness even before we went to P.V.

''He doesn't play anymore, Emerson. For the last two years, he's been working like a dog. Business is better than it's ever been, but he's always taken time out before. He's always managed to juggle jobs so that he has free time. I mean, he used to surprise me sometimes by coming home at noon with a picnic basket full of goodies and a bottle of wine, and we'd walk up the street to the park and have lunch in the shade of a tree. It wasn't much, just lunch hour. But he'd steal time away from the studio to make an hour in the park seem like a vacation.

''Photography is the one true love in his life. I've never

kidded myself about that. But Brady never made me feel like a second-class citizen. If anything, I think he went out of his way to make me feel that I was the most important thing in his life, even though I know I'm not. Now, he tries, but..."

She lapsed into silence, and I thought for a moment.

"Okay, so we know something was bothering him. Somebody also tried to kill him last night and managed to ruin a perfectly good tuxedo in the process. Has he made any enemies lately?"

"No, not that I know of." She paused. "I don't know. You know the story. People who don't know him feel threatened by him, feel like they have to fight him to get what they want. People who know him want to take him home to their kids to play with, like some big stuffed carnival bear. I suppose he has enemies, but ones who would want to kill him?"

"I know it doesn't make sense, Kitty, but Puppy called me last night for help. He's got some trouble at the studio that may have something to do with what happened. I don't know."

She looked at me in shock. "Serious trouble?"

"Well, serious enough. Puppy called to see if I could help out before it gets too bad. I don't want to worry you with all the details until I find out what's going on."

"That's not fair."

"You've got enough to worry about here. You need to talk that man over there back to the land of the living and let him know you're not ready to let him go yet. I'll take care of things at the studio. Whatever the problem is, I'm sure we can straighten it out. Okay?"

"You're still trying to take care of me after all these years. I have a right to know, Emerson."

"All right, we'll talk about it, but not right now. Let me do a little digging first."

"You will tell me, though. If you won't, I'll make Brady tell me." She thought for a minute. "You know, it really makes me angry. Brady and I have never had secrets. I think once we knew we were right for each other, a lot of the walls did come down. I feel like I know his life story inside and out, and there's nothing he doesn't know about me. So why is he holding back? Why now?"

"From what he told me, there's nothing you can do, Kitty. Let me handle it, and we'll talk about it tomorrow, I promise."

She looked as if she wanted to say something, but her attention was diverted by the squeak of rubber-soled shoes on the tile floor as a nurse came in the room to check on Brady. She glanced at us without expression then turned to look at Brady's chart.

"I'm going to take off," I said quietly as the nurse started changing the IV bottle hanging from the pole next to Brady's bed. "Is there anything you need?"

"I'm fine. You've already been a tremendous help. I'm glad we had some time together, Emerson."

"I'll be back, don't worry. You'll call if anything changes?"

She nodded and gave my hand a squeeze, then rose to get a closer look at what the nurse was doing. Her attention and concern were again focused on her husband, and my silent departure went unnoticed by all three souls in the small, sterile room.

THREE

A SHARP-FACED YOUNG WOMAN stood at the nurses' station, dressed in green khaki shorts and a white cotton blouse that hung loosely on her thin frame. Her mouse-colored hair fell limply past her shoulders, too thin to hold a curl in the heat. The plain features would not have elicited a second glance were it not for the fact that her eyes met mine as I came out of the room in ICU, then furtively looked away. The movement bothered me, made me wonder on the way out what had attracted my attention. There had been something in her look. Surprise? Recognition?

Ten steps past her I had it—I knew her. I turned around, took two hesitant steps, and cocked my head. She looked intently at some papers on the countertop in front of her, ignoring my presence.

"Sue Kaminski?"

I heard a soft "damn," then she heaved a sigh and turned to face me. I stepped closer.

"Chicago *Sun-Times?* We met at the writer's conference at Northwestern in June, right?"

"I was hoping you wouldn't recognize me," she murmured.

"What are you doing here?"

She shrugged. "Nothing better to do on a Sunday except follow up leads."

"Such as?"

"Human interest story on Brady Barnes, the photographer. He was shot last night."

"How the hell did you find out?"

"From you, just now." She flashed a self-satisfied grin.

From what little I knew about her, she was a smart reporter with good, aggressive instincts, but I didn't know she was *that* good.

"I'm a little slow. Explain, please."

She shrugged. "Doug Woodall reported a shooting on WGN radio last night. I guess he got it off the scanner when the victim was brought in. TV's already had it on the early news editions this morning."

"But the police haven't released his name."

I think she took delight in letting me know how smart she was. "I figured I'd see if there was a story, so I came down. I saw Barnes' wife in the hall and wondered. You just came out of the room she's been in and out of and confirmed it. What are *you* doing here, by the way?"

"Friend of the family." I paused. Like a pitbull with a porkchop, she didn't let go of a story easily, I knew, and I could see her impatience to see me leave so she could get back to the hunt.

"Come on, let me buy you a cup of coffee."

She hesitated, but when I gently put a hand on her shoulder, she acquiesced and turned to walk down the hall with me.

The hospital cafeteria was becoming an all too familiar place in such a short time. We made our selections—Kaminski got a large coffee, but feeling the effects of too much caffeine, I opted for seltzer water—and made our way up to the registers where I paid.

"Look," I said as we eased into chairs at a table off to the side near the windows, "I pulled you away because there isn't any story here."

"There's always a story," she replied, slowly stirring her coffee. A small notebook and a pencil sat on the table next to her cup.

"Barnes is still out of it, and his wife is in no mood to talk to reporters. Besides, there's nothing she can give you. Get the hospital to give you an update on his condition, talk to the police about what happened, and file your story."

"Not much human interest. 'Just the facts, ma'am,' is that it? What's your part in all this?"

I sighed. "Off the record, okay? I'm not wild about publicity, not this kind." I waited, watching the wheels turn behind the clear green eyes.

She chewed her lower lip. "Trade?" she asked finally.

She wouldn't let it go, I realized. She was fishing, trying to find out if there was anything she could buy with her silence. It occurred to me that we might find each other useful.

"All right. There may be a bigger story in all this than what you're after right now. I don't know. If I find it, it's yours."

"Deal." She put the pencil and notebook back in one of the big pockets in her shorts. "What have you got?" Her eyes were bright, and a small smile of triumph passed her lips.

"I was there when Barnes was shot." I told her what had happened the night before. She listened intently, and when I was done, her mouth had turned down into a small frown.

"That's it? I mean, it's nice to have an eyewitness account and all, but I got almost that much from the police report."

"Barnes *was* nearly murdered last night," I said.

"What, some guy, probably coked up, gets nervous and shoots a man before robbing him? Not much news there.''

"I don't see it that way.''

"You think the guy had a contract on Barnes?''

"He was hiding in the bushes, waiting.''

"Why would anyone put out a contract on Barnes?''

"Juice money? Maybe he pissed someone off. That's what we have to find out.''

"We?''

"You wanted a story, a trade. I'm sure I'll be able to think up some favors you can do for me down the road.''

"I don't know. It's not much of a trade so far.'' She paused. "What about you? Maybe you were the guy's target. Hiding any dirt these days, Ward?''

"It crossed my mind. I'm sure I'm not as popular as I'd like to think. But the guy would have had no way of knowing I'd be there. He was waiting there. It's a simple enough hit if it goes right—wait for the victim to come home, pop him on the way up the walk and fade away into the shadows. The guy just didn't figure I'd be stupid enough to chase him.''

"What do the police think?''

"They're probably figuring it the way you did.''

"But you really think there's something to this.''

"I have my reasons.''

She looked up at me intently, then toyed with the stir-stick in her coffee cup.

"All right. I'll go with you on this. You haven't given me much, Ward.''

"I don't have much to give right now, but I'm sure I will. I have a bad feeling I'm about to get into something messy.''

"You get this feeling often?''

"Often enough.''

She looked at me again, then nodded, as if in confirmation. She reached into a pocket.

"Here's my card, Ward. I want to know what's going on. You be sure you call."

She rose from the table, taking her coffee with her, and I plucked the card from her outstretched hand.

"Count on it."

THE ORNERY FEELING had not gone away. If anything, it was made worse by too little sleep and too much worry for a friend in the hospital. The joggers and sun-worshippers were out in full force enjoying the summer day as I drove up the lake toward home. I lit a cigarette in defiance, blowing the smoke out the open windows with a sneer.

Despite the fact that I'm an on-again-off-again smoker, more off than on, I like to smoke. I like the feeling of the constriction in my chest as the smoke is drawn deep into the lungs. I like the slightly giddy feeling as the nicotine and carbon monoxide hit the bloodstream, racing from fingertips to the brain. I like the smell of a freshly lit cigarette, and the unique smells of a cigarette smoked in the warm salt air of the tropics as opposed to one smoked in the still, dry crackling air of a frozen day in the snowy north woods.

Why do I feel these terrible paranoiac pangs of dread when I see the muscular, clear-eyed, pink-cheeked, al-falfa-sprout-eating health addicts strolling out of the aerobics clubs or the natural food stores? Why do I surreptitiously thumb my nose at the bikers, Rollerbladers and joggers as I drive up the lakefront?

Some friends invited me down to the Moosehead one night after work to listen to some jazz and drink a few beers. I remember being introduced to a young patent attorney named Steve Heller. Thin and wiry, he was impeccably dressed in a Ralph Lauren suit. While he'd obviously just come from work, I got the impression that he was just as fastidious in his personal life as he was professionally. Rather than hang out in jeans and a torn T-shirt (as I'm prone to do on weekends), I laid odds on the fact that casual dress to him meant L. L. Bean. I imagined that if I walked into his home I would find nothing out of place—no dirty dishes in the sink, no clothes on the bedroom floor, no dust on the tops of picture frames, underwear neatly folded in drawers, and all the carpet pile carefully vacuumed in the same direction.

I was interested in his job, but what I found out about him from the conversation around the table was that he liked jazz, enough that he could speak knowledgeably about who wrote what piece, when it was originally recorded, and by whom. I found out that he didn't like to talk about his work, though no one seemed to quite know why. And I found out that he was a fitness buff, the kind who liked to compete in triathlons, the kind who liked to compare notes with friends on his training program. In fact, I found out more than I wanted to know about his workout regimen, and he talked about it with such passion that it made me nervous. I liked him, but maybe it was the competitiveness and intensity he personified that put me off just a tad.

Okay, I run a mile or two every so often. And once in a while I swim a few laps. And yes, I've been known to drag the weights out of the closet and pump them until the sweat runs down my nose and the small of my back, and my heart feels like it's about to burst.

I don't want to be a Yuppie. I don't want to be a health nut. But I feel the stares of those who live on oat bran and endorphins, of the holier-than-thou, stares that burn with the intensity of an argon laser, daring me to call myself fit, worthy of their esteem. Even the fat ones will look at you with self-righteousness. At least they're on the regimen, the look says. At least they have the will-power to stop eating, stop smoking, and start running for their lives.

"But my knees," I complain. "And my strained back," I implore. "Besides, I'm not overweight," I try. But it falls on deaf ears.

It wasn't until later in the evening, after fixing a light (healthy) supper of mixed greens with some leftover cold, sliced grilled pork tenderloin and a honey-mustard dressing on top, that I began to sense what was bothering me. Some of the old familiar self-pity was beginning to settle in. The day's events, and Kitty's words, were having an impact, putting some of the intangible feelings into perspective.

I was not quite a decade younger than Katherine Barnes, and while my biological clock ticked off the minutes of life left to me, not my ability to sire children, I felt the same detached quality about my life that she had before meeting Brady. I padded aimlessly around the empty house, pacing like a panther in a cage, hearing the soft tread of my footsteps echo hollowly in my mind.

The confines of my cage, my life, were self-created. I was normally comfortable with me, with solitude, with what had probably become fussy bachelor ways to an outsider. But every once in a while, my carefree, irresponsible existence grated on even me. Some nagging guilt would not let me enjoy life as it came. I'd worked hard at creating this lifestyle, making it possible to take retirement in small chunks along the way, forsaking the American tradition of working now and playing later. Now, like bonnie Prince Charlie, I craved a small piece of responsibility, of justification for living the way I do. A cause, to care for another human being—it probably didn't matter. Involvement, attachment was the thing.

No girl? No sexual outlet? Then it was probably time to swing into the saddle of the sway-backed steed, run up the family crest, and totter off in search of dragons.

And maybe one more night's sleep would make the feeling go away.

PUPPY WAS AWAKE when I went to visit early Monday morning. He looked like shit, but there was a wan grin on his face that suggested he was happier alive and feeling pain than dead and feeling nothing. Kitty looked haggard, blond hair now tousled and dull, eyes puffy and smudged. The worry and lack of sleep was beginning to take its toll, making her look much older than she had the day before. But she, too, was smiling. Someone was dispensing good news this morning.

"Ho, Emerson," Puppy said when he saw me, his voice thin and weak. "I told you they couldn't kill me."

"They came close, Brady. I take it you're not planning on leaving us anytime soon."

"What? And miss all this fun?"

"He wiggled his big hairy toes for us this morning," Kitty said, gazing at him fondly. "A couple more days, and they may let him out of ICU, they tell us."

"That *is* good news. Have you had any breakfast yet?"

"He doesn't get any breakfast, and I guess I haven't eaten since sometime yesterday afternoon."

"I hate to say it, Kitty, but you look like hell, and you're not going to do anyone any good if you end up in a bed next to Brady. Why don't you go home, get something to eat, take a shower, and sleep for a while?"

She looked at Brady hesitantly.

"Go on," he said. "I'm not going anywhere."

"I'll stay with him," I said, gently steering her toward the door. "Take a break. Take as long as you like."

"All right. But no wheelchair races in the halls or anything like that while I'm gone."

Brady stifled a laugh, holding his arms across his chest, pain showing through on his face.

"Oh, sorry, sorry," Kitty said with consternation, rushing to the bed.

"I'm fine," Brady smiled. "Now git," he said with a mock growl.

She kissed him on the forehead, grabbed her purse, and left. When she was gone, I hitched a chair up next to Brady's bed.

"Hurt?"

"Like a son of a bitch. But they've got good drugs here. I don't know what they've got me on—Demerol, maybe morphine—but I keep sliding in and out. All I seem to be able to do is sleep. At least the pain isn't too bad." He paused.

"Look, I want to thank you," he continued slowly. "I don't remember much after getting hit. I didn't even know I'd been shot until I guess I heard the gun go off the second or third time. Kitty tells me you almost got the guy."

"Horseshoes. Close doesn't count."

"At least you tried."

I shrugged it off, embarrassed by the sentiment he obviously felt. "Temporary insanity. I'm normally not that stupid. Look, Brady, you've got a problem, a bigger one than you mentioned the other night."

"What do you mean?"

"The guy tried to kill you, that's what I mean."

"Who was he?"

"You tell me."

"How the hell should I know? I was on the sidewalk bleeding, remember? What did he look like?"

"I don't think you know him, Brady. He was a black guy, probably late twenties. Drove a purple car. That's not the point. I think someone hired this guy to hit you. Could it have anything to do with what you told me the other night?"

He looked bewildered. "Christ, no. Why would they want to kill me?"

"They? They, who?"

He shook his head. "I'm sorry, Emerson. I'm not tracking well. My head feels like it's stuffed with cotton. I don't know why anyone would want to kill me."

"No enemies?"

"Well, sure. But I can't think of anything I've done that warrants a bullet."

He seemed to be tracking fine to me. "What did you mean when you said 'they' wouldn't want to kill you?"

"I don't know. I didn't mean anything."

"You've got to be straight with me, Puppy. You're not into drugs or juice or anything like that?"

"No, damn it!"

"Okay. I had to ask. It happens to people. You remember what Peter Harriman was into? I got sucked into that mess, if you recall. It still gives me nightmares."

"I'm not Peter Harriman. That's not a fair comparison, just because he was a photographer."

"You're right. Sorry. But you get my point. People are not always what they seem. Sometimes they have something to hide. If you're hiding something, then I'm not the guy to help you out. I don't like getting shot at. It scares the piss out of me."

"Honest to Christ, I don't know why somebody took a

shot at me the other night." He spoke slowly and somberly, his brow furrowed, and I believed him.

"Well, think about it. The police will ask you the same thing, and this is an added complication we don't need right now. As for the other matter, checking out your people shouldn't be too much of a problem. In fact, this could make things easier. I can say that you asked me to hang around the studio to keep an eye on things while you're in the hospital. But I'll need to check out the ad agency, too. Who's the account rep?"

"Tom Bruce. But Jack Thane always has his finger in the pie on this account."

"Any ideas on how I might get in there?"

"Talk to Nell. She'll know what's going on. The agency might need a writer on a project. You might be able to swing a freelance assignment. That would put you inside."

"All right, I'll try it."

Brady yawned widely, then winced in obvious pain. He'd overextended himself, and I realized that I shouldn't have pressed him so hard.

"You'd better save your strength. If the nurse finds out I've had you talking this long, she'll kick me out of here. Why don't you get some sleep? I'll go to the studio when Kitty gets back and let them know what's happened."

"Okay." He yawned again, and his eyelids drooped. "Oh, Emerson? Don't let Nick give you a hard time." With that, his eyes closed, and he settled into sleep.

NELL REILLY SAT behind the reception desk in the foyer of the loft studio on west Ohio Street. The bottle-thick lenses of her glasses magnified her enormous, pretty hazel eyes as she glanced up. She wore a white cotton sleeveless sundress dotted with a pattern of tiny pastel flowers, and an unbuttoned sweater covered her bare shoulders against the chill of the air-conditioning. A smile lit up her face when she saw me, the kind of smile that makes you feel good inside no matter what your mood.

"Hello, Nell."

"Hello, stranger," she cried with delight, quickly rising and rounding the corner of the desk. She took both my hands and rose up on her toes to give me a light kiss on the cheek. "It's been too long, Emerson."

She stood close for a moment looking into my face, then flushed with sudden self-consciousness and dropped her gaze to the floor. The flush crept from her cheeks down her long, graceful neck, slowly reddening the milky skin, and ended with a small pink blotch at the top of the V-necked dress. She took a hesitant step back and let my hands drop gently from her grasp.

"We've missed you around here," she murmured, almost shyly. Then she looked up at me and smiled again, composure regained. She leaned back on the edge of the desk and folded her arms across her chest.

"What brings you down here, anyway? Brady's not in yet. I haven't heard from him this morning, but I'm sure he'll be in any time now."

"You haven't heard, then."

"Heard what?"

"Brady was shot the other night."

"Oh, no!" A hand went to her face, slender fingers covering her mouth. "Is he…?"

"He's all right. He's in ICU, but he's going to be fine."

"My god, what happened?"

I explained briefly, then put a hand on her shoulder. "Brady asked if I could spend a little time here, keep an eye on things. Okay with you?"

"Of course. It's so hard to believe…" She shook herself then, pushing aside her emotions, and stepped back into character, becoming the model of efficiency and organization Brady had recognized so many years before. "I'll have to check the calendar and see if we can juggle the shooting schedule for the next week or so. You'll want to use Brady's office, so I'll get that straightened up in a minute. And we need to tell everyone. Oh, and flowers for Brady's room and another arrangement for Kitty at home."

She had rounded the desk again, and was busily scribbling notes on a scratch pad.

"He's not allowed visitors yet, I take it."

"Just family. He should be out of ICU in a day or two, though."

"Fine. Emerson, have you met everyone here?"

"No, but I know some of the folks." I hesitated a minute. "Look, Nell, I don't want anyone to think I'm moving in and taking control. You people know what you're doing, and it should be business as usual. I'm just here to make Brady feel better."

"I understand. No big deal." She looked up from her writing. "Okay, let's go tell the staff."

She led me through a door behind the desk into a corridor of offices and open cubicles that held light tables and libraries of comp sheets of models of every shape, size, sex, and expression.

"Brady's office, if you remember, is down in the corner," she said over her shoulder, gesturing down the hall. She pushed through a wide set of double doors into the studio proper.

It was a cavernous expanse, divided into a half dozen or more photography bays on the right and support areas on the left, including a darkroom for black-and-white photography, more light tables, prop rooms and storage. The high ceiling faded out of sight in darkness, leaving the space eerily lit by the staged sets in only two of the bays. The first bay on the right was a full kitchen used both for food photography and as a company cafeteria and common area for the staff.

A loud angry voice emanated from somewhere close by as we entered the studio. "Goddamnit, Marty! That lab is butchering our chromes! I don't care what you say."

"Coffee?" Nell asked as though she hadn't heard, leading me into the brightly-lit kitchen.

She pushed past two men standing on opposite sides of the island in the center of the kitchen. The one standing closest to me was small—only five-foot-eight or so—but obviously once powerfully built with wide shoulders and a slim waist. A scowl darkened his olive complexion, eyes as hard as onyx under a thick sheaf of carefully groomed and oiled black hair. The lines in the chiseled face and the gray at his temples suggested he was older than he appeared. Nick Fratelli, I knew, had to be in his early sixties, though he looked to be still in his forties.

"It's not their fault," the other man said quietly as we entered. His voice was a nasal tenor, and it fit the thin acerbic face framed by horn-rimmed glasses. He was tall and slender, the lack of meat on his bones accentuated by the fact that his clothes—a dark plaid button-down shirt and gray cotton slacks—were baggy on him.

"If those fucks can't get it right, we shouldn't be using them," Nick growled through gritted teeth.

In the corner of the kitchen, a young woman stood with her back to us, busying herself at the counter, trying to ignore the argument. As I followed Nell to the coffee brewer I could almost see the woman wince as her shoulders tightened.

"Where the hell's Brady, anyway?" Nick said, whirling toward Nell. As he turned, he bumped into me, and I backpedaled a few steps to avoid getting under his feet. "And who the hell are you?" he growled again, throwing an ominous look at me.

"Nick, you remember Emerson Ward, Brady's friend?" Nell said sweetly, reaching past him to hand me a mug of coffee.

"Oh," he grunted, glancing at me again with a flicker of recognition. Just as quickly, his attention turned back to Nell. "Where's Brady? We've got a real problem here. We're going to have to re-shoot half the goddamn catalogue shots because the lab fucked up the color."

"Brady won't be in today," Nell said calmly, Nick's anger and abuse sliding off her like butter off Teflon.

"Why? What's *his* problem?"

"I have an announcement. Nancy, where's Sarah?" Nell turned to the girl at the counter.

The girl called Nancy started like a frightened fawn and turned, quickly swallowing a mouthful of what looked like a buttered croissant with jam, judging from the ingredients on the counter.

"I think she's in the prop room," she said. She was a pretty girl in her early twenties, but her large eyes and pale skin made her seem a little spooky, as though she was only half-girl, half-wraith.

"I'm here," another female voice called out loudly. A woman a little older than Nancy strode into the kitchen and over to the coffee machine. Tall and blonde, she, too, was attractive, but her earthy presence and obvious self-confidence made Nancy seem to fade even more from sight.

"Okay, that's everybody," Nell said. "Brady's not coming in because he's in the hospital. He was shot."

I took in their reactions. I suppose I hoped one of them

would look guilty or triumphant or *something*. Nancy and Marty looked shocked. Sarah looked curious. Nick still looked angry. I didn't see any sort of confession written on anyone's face.

"What? You're kidding, right?" Nick said impatiently.

"That was him?" Sarah murmured. "I wondered about that. They said the man was shot right outside Brady's house."

"He went to the emergency room Saturday night and had major surgery," Nell said, ignoring them, "so he probably won't be back for a couple of weeks. I'll send flowers from all of us. He can't have visitors yet, so there's no reason to go down there."

"Will he be all right?" Marty asked.

"Yes, he'll be fine," Nell reassured him. "Anyway, I checked the book this morning, and it doesn't look as if his absence will cause us too much trouble in scheduling."

"Great. Fucking great," Nick said, disgust in his voice.

"The only project he was really involved in was the sparkler shot, right, Nick?"

"Well, yeah," he said grudgingly.

"Then I'll call Irv and see if we can reschedule and push it back a week. That's simple. Any other problems?"

"Just these damn catalogue shots. I'm telling you, I'm not using that fucking lab anymore."

"Nick, the sets are still up, and if you want to switch labs, I'm sure Brady won't have any problem with it," Nell said soothingly.

"Yeah, right." Fratelli hesitated a moment, realizing that his anger was misspent—Nell had defused him. He shrugged. "All right, girls, get the sets ready. Marty, do the set-ups, pop some Polaroids, and let me know when

we're ready to go. Let's see if we can get this done without wasting the whole fucking day. I'll be in my office.''

Nick stalked out of the kitchen, residual anger tight-
ening his jaw. Nancy followed, bolting toward the depths
of the studio as though afraid of another reprimand. Sarah
sauntered after her, a small smile of amusement on her
face and a hint of strut in her walk. Marty just stood at
the island, shaking his head.

''It's not the lab,'' he muttered to himself.

''Why do you say that?'' I asked, curious now.

He started and looked up as though seeing me for the
first time, pushing his glasses back up on the bridge of
his nose with a forefinger.

''Marty Hopkins,'' he said, extending his hand. ''We've
met before.''

''Sure, I remember.''

''You know anything about photography?''

''A little. I use a camera on assignment occasionally.
Travel pieces and stuff.''

He nodded. ''Here, let me show you what I mean.'' He
picked up an eight-by-ten color transparency off the island
in front of him and walked over to a small light table on
the counter in a corner of the kitchen.

''See that?'' He made room for me and pointed to the
backlit photo. ''The lighting's flat, and there's not enough
depth to it. The color's fine; the lab had nothing to do
with it.''

''Can you fix it?''

''Sure. Pop the lighting here and here.'' He gestured
quickly at small areas of the transparency. ''Stop it down
to get more depth of field, and the whole set will have
more contrast, more richness. Nick's losing his touch. It's
not like him. This is simple stuff.''

He shook his head slowly, then shrugged, the bony

points of his shoulders showing through the fabric of his shirt.

"Well, I've got work to do." He picked up the transparency. "You going to be around?"

I nodded.

"Then I'll see you later. Nice talking with you." He ambled off with a slight stoop, as though his head was too heavy for the slender frame to carry.

"Marty appreciates it when people take an interest in his work," Nell said quietly, coming up behind me and taking my arm. "Come on, let's get you squared away."

"Will Nick get upset when Marty changes the lighting on the sets?" I asked as she led me back into the suite of offices.

"Maybe. Nobody knows what he's going to do these days," she said, then put a finger to her lips as we walked down the hall.

Brady's spacious office was furnished like his home, with big, comfortable pieces. An old oak desk, oak file cabinets and bookshelves dominated one half of the space. The other half was given over to a sitting area with a couch against the wall, a coffee table strewn with magazines and books of photography, two wing-backed chairs and end tables with antique lamps. Framed photos and artful posters covered the walls. I plunked down in the high-backed leather swivel chair behind the desk and watched Nell move to straighten up the coffee table.

"You didn't tell them why I'm here."

"They would have asked a lot of questions." She paused, and straightened to look at me. "Goodness, I don't even know why you're here. I mean, I understand Brady's concern, but we'll manage to muddle through without him for a time. He's wonderful to have around, even when he's not shooting. Everything seems to, well,

work better when he's here. They all know their roles and
stick to their jobs when he's here. And if they have problems, he fixes them. Things get a little more confused
when he's not around, as if people forget what they're
supposed to do, but we manage. They're all good at what
they do.''

''Is that everyone?''

''You mean on staff? Yes, except for Sharon, who
freelances for us when we need a food stylist. Oh, and
Billy, who we use sometimes on big projects as a 'go-
fer,''' She turned back to the coffee table.

I sat silently, digesting what she'd said. I could see how
Puppy's larger-than-life presence would have a calming
effect in the studio, sort of like a parent in the family.
When the parental figure is gone, the hierarchy changes,
and there's more jostling for position among the children,
more personality showing through, more demand for recognition. I realized, too, that Nell wielded a lot of influ-
ence, despite her modesty. She'd handled the announcement of Brady's absence adroitly, preempting questions
and keeping everyone focused on their tasks. But there
had also been a surprising lack of concern about Brady.

''Is there anything I can get you?'' Nell asked, interrupting my thoughts.

''Not that I can think of. Are you free for lunch?''

''Well, yes, I guess so.'' She blushed again suddenly,
as if startled by the idea. ''I'll see if Sarah can cover the
phones for an hour.''

''Great. Let me know when you're ready to go.''

I spent the morning wandering around the studio, getting a feel for the place, exploring the nooks and crannies.
No one paid much attention to me, but they were too busy
on the sets to notice much. At one point, I stood and
watched Marty wheel studio lights on stands around a set,

adjusting them, then coming back to the camera to get a view through the lens before returning to make more adjustments. All the while, Nick was busy in another bay ordering the girls around to fix this and straighten that. Finally, he wandered into the bay where Marty was working. He glanced wordlessly at the new lighting arrangement, but there was a grim set to his mouth as he stepped to the back of the camera. He took two steps up the short ladder set up next to the camera stand and pulled the cloth over his head for a long minute before emerging to eyeball the set again over the top of the camera.

"It'll do," he grunted. Then he turned and yelled, "Come on, girls! We haven't got all day to screw around!"

I saw Marty throw me a small conspiratorial smile and a brief nod as I walked away from the set. I admired his gumption. He didn't appear to be the sort to stand up to a man like Nick, but perhaps Fratelli was more bluster than bite.

Nell found me just after noon, and we walked up Franklin Street under the harsh weight of the July sun to a little deli a few blocks north. Nell carried her sweater over her arm, exposing her soft round shoulders to the sun, and I could almost see them slowly burn to pink in the heat. Her thick auburn hair was cut short, framing an attractive face with a pert nose. It could have been a very pretty face, but like the archetypal librarian or grade school teacher I always fell in love with as a child, she downplayed her looks, hiding behind the glasses and a lack of makeup, a straitlaced no-nonsense attitude and conservative taste in clothes. But she had an easy smile, and her occasional step out of character—like her greeting that morning or the way she sometimes moved—suggested a greater depth. I made a couple of silly comments on the way to lunch, and she laughed freely, spontaneously, then caught herself short each time, as though she thought her behavior inappropriate. Her combination of shyness and purpose intrigued me; I wondered what sort of passion lay beneath the surface.

We selected sandwiches and cold drinks, and I paid over her protestations. When we found a corner table away from the lunchtime crush, I held her chair while she got seated. Before she unwrapped her sandwich and began eating, Nell dug into her small purse and handed me two keys.

"Before I forget, you'll need these, I'm sure. This one is to the building, and the other is to the studio. I'll show you how to work the security system when we get back."

I held the keys over the table in surprise for a moment. "Are you always this free with access to the studio?"

"Emerson, please. You're Brady's friend. He sent you to keep an eye on things, so you should be able to get in and out when you want to. Should I not trust you?"

"Seriously, how many people have sets of keys to the studio?"

"Well, everyone on staff—Brady, Nick, Marty, Sarah, Nancy, and me. I give a set to Sharon when she works with us because she sometimes stays late to clean up the kitchen after a session with food. But she always returns them after a job. Let's see, who else? Billy doesn't have keys. Oh, Rosa, of course—she's the cleaning lady. And that's it."

"Sounds like a lot."

"Not really. Besides, sometimes people like to come in early; sometimes they stay late. It's not really a nine-to-five job all the time, and I'm certainly not going to be at everyone's beck-and-call when they want to get in. Why shouldn't they all have keys?'' She looked at me curiously.

"I guess you're right. I just never really thought about it. Thanks.'' I slipped the keys into my pocket. "How's Darlene?'' I asked, changing the subject.

"Oh, gosh, a typical teenager, I suppose. She's fine, but you remember high school…''

"Nope, don't remember a thing about it.'' Nell laughed, and I smiled with her. "I think that's one of those difficult periods of life that I have simply blanked from memory.''

"Well, I'll remind you. There's this thing called dating, and there's peer pressure, and there are clothes, and girlfriends, and the telephone, and curfews, and a lot of disagreement about all of those things, including some close to knock-down-drag-out fights. But she's a pretty good kid, and for the most part, we get along okay. It's not easy, but we've managed to stay friends through all of this. Raising children isn't easy, I can tell you. Just when you think you've got it figured out, they grow up a little more, and there's something else to deal with, until finally they're just gone out of your life. I can't believe she'll be off to college soon.''

I smiled. "What is she now? Sixteen? I'll bet she's breaking a lot of hearts.''

Nell rolled her eyes. She was a young mother, having married and gotten pregnant early, probably before she was twenty. The marriage hadn't lasted long, and she'd raised her daughter by herself ever since.

"Amazing,'' I murmured. "You've worked for Brady that long?''

"Almost,'' she said with her mouth full, then paused to swallow and lick a dab of mayonnaise from the corner of her mouth with the tip of her tongue. "It's been fifteen

years. I got the job when Darlene was just a year old. Vic
hated the thought of me working, but we needed the
money, and I liked the job. I told Vic I wouldn't quit, and
I think that was the final straw. We broke up after that.
I've been there longer than anyone except Nick.''

"Really?"

She nodded. ''Nick's been there from the start. He and
Brady go back nearly forty years. I'm not sure how they
met, but I think Nick had learned photography in voca-
tional school, and was freelancing whatever he could for
the newspapers back then. Brady liked his stuff and took
him in.''

''That must have been tough when Brady was just starting out. Nick is good, I take it.''

''Technically, yes,'' she said, chewing another mouthful of food. ''He's an excellent technician—lighting,
framing a shot... But Brady has the eye. He could have
been another Ansel Adams or Helmut Newton, but he
didn't have the ambition. Well, that's not quite true. I
guess it's more as if he didn't have the passion. He decided he wanted to make money, not create art, so he went
commercial. He and Nick sort of complement each other,
but Brady would be successful with or without Nick. Nick
needs Brady.''

''What about Marty?''

She smiled. ''I like him. He's been with us for about
eight years. To tell you the truth, I think he's almost as
good as Brady. Better, maybe, because he's as good a
technician as Nick *and* he has an eye. But no one's given
him a chance. But it doesn't seem to bother him. I think
he knows he's good, but he's not egotistical about it. I
don't think it's ever occurred to him that he could be more
than what he is. He's comfortable doing what he's doing,

and he doesn't seem to mind letting Brady and Nick take all the credit.''

"What, exactly, is he?"

"You mean his title? Chief Assistant, but we don't pay a lot of attention to that sort of stuff. Titles might make a difference in a big company, but not with a staff of six. We all know what we do.''

"And the girls?"

"They're all right.'' There was a momentary look of distaste on her face. "Sarah is a little too smart-mouth for her own good. It will probably get her in trouble one of these days. And poor Nancy... Well, you saw her—as timid as a rabbit. She used to do window displays for one of the department stores down on State Street. You know, late at night when no one was around. She's not good around people, but she's good on the sets. I just don't know if she'll last. When the studio gets really busy, she runs around in near panic.''

"She seemed all right this morning. I mean, I can see she's the nervous type, but she seemed in control.''

"We're quiet today. These catalogue shots are easy; we've been doing them for years. The client doesn't even come in for the shoot anymore, except maybe for a planning meeting and lunch with Brady. Usually, during a shoot like this, the studio is crawling with people—clients, agency account executives, art directors, sometimes models. It can get to be a real zoo. We try to limit the number of people, but clients and agency people love to get out of the office. They think what we do is glamorous.''

"Isn't it?" I smiled.

She laughed. "Stick around a while longer, Emerson. You'll get bored to tears. It's a lot of physical and tedious work getting the shots set up, and a lot of sitting around and waiting while film is developed to see what you got.''

"A little like sex, huh? All that work, and bang, with a click of the shutter, it's over in a fraction of a second."

Her eyes widened, and she laughed again, but her blush turned her cheeks crimson this time. She was good company, and we chatted about nearly everything it seemed for the better part of the hour we had. The time passed all too quickly, but when I saw her glance at her watch a second time, I knew she was feeling guilty about being gone so long.

"I'm sorry," I said. "You want to get back, and I'd better head for the hospital. I promised Kitty I'd stay with Brady while she got some sleep. I'm neglecting my duty." I rose and walked around the table to hold her chair for her while she got up.

When we were out on the street, I broached the other subject that had been on my mind during lunch.

"I wonder if you could do me a favor, Nell."

"Of course."

"I'd like to get to know the folks over at Thane Communications, but I need an excuse to hang out over there. Is there anyone you could call to find out if they need a writer on a project?"

"I could talk to Peggy McNeal. She would know."

"I'd really appreciate it."

She stopped walking and looked at me curiously, silent for a moment. "What are you up to, anyway?" she murmured.

There was no good answer except the truth, and I wasn't ready to share that with her. So I said nothing.

"All right," she said, walking again.

She'd accepted my silence in lieu of an explanation, but I sensed a sudden distance between us that hadn't been there moments before. Sometimes I wished I didn't have this need to fight other people's causes.

FOUR

I SHOWED UP BRIGHT AND EARLY Tuesday morning in front of Peggy McNeal's desk, wearing a light blue two-piece summer suit, tie, and stiffly starched shirt that had already wrinkled in the heat on the way downtown. She looked me up and down slowly with cool green eyes. Her pixie face was framed by short, straight brown hair in a pageboy cut above the open collar of her blouse. A small gold and ivory cameo, hanging on a delicate gold chain in the soft hollow of her throat, stood out against her tan skin. Her slow appraisal caused a corner of her mouth to turn up slightly in approval, almost making me blush.

"So, you're the new guy." She stood up and came around the desk, giving me the chance to eyeball her in return. She was slim and athletically built, but small, making me think of a teenage gymnast.

"Come on, I'll give you the tour and show you where you sit." She grasped my arm above the elbow and gently pulled, letting me know in no uncertain terms who was in charge.

Thane Communications took up one whole floor of the Michigan Avenue office building. Peggy led me around the floor, stopping briefly in each department—creative, account staff, media, mail room, et cetera—explaining office services and policies with running commentary. She finally ushered me into an airless, windowless inside office that was bare save for a desk, two chairs, computer terminal, and a few forlorn scraps of paper adorning a small wooden bookcase on one wall. The cold, blue-white light of the overhead fluorescent fixture made the space even less welcoming.

"This is where you'll sit. Your extension number's on the phone. I'll get you a procedures manual to explain the phone system and faxes and stuff. If you need anything else—paper or supplies or anything—just yell. I'll be back in a while."

I took off my jacket and sat, rocking gently in the swivel desk chair, shivering a little as the cool wind from the air-conditioning vent dried the last vestiges of sweat that had kept patches of shirt fabric stuck to my skin. I stared thoughtfully at the blank walls, grateful that I had enough business of my own to preclude a daily eight-hour stint in an atmosphere as stifling as this. Sure, it was fun to play dress up and put on a coat and tie once in a while like the lawyers and investment bankers on LaSalle Street or these ad goons on Michigan Avenue. And I sometimes missed the office camaraderie, the human contact. But I'd done my suit-silk-tie-and-suspenders tour as a stockbroker years before. I found that I'm more comfortable in casual clothes, and that I'm my own best company. The consulting and writing I did afforded me perhaps the best of both worlds—an occasional expense account lunch or dinner with a client, the freedom to say no to a job, a close circle of personal friends, and no need to play office politics.

Shortly after Peggy left, a tallish woman with a mane of dark, nearly jet-black hair staggered in on spike heels under the weight of a large stack of books, file folders and papers. I quickly rounded the desk to help. I got my hands under the stack, and she leaned forward, almost brushing my cheek with her hair, tipping the whole pile into my arms. I put the pile on the desk then turned to face her.

"Thanks." She extended a slender hand. Her long fingers were tipped with flame-red nails. "Jayne Thompson."

"Emerson Ward."

She held my hand a moment longer than she had to, and again I had the feeling I was being sized up. Beneath the halo of dark hair was a striking heart-shaped face with baby cheeks and a mouth and eyes that both turned down at the corners, giving the impression she was about to cry at any moment. The full lips were emphasized with the same shade of red she wore on her fingernails. She wore a filmy, white, long-sleeved silk blouse with straight lapels that barely revealed the outline of a lacy white bra underneath. A single strand of pearls circled the long neck. Dark stockings, and a tight, short silk skirt that was obviously part of a suit completed the outfit.

She glanced behind her to find a chair and pulled it up close to the desk. I took it as an invitation to sit.

"I hear you're good. Ever written annual reports before?"

"Plenty."

"Good. We're up against it." She spent the next ten minutes briefing me, then left me on my own.

I spent most of the day going through the files Jayne had dumped on my desk. I took frequent breaks, though, to wander the halls and hang out in the lunchroom. It felt good to stretch my legs, but I had an ulterior motive—eavesdropping on office gossip.

Peggy invited me to lunch. We kept the conversation light, and I enjoyed her company, but I had the distinct feeling that she was sizing me up as potential mating ma-

terial. Everywhere I went these days the ticking of biological clocks seemed deafening. Feigning natural curiosity, I gently pumped her for office dirt. She seemed to
relish the opportunity to dish it.

It was late afternoon when a knock on my office door
made me look up from the files strewn across the desk.
Peggy leaned around the door frame.

"You have everything you need?"

I nodded.

"Well, I just stopped by to say goodnight. See you
tomorrow."

I looked at my watch. It was after 5:00. "I didn't know
it was so late. Yeah, see you tomorrow."

When she left, I rose and stretched, then tried to tidy
up the desk before shrugging into my suit coat and heading out the door. I hadn't learned much. Two people were
being let go because their account was changing agencies.
Yet Thane had just won a big piece of business. It didn't
make sense. Other than that, I hadn't picked up anything
juicy from the office grapevine.

Wednesday morning, after getting up early for a lei-
surely cup of coffee and taking the Michigan Avenue bus
down to the office, I called Chris Ruys to see if she was
free for lunch. She agreed to meet me at noon, so I called
Avanzare for reservations. I met with Jayne Thompson
and let her know that I thought I had everything I needed
for the time being. And for the next few hours, I pushed
aside all thoughts of anything except the project at hand.
By 11:30, I'd written copy for two of eight spreads in the
annual report, with only one brief time-out to refill my
coffee mug and make a phone call. I reread the words on
the computer screen as they scrolled past, then filed the
copy with satisfaction. On my way out, I let Peggy know
I was going to lunch, and walked the few short blocks

over to Avanzare. The day was a carbon copy of Tuesday, and I was glad I'd opted for baggy cotton slacks, white sport shirt and seersucker sport jacket instead of a more formal suit and tie.

I waited only a few minutes near the bar before Chris showed up. She ran her own successful public relations firm out of offices in the building next door on St. Clair, so she hadn't had far to come. Her face lit up when she saw me, making me smile, and we brushed cheeks in greeting. A tall, elegant, and slightly blond Chris had an oval face with high cheekbones, button nose, and wide smile. We'd known each other for some time, but saw each other only occasionally. At one point, we'd almost become romantically involved, but some instinct had warned me off, a feeling that we were better off as friends. At first she'd felt slighted, and I felt like a cad for turning down the opportunity and hurting her feelings, but my instincts had been right. We were still friends.

"It's great to see you," I told her as we were shown to a table. "You look fabulous."

We ordered drinks—sparkling water for both of us— and caught up on each other's news while looking over the menu. She'd warned me that she didn't have much time, so when the waiter returned, we were ready to order lunch.

"How's your love life?" I asked when the waiter left.

"I'm actually dating a guy," she laughed. "I even like him, which is saying a lot. These days, if they're single, disease-free, and likable, you're doing pretty well. We'll see. Men are so scared of commitment, I'm not going to get serious about this guy."

"I hope things work out. You deserve it." I paused for a moment. "Chris, what do you know about Jack Thane?"

Besides being one of the best publicists in Chicago, Chris knew a lot of people in town and often had a line on the latest gossip.

"Other than the fact that he's an egomaniac, and most people I know think he's a jerk, what do you want to know?"

"How's his business going?"

"Not that well, from what I hear. He lost that big food account last year, you know."

"Yes, I heard. I also heard yesterday that they just picked up another food account worth about twelve million."

"That's right. I read in *Ad Age* that they were pitching the business. Grabel Foods, isn't it?"

I nodded. "So if he's winning all these accounts, why isn't he doing well?"

"He's overextended. He opened the Chicago office about four years ago, but last year Thane acquired another small agency here in town, merged the two, and moved his people into the other agency's offices. And, before they lost that big account, he closed on the acquisition of an agency down in Atlanta. The rumors I hear are that the Atlanta office is doing horribly, losing accounts right and left. Despite the buyout, Thane hasn't been able to stop the bleeding down there. So, he's got some serious financial troubles."

"Cash flow, mostly?"

"I suppose. I mean, I'm sure it's great he just won a big new account, but it won't generate much income for a while. These things take time. In the meantime, what I hear he's losing in Atlanta has got to be hurting."

"Interesting," I murmured.

"Why do you ask?" She looked at me with curiosity for the first time.

"I'm over there doing a freelance job, heard rumors, and wanted to be sure Thane could pay my bill."

She laughed at the joke, then turned serious a moment later. "Emerson, you know that all I've heard are rumors, too."

"I know—I didn't hear it from you. I always protect my sources, Chris. You know that."

"Thanks." She smiled again.

The rest of lunch was enjoyably spent trading gossip about mutual acquaintances, and after parting ways at the front door, I walked back to my temporary office with a smile on my face, glad that I'd taken the time to meet with her. We didn't see each other often enough.

When I got home from work, there was a voicemail message from Lanahan. They'd traced the gun to an old man in Ukrainian Village named Milan Kulas. He had reported the gun stolen two weeks earlier. The gun, it seemed, was a dead end.

"HOW'S IT GOING?"

"Not very well, I'm afraid."

Nell sat at her desk in the studio reception room, brows furrowed in a look of confusion and concern, staring intently at a ledger in front of her. She glanced up at me, and her expression softened only a little on seeing my smile.

"Irv Steinmetz just walked in and he's furious about rescheduling the shoot. He's threatening to pull the job and go to another studio. Nick is in one of his black moods, and if he could, he'd blame me for the fact that Brady's in the hospital. Nancy is terrified, so she's no help. She's hiding somewhere; she always does when Nick gets this way. And Sarah, I think, has PMS. She's been irritable and mean all morning. When I asked her to help make coffee and set out sweet rolls and fruit, she told me to go...well, do something with myself."

She flushed at the mere thought of the expletive that had come to mind, making her even more endearing.

"So," she continued, "what more could be wrong?"

"I don't know. But it sounds as if those are just annoyances. You have something else on your mind."

"No, those aren't just annoyances," she countered firmly, eyes sparking and nostrils flaring. "My goodness, when a client says he's going to pull a job, that's a real problem. I'm just so tired of baby-sitting these people. I'm not their mother, for goodness sake, and they can't expect *me* to solve all their problems. Even Brady..." She let it go, suddenly aware that she had lost her usual composure. "I'm sorry."

"I can guess how hard it must be without Brady here."

"It's hard enough sometimes when he is here," she said calmly now. "He can be as big a baby as the rest of them. And you're right. I do have a more troublesome problem."

"What is it?"

"I don't want to bother you with it." She spoke demurely, as though embarrassed by her outburst. I'd never seen her angry before.

"Please. Maybe I can help."

"Well, it's the books. Things just aren't adding up. Here, look."

I came around behind her, put a palm on the edge of the desk and leaned down to peer over her shoulder at the ledger. She smelled faintly of baby powder, clean and fresh.

"It's time to write checks for bills, see, and the checking account is short this month. Clients have been slow to pay invoices lately for some reason, but I try to pay our suppliers on time, no matter what. When cash flow is good, we siphon off money we don't need and put it into a money market account to earn interest. When there's an excess in the money market account, Brady sometimes moves money into longer-term CDs, which pay even better interest. If cash flow is tight, like this month, we just move funds from the money market account back into the checking account.

"This morning, when I started to write a check on the money market account so we'd have funds to pay bills, I noticed that the balance is almost zero, well below the minimum."

"Maybe Brady moved money into another CD."

"Why would he do that when the checking account is so short?"

"Maybe he didn't realize how low on cash you are. Or maybe he expected a check from a client. How are your receivables?"

"Well, we do have a lot outstanding, and payments for some invoices should be in any day now."

"There you have it. Can you wait on the bills for a few days?" I straightened up, and she swiveled the chair to look at me.

"I suppose so. We're current with everybody, so none of them will cut us off, I guess."

"I know, I hate to make payments late, too. In the meantime, why don't I ask Brady what he did with the money market funds when I see him?"

"Would you?" She looked relieved. "I didn't think I should bother him in the hospital."

"Sure. Anything else I can do?"

"Goodness, I'm not sure you want to go in there, but you might want to see if you can mollify Irv. You've seen Brady. Maybe you can convince Irv that he really *was* shot. Despite the fact that it's been in the papers and everything, Irv seems to think I'm rescheduling the session to give Brady a vacation." Her sweet smile couldn't disguise the exasperation in her voice.

"Gladly, ma'am." I gave her a short bow.

She laughed. "Thank you, Emerson. What would I have done without you this morning?"

Beyond the reception room door, the muffled sounds of angry voices reverberated through the hallway. When I pushed through the double doors into the studio, the voices became loud and clear. The scene in the large kitchen bay was not a happy one. A small man with a bald pate encircled by a fringe of gray hair sat at the oak kitchen table. He had too little chin and a large nose that was red at the tip. Perched on the bridge were wire-rimmed spectacles with thick lenses that magnified bulging eyes.

"God damn it, Nick!" he was saying. "You know we're on a tight schedule with this one. It's a new campaign, and we have to have film to twenty national magazines and god knows how many regional magazines in less than four weeks! We can't push the shoot back a week! It's just not possible. You must be able to do something!" Flame-red spots high on his cheeks and taut tendons in his neck were evidence of his anger. Nick was seated across from him, fingers laced around a cup of coffee, eyes glumly on the table in front of him, taking the harangue in silence.

Leaning against the island in the center of the kitchen, ankles casually crossed and arms folded across his chest, was Tom Bruce. His suit coat, I saw, was hanging on the back of a chair at the table, and his shirtsleeves, to no surprise, were carefully rolled up one turn of the cuff. He faced the men at the table and wore a serious look on his face. Marty was on the other side of the island, leaning over some papers, seemingly oblivious to the voices. And on the far side of the kitchen, sitting cross-legged on a stool at the counter, was Sarah, looking sullen and resentful.

"Good morning, campers." I said it quietly, but cheerfully, making my way over to the coffee brewer. "Anyone for more coffee?"

"Who the hell are you?" Steinmetz snapped.

"Oh, Jesus," Nick groaned. "We're in a meeting, Ward, as if you hadn't noticed. Go away."

Bruce had glanced at me sharply in surprise, Marty hadn't appeared to notice my entrance, and Sarah continued to look sullen. I grabbed a full pot of coffee off the warmer and took it over to the table to refill the mugs in front of Nick and Steinmetz.

"Who *is* this guy?" Steinmetz directed the question to Nick.

"Emerson Ward," Nick said wearily as I turned to pour more coffee in Bruce's cup. "He's a friend of Brady's."

I could feel Bruce's eyes on me as I carefully tipped the coffeepot. When his mug was full, I met his gaze.

"You were in the office the other day, right?"

I nodded. "I'm working on the NLMB annual report with Jayne."

"I thought I'd seen you." The look was smug, self-satisfied. "So, what are you doing here?"

"Like Nick said, Brady's a friend of mine. He asked me to drop in occasionally, see if I could help out, be a messenger while he's in the hospital."

"Yeah, well you can tell the S.O.B. I don't care if he's dying," Nick growled at me. "He should get his ass out of bed and back here in the studio." He paused and sighed. "Ah, shit, don't tell him that. I take it back."

He turned back to face Steinmetz, and his voice took on a pleading quality. "Look, Irv, the fact is we can't get the lighting right on the shot without Brady. Not the way Tom's people have it laid out, anyway. You've got to give us a few days, at least until Brady's well enough to give us some advice on this one."

Steinmetz glanced up at me. "He's bad?"

I shrugged. "Brady's tough. But they pulled a thirty-eight slug out of him that did a lot of damage going in. He'll be out of action for a while. Nick's got a good idea, though. A few more days, and Brady might be up to some consulting."

"I think I can do it," a voice said softly behind me. We all turned to look at Marty. He looked at each of us in turn.

"Without special effects?" Nick asked sharply.

"I still don't see why you can't play with the chrome in the lab and add the effects later," Bruce interjected.

"Any decent studio can do that," Steinmetz said coldly. "We're here, Tommy, because Brady and Nick have worked magic for us for years. It gives us bragging rights, and it's won us—and them—a lot of awards over the years."

"Shit, this layout will still win you awards, no matter how you shoot it," Bruce grumbled, angry at the patronizing tone.

"What do you have in mind, Marty?" Steinmetz asked, ignoring Bruce.

"The layout's easy if you use effects, no doubt about it," Marty said in his calm, nasal voice. "Tough, of course, if you don't. But I've got a couple of ideas that might work. Give me a day, two at most, and let me play with it. I'm pretty sure I can make it work."

Nick turned to see Steinmetz's reaction. "What do you say, Irv? Give us two days."

In a curious gesture, Irv leaned forward, elbow on the table and softly patted the top of his bald head, as though it would help him think. "You really think you can handle it?" he asked, glancing at Marty.

"If Marty says he can do it, then he can do it," Nick said. I was surprised that he would stick up for Marty with such conviction.

"All right. Two days. You show me what you've got, and we'll see where we go from there. Tommy, let's go back to the agency and talk to Hank. I want to go over the media plan again. I'm not sure he's making some very smart buys for us."

"Sure, Irv." Annoyance passed over his face like a cloud, and then he was all smiles again, eager to please his client. He pushed himself away from the countertop and walked to the table to get his coat.

I strolled over to the counter to find a clean mug, since I still had the coffeepot in hand. By the time I fixed a cup and turned around, Bruce had made his way to the double doors and was standing patiently, waiting for his client. Marty had taken all the papers on the island back into the depths of the studio with him. Sarah had quietly disappeared, and Nick and Irv stood talking at the table while Irv got his things together.

"Why didn't you tell me that Marty could help work this out?" Steinmetz asked in a low voice.

"He's never even seen the layouts until now," Nick replied peevishly. "He's been busy on other projects, and you've always insisted on Brady for this shoot."

"I've seen Marty's work. He's good. If he's free, let's see what he can do. I'm surprised at you, Nick. You could have stepped up to the plate on this one."

"Hell, if I'd known you didn't care *who* shot the damn layout, we could have settled this first thing without a pissing contest. If you want Marty on this one, you've got him."

"You said you couldn't handle the shot without Brady. Marty says he can. Sounds like you're losing your touch, Nick." Steinmetz hefted his briefcase and walked out of the bay, then stopped and turned. "I'll be back day after tomorrow," he called.

Nick waited motionless until Steinmetz left with Bruce at his heels like an obedient puppy, then stalked out of the kitchen with a look of disgust on his face. No, the House of Barnes was not a happy campground right now. If Brady had known what was happening in the studio, I think he would have preferred being in the hospital.

I took another swallow of coffee and wandered back to Brady's office to sit and think for a minute. After a few moments of indecision, I buzzed Nell on the intercom and asked her to come in. She stepped in the office a minute later with a quizzical look on her face. I motioned to a chair, and after a moment's hesitation she sat down.

"It's obvious that you run things here," I started slowly, pacing in front of her. "You keep the books, schedule the photo sessions, answer the phones, pay the bills and handle payroll, and who knows what else. And despite the fact that Brady's boss, from what I've seen you're the glue that holds this place together. What does Brady pay you for all this?"

The question surprised her, but she responded politely, with no defensiveness in her voice. "That's none of your business."

"How much?" I asked firmly.

Her expression turned quizzical again. "Seven hundred a week."

I did a quick mental calculation. "Is it enough?"

"Well, no, not really. Not with tuition for private school for Darlene. But we manage just fine, thank you."

I nodded. "You're worth more. Look, I'm sorry to have put you on the spot, but I have to trust someone in this place, and you're it. I don't know you that well despite the fact that we've said hello for years. That's my fault, and my loss, and I'd like to start making up for that. But I think I know you well enough to trust you."

Her skin was flushed, with anger now, not because she felt flattered. I could see she was about to speak, but I held up a hand.

"I'm being presumptuous to make a point. You know the business and the people here better than anyone, except maybe Brady. And we both found out today that Brady can still keep secrets even from you.

"If you think you had trouble here today, you've just seen the beginning. The real reason I'm hanging around these days is because somebody stole the entire Winton collection out of the safe and replaced it with fake gems. Brady discovered the switch last week and asked me if I could help out before calling in the police."

She paled as fast as she'd blushed, but there was no sign of guilt on her face. I'd made the right decision.

"I don't know if Irv told you on the way out, but Marty is going to try to set up the lighting for the shot and do the photography. Which means that in a matter of days, it's possible that Irv will find out the gems are fake. If that happens, this place will be up for grabs."

"Oh, my god," she murmured. "You don't know how it happened?"

"Nobody does."

"How did Brady find out?"

"One of the stones was smashed on the set last week,

so Brady had them checked out by a jeweler. The reason I'm telling you all this is because if someone else discovers the theft, you're going to have to work extra hard to hold this place together. It's not going to be pretty. I know that's going to be tough on you, but you have to hang in and keep things going.

"The other reason I'm telling you is because I need your help. I want you to think of anyone who could have had access to the studio—former employees, for example."

"You don't think one of us did it, do you?" She looked startled, and a little frightened.

"Frankly, I don't know. I told you, I trust you. But I can't rule anyone else out. And I need to find people with a possible motive. Like someone who used to work here who might hold a grudge against Brady, or who knew about the shoot and saw a chance to get rich quick."

"I guess it could be possible," she mused. The shock was wearing off, and she was back in control. "We haven't changed the locks in ages, and I don't think we've ever changed the alarm code, not since I've been here. When people leave, I've always made sure they give back their keys to the studio."

"Keys are easy to duplicate." I paused. "Anyone come to mind?"

"No. We've had a couple of reps over the years, but they never had keys. Most of them handled more than one client, so they worked out of their own places, and came in only occasionally. But I'll think about it."

"That's all I ask. I'm sorry to lay all this on you. Something about this whole situation doesn't feel right, and right now I'm just poking around. I could use your help."

"I'll try."

MICHAEL W. SHERER   87

"Thanks. I'm going to go see Brady. I'll ask him about the account, okay? And remember, not a word to anyone."

"Goodness, no. I won't tell a soul."

FIVE

I TOOK A CAB over to the hospital. It was too hot and sticky to walk. The staff in ICU told me Brady had been moved upstairs, which I took to be a good sign. But when I found the private room, he didn't look good. He seemed to have shrunk, withered by the lack of real food and the internal struggle his body fought to heal the massive wounds. His graying hair was tousled and greasy, and the beard was scraggly and unkempt. A sheen of oil and perspiration covered his forehead. Despite the fact that the room was cooler than it was outside, the air-conditioning couldn't dissipate the mugginess of July. Hospital sponge baths, I knew from experience, could help prevent you from turning up your nose at the overripe smell of yourself. But there was nothing like a shower to speed the healing process. Brady would be begging for one soon, if he hadn't already.

Kitty was in a chair by the window reading a magazine when I walked in. She looked up and put a finger to her lips when she saw me. I tiptoed over to the window and sat in an empty chair across from her.

"How is he?" I asked in a low voice.

"I don't know," she whispered. "I guess it's good that he's out of ICU, but he's in a lot of pain. And you can see how awful he looks. He seems so much older somehow. Like he's tired of fighting. I never thought about the difference in our ages, but now it shows. I can't help thinking about how my father looked when he died. It scares me, Emerson.''

I reached over and patted her hand. "How about you? How are you holding up?"

"I'm okay. Tired, that's all. And worried, of course. He's been asleep all morning, and I can't help wondering, what if he doesn't wake up? What will I do then?"

She searched my face with her eyes, but I didn't have an answer. After a moment, she bit her lower lip and looked out the window, then turned silently back to her magazine.

There was another half hour of silence, broken only by the labored sounds of breathing from the bed and occasional muffled voices from out in the hall before Brady groaned and stirred in his sleep. A few moments later, his eyelids fluttered open, and Kitty was at his bedside when they did. She was all smiles now, radiating warmth and cheer, giving Brady the only medicine she could offer. She took his hand and gently kissed his temple.

"Good morning, darling. How do you feel?"

"Like two-day-old dog-do." His smile was wan, but showed he still had spirit. "Thanks for asking."

"Are you in pain?"

He nodded. "A lot. And I'm thirsty." His voice was gravelly and weak.

Kitty glanced at her watch. "You're due for a shot. I'll talk to the nurses. Emerson's here. We've been visiting while you were asleep." She poured a glass of water from a plastic pitcher on the nightstand next to the bed while she talked, and helped him take small sips. Then she carefully tugged and pulled him a little more upright, fluffing his pillows and rearranging the sheet that covered him.

When he was comfortable, Brady turned his head to look at me. "So, do I still have a business?"

"Of course. Nell's got everything under control."

"I don't know what I'd do without her."

"Now don't get him thinking about work," Kitty admonished me. "I'm going to see the nurses. Find something nice to talk about while I'm gone. Tell him some dirty jokes or something."

"Sure." I smiled.

When she left the room, I got up and walked over to sit on the edge of Brady's bed.

"Okay, tell me what's going on," he rasped.

"You sure you're up for it?"

"The pain's pretty bad, but better now than after they give me another shot. I can't think straight when I'm doped up."

Briefly, I told him what had happened that morning, that Nell had tried to reschedule the photo session. I told him about Irv's reaction, and Marty's offer to help.

"Christ, I guess I should have expected we couldn't stall for long."

"Can Marty do the job?"

"You know, I think he probably can." He looked surprised, as though he'd never considered the possibility.

"Sooner or later, someone's going to notice that one of the gems is missing. There will be a whole lot of questions."

"Then you don't have much time. Have you got anything yet?"

"Jack Thane's in financial trouble. Could be a motive there for some quick cash. But he wouldn't have made the switch himself, and my gut tells me that Tom Bruce didn't do it. I think he'd lie and cheat to get ahead and maybe help Jack out, but I don't think he has the balls to steal, not like this. Anyway, Nell put in a word for me, and I've got a project over at the agency, so I'll keep nosing around.

"Steinmetz? I don't know. Seems to me he'd go along with a delay if he took the stones. Unless he wants to draw attention away from himself by being the one to discover the switch and raise the alarm. You know, play the indignant client. As for your people, the only one I'm sure about, the only person I trust, is Nell."

I paused. Brady looked at me silently, without expression.

"You know, I can't help feeling that whoever did it had to have had inside help, Puppy. What about someone who used to work for you? Someone who might still have a key to the studio?"

"I'll think about it," he said quietly, frowning.

Watching his face, I had a sudden sense that he was disappointed. I couldn't put my finger on it exactly. It was almost as if he knew something that I was supposed to discover, but hadn't. I didn't like the feeling. It left me a little queasy in the gut.

"By the way," I said after a moment, "Nell says she's short in the checking account, and wanted to know why you moved funds out of the money market account."

For an instant, he looked startled, then he waved a hand feebly. "I needed the money. I thought I could cover it before Nell wrote checks for the bills."

"What for, Puppy?"

He blinked before answering. "Kitty's birthday is coming up. I've had my eye on a diamond necklace for her, and I was a little short. Besides, *Urban Living* owes us for a big session last month. The check should be in any day. It's more than Nell needs. Tell her not to worry so much."

"All right." He'd been quick and convincing, but there had been something in his eyes. Maybe just pain. I shrugged it off.

Brady yawned and sagged back into the pillows.

"Sorry. I shouldn't have kept you talking so long. Don't worry about any of this. I'll handle it. You just worry about getting well."

"Thanks, Emerson. I'm sorry I'm so drained." He sighed. "Look, if you want to check out people who used to work for me, the personnel files are in the locked file cabinet in my office. Keys are in my top desk drawer. Bring them in and I'll go over them with you."

"Okay." The concession made me wonder if my feeling had been wrong.

He'd talked too much, overexerting himself, and he winced suddenly. "I'm starting to hurt pretty bad again. Could you find out where Kitty is with that nurse?"

"Sure. I'll see you later, okay?"

He gave me another feeble wave and a flicker of a smile, his attention already diverted by pain. I walked out to find Kitty and have a couple of words with her before I left. I suggested bringing dinner over to her house, figuring she probably wasn't getting too many regular meals, and after some convincing, she accepted.

I SPENT THE AFTERNOON back at the agency immersing myself in the annual report, putting everything else out of my mind. It was a little trick I'd learned. Writers can be among the foremost procrastinators in the world. We come up with a brilliant story idea, we figure we deserve a break. We write a couple of paragraphs that really sing, we reward ourselves with a break. I'd learned to compartmentalize; when I had a lot of projects going at once, I mentally juggled them, switching from one task to another with ease. But when it was time to write, it was a matter of clearing the slate, emptying the mind of everything but the topic at hand.

By the time the five o'clock whistle blew, I'd finished another three spreads, and I pushed away from the desk in satisfaction. It was a good day's work, and *now* I deserved a break. I stopped at the Treasure Island on Elm on the way north and picked up a pound of Greek salad, some marinated asparagus wrapped in prosciutto, a package of boneless chicken breasts, a bottle of wine for Kitty and beer for me. I walked the rest of the way up Dearborn to the Barnes house with my grocery bag.

Kitty met me at the front door when she heard the bell, and led me back to the kitchen to unload my supplies. She'd showered and changed into shorts, sandals, and a sleeveless blouse, and had merely brushed her hair back wet and touched up her face sparingly. She looked better than she had in days. I uncorked the bottle of wine and poured her a glass and opened a beer for myself before putting anything away. Kitty gave me what I needed to cut up the chicken and I put it in a pan with lime juice to marinate. When the initial preparations were finished, Kitty suggested we sit outside.

Cushioned, wrought iron chairs and a glass-topped wrought iron table stood under a tree in the small back yard, and we took our drinks out with us. I lit the gas grill standing next to the foot of the porch stairs before joining Kitty at the table.

"Ah, this is a lot better than being in the office," I sighed, leaning back in the chair and taking a sip of my beer.

"It's nice to have you here. I wish Brady could be with us. It would be like the old days when you came around more often."

"I don't know why I haven't. Just busy, I guess."

"Is Brandt throwing a party again this summer?"

"I would imagine so." Brandt's annual August bash was the stuff legends were made of, a rollicking affair that started at noon on a Saturday and usually rolled into Sunday brunch. It was the kind of party where the beer and margaritas flowed incessantly, and just when things seemed to be dying down, a new batch of revelers would arrive and join in to liven things up.

"Maybe Brady will be up and around by then."

"I hope so, Kitty."

She was silent, and I tried to think of something that would take her mind off Brady, if only for a little while.

"I'm curious about Nick," I said finally. "What's his story?"

"Nick's, well, Nick. I don't know. How do you describe someone who's been with your husband longer than any of his wives? You know, Brady without Nick is like Johnny Carson without Ed McMahon; you just can't imagine it. Brady's big, sometimes loud, boisterous. Nick's small, dark, serious, moody. They're perfect foils for each other.

"I guess they used to be pretty close. Nick was a family friend, not just Brady's assistant. They don't seem to socialize much anymore. Nick's been to the house only two or three times since we've been married. I don't know what I can tell you. You know I don't spend much time at the studio. And Brady doesn't really bring his work home."

"Is he married? Any kids?"

"No, I know he was married once, a long time ago, but he doesn't have any kids." She thought for a moment, knitting her brows. "Okay, I know Nick came from a big Italian family, and grew up on the west side. You know, around Taylor Street, near Circle Campus. I guess when Nick's father died, the family drifted apart. His older brothers and sisters married and moved away, leaving Nick, his mother, and a kid sister he apparently doted on. Maria, I think. She's a nurse somewhere here in the city. That's about when Brady met him. Brady hired him, and they've been together ever since. What else can I tell you?''

"Does he still live in the old Italian neighborhood?''

"Oh, no. He's got a big condo up in Lincoln Park, on Lakeview, I think. In fact, I think he still lives with Mama Rosa. Or, I guess she lives with him.''

"Rosa? You mean the cleaning woman at the studio?''

"Yes, I'm pretty sure she's still there. I remember some years ago Brady telling me that she was driving Nick nuts. After raising that big family, she felt old and useless living with Nick in a big condo with no one to take care of. She wanted something to do, so Brady let her work in the studio. She cooks for all of them occasionally, and keeps the place clean.'' She paused for a moment. "Say, speaking of cooking, are you going to feed me or not? I'm hungry.''

"I'm sorry,'' I smiled. "Coming right up.''

I went into the kitchen, got a fresh beer and brought out the chicken to put on the grill. I helped Kitty finish the bottle of wine during dinner, and later we had coffee in the kitchen while I cleaned up and loaded dishes into the dishwasher. We talked about old times, and she laughed at some of the memories. By the time I left, she seemed more relaxed, and I was glad that I'd been able to cheer her up a little.

I walked home around 9:00, and decided to run an errand before turning in. I took the Alfa out of the garage and drove down to the studio, knowing there would be a place to park somewhere nearby that time of night. The keys Nell had given me worked smoothly, and a little green light on the security panel blinked on when I punched in the code. There was enough light emanating from the exit signs in the hall to find my way to Brady's office, and when I got there I found a wall switch.

The keys to the file cabinet were right where Brady told me they'd be. There weren't more than twenty manila folders in the drawer marked "Personnel," not a lot given the time the studio had been in business. Some were skinny, others fat. I put them on the desk and randomly opened a few. The fat ones recorded employment of those who had stayed with Brady for some time, containing copies of memos on raises and evaluations. The skinny ones usually held only a resume and a few sheets of paper, interview notes and such. I sighed and put them all back in a neat stack. I would have to take some time and weed them out. Recent employees would be more logical suspects than those who hadn't worked there for a while, but I might have to check all of them. A thought I didn't relish.

I got ready to leave, but was struck by a sudden impulse. I left the files on the desk, walked out to the reception area and turned on the overhead lights. I stood for a moment, thinking, putting myself in Nell's shoes. She would have the combination to the safe committed to memory, but she was too organized. She would have it written down some place, too, just in case memory failed. I searched the top desk drawer, then flipped through the pages of the address book on top of the desk. Nothing. There was a writing board recessed into the wooden desk. I pulled it out. A list of neatly typed phone numbers was taped to the surface. I started to push it back into place, then stopped and pulled it all the way out instead. A scrap of yellow paper was taped above the phone list. Three numbers were handwritten on it.

It took only two tries to open the big safe in the studio "library." The door was heavy, but swung open easily. There was only one flat, black velvet box inside about twelve by eight inches. I'd somehow expected something bigger. I took it over to a table under a hanging light fixture, and was dazzled by the brilliance and color of the gems inside when I opened it. They glittered, reflecting the light, whenever I turned my head even a fraction of an inch. They looked real enough to me, and they held me hypnotized for a long minute. It was easy to see why someone had been tempted by them. I closed the box and put it back in the safe, spinning the tumblers.

"Who's-a there?" a voice called out behind me in a singsong Italian accent.

I whirled around, startled, and saw a shape in the dim light by the double doors to the studio.

"It's Emerson Ward," I said loudly.

The stooped figure advanced slowly until I could see her in the halo of light cast by the fixture over my head. She was an old woman with gray hair and a lined face that had once been very pretty. She wore a dark, floral print dress that came down to the socks covering her ankles, sturdy work shoes, and a long-sleeved cardigan. She was small, but plump around the middle, and she held a mop handle menacingly in two hands.

"What are-a you doin'-a here?" She looked at me suspiciously.

"You must be Rosa," I said smiling, trying to disarm her. "You nearly scared me to death. Brady asked me to come by and get some things from his files."

"Oh, you're-a the friend of-a Mister Brady." She lowered the mop handle just a little and took another step forward. Her eyes were clear and bright, looking strangely young in the old face.

"That's me. I'll probably be around a lot until he's out of the hospital."

"I'm-a sorry. I thought it was-a maybe a burglar or something."

"That's okay. What are you doing here so late?"

"Always-a work. These-a people are-a so messy." She shook her head disdainfully.

"Well, I won't keep you. I'm sorry if I startled you. I got what I need in Brady's office. Do you want me to lock up when I leave?"

"No, I take-a care of-a that."

"Okay. Well, goodnight, Rosa."

She watched me wordlessly as I brushed past her, and I could feel her eyes on me until I pushed through the double doors.

FRIDAY, AFTER A FULL MORNING of working at the agency, I got the car and drove to the near west side in search of Milan Kulas. Ukrainian Village was a typical Chicago pocket neighborhood. Bounded by busy, dirty commercial streets—Division and Chicago on the north and south, and Damen and Western on the east and west—the tree-lined side streets were populated primarily by single-family homes, two-flats, and an occasional four-story apartment building. Though not ritzy, the houses and tiny front lawns were well tended, clean and neat. The area was heavily Hispanic, but the neighborhood itself was mostly first- and second-generation Polish and Ukrainian families, and the properties were slow to turn over.

I parked under the shade of a tree on one of the side streets and looked for Kulas' address on foot, admiring the small flower gardens and window boxes at each residence. The street was quiet. An older man sat on the steps of the house I was looking for. He had silver hair combed straight back, and wore nothing but a pair of shorts and thongs on his feet. His skin was darkly tanned.

"Hello," I said as I sauntered up the sidewalk. "Nice day to be out in the sun."

"Hey, dere, young fella." He spoke with a thick accent.

I leaned against the wrought iron stair rail. "My wife and I are trying to buy a house," I lied. "We heard this was a good place to look. It seems like a nice neighborhood."

"Yeah, we got lots of nice people living here." He pointed across the street to a big brick house on a double lot with a gabled porch roof. "Dat house dere? A judge. Down dere? A banker."

"You live here?"

"In the basement," he nodded. "Dis is my son Casey's house." He said it proudly.

I noted the side door into what Chicagoans call an "in-law" apartment.

"Emerson," I said, stretching a hand up the stairs.

"Milan." He reached down to shake my hand.

"You don't have any trouble around here? It's so hard to find a safe neighborhood in the city."

"Nah. You gotta watch what you leave out. You got kids? You got kids, you tell 'em not to leave their bikes out where dey get stolen. And sometimes da Mexican kids down at de end of da block get noisy. I hear 'em going through my garbage one night. I take out my gun and scare da hell out of da little buggers."

"You've got a gun?"

"Yeah, had a big gun, a pistol like this." He spread his hands. "Just to scare the Mexicans, you know."

"What happened?"

"Got stolen. Broke into my house. Some nigger, the cops told me."

"You got robbed? Did they take anything else?"

"Nah," he said with disgust. "Ain't got nothing else worth stealing."

"They didn't hurt you, did they?"

"Wasn't even home."

"The neighborhood doesn't sound too safe to me."

He waved his hands. "No, no. It's okay. Usually, we don't see dose kind here. De only problem is dem Mexicans, and dey stay down dere where dey belong. Dey come up dis way, I chase 'em away, send 'em home."

"I don't know."

"Really. It's okay."

I shook my head and smiled. "What do you do, Milan?"

"Tend bar two, t'ree nights a week. I do a few odd jobs and garden for some people." He waved his arm. "I do all the gardening for Judge Wroblewski dere, across da street."

I turned and looked at the big house, then faced Kulas again. "Well, it was nice talking to you, Milan. I've got to get back."

"You, too, young fella. You tell your wife dis is a good place for a family. You'd like it here. You'll see."

"Okay, I will. Thanks."

A harmless old man, I thought as I drove home, just like Lanahan said. But it was curious that whoever robbed him had only taken the gun. Maybe he'd hoped to find more, but Kulas really didn't have anything else worth stealing.

My phone was ringing when I walked in the back door,

and I grabbed the kitchen extension and said hello before the voicemail clicked on.

"Emerson?" It was Kitty. "Emerson, you've got to come down here to the hospital."

It was the most plaintive voice I'd ever heard.

SIX

I SAT IN THE PATIENT LOUNGE cradling Kitty's head against my chest as she sobbed softly. Puppy was dead, a forever death this time, not some out-of-body flirtation with a blazing white light at the end of a long dark tunnel. He was gone for good, and Kitty's grief rent my heart. His loss left a hole in our lives as big as Brady himself. It would take time to close over, and in Kitty's case, I was afraid it might never heal completely.

One of Brady's attending physicians strode purposefully into the lounge with a clipboard in his hand and a concerned look on his face. I gently straightened Kitty up, and rose to meet him a few steps away.

"What the hell happened?" I whispered fiercely. "I thought he was doing fine."

"He was," he replied in a low tone. "We're not sure what happened, but it looks like massive cardiac and respiratory failure."

"Why?"

"Look, your friend just underwent major surgery after getting shot in the chest. He was getting on in years. These things happen sometimes. We think they're doing fine, but the trauma is just too much and the whole system shuts down. We did what we could." He shrugged.

"I want to know why he died." Call it shock, or denial, but I just couldn't accept that Brady had given up fighting, that his body had refused to cooperate with his will to live. There had to be a reason.

"So do we. I need to speak with his wife."

"Okay."

He approached Kitty and sat down next to her. She looked at him balefully.

"Mrs. Barnes, I'm terribly sorry about your loss," he said gently. "It's a shock to us all. I hate to ask this now, but it's customary in cases of sudden death like this that we perform an autopsy. We have to know if his death was the result of the gunshot wound or some other cause. We need your consent."

She searched his face with her eyes, and signed the consent form wordlessly. He mouthed his thanks, expressed his condolences again and rose to leave. I touched his arm on the way out, stopping him.

"She's going to have a hard time getting through this. Is there something you can give her to help her out?"

He hesitated, then reached into the breast pocket of his long white coat and pulled out a prescription pad and a pen.

"Sure. This is for a mild sleeping tablet. I'll give her a few days' worth. That should do it." He tore off the prescription and handed it to me. "It's not refillable. I don't want her to start relying on these. This will be a bad time for her, and I don't want to make it any worse by giving her a crutch."

"Thanks. I'll make sure she's careful."

I filled the prescription at the hospital pharmacy on our way out, and took Kitty home. Once there, I went to the kitchen to make drinks for both of us, and found Kitty in the living room slowly walking around, pausing occasionally to look at a picture or a knick-knack, tracing a finger across the edge of the grand piano.

"You okay?"

She turned to look at me. "It already seems empty without him. There's so much of him here, so many reminders."

"Here, have some wine, and let's talk. We have a lot to do."

She took the glass from my hand, nodding, and sat on a couch.

"First off, do you have money? They're going to freeze all of Brady's accounts until the IRS gets a handle on the estate, and I don't want you to get caught short."

She thought a minute. "I've got a few hundred in my checking account, but I have a savings account that has more than five thousand in it."

"In your name?" She nodded again. "Good. That should be enough to carry you for a while. Now, do you know who Brady's executor is?"

"Arthur Ryan."

"I know him. I'll call in a minute. What about life insurance? I assume Brady had a policy."

"Wait a minute." She went to the old rolltop desk in the den and came back a moment later with a policy in her hand.

"Okay, hang on to that. The company won't pay off without a death certificate, and we won't be able to get that until after the autopsy. I'll take care of it next week." I paused. "You have to plan funeral arrangements, too. I'll help you take care of the details, but you have to decide how you want to handle it."

She sighed. "All right. Give me a little time to think about it."

"Okay. I'm going to go call Ryan. You sure you're all right?"

"No, I'm not, but I'll survive, Emerson. We had a lot

of great years. I'm going to miss him terribly, but I lived without him once. I can learn to live without him again.''

''That's my girl,'' I said softly.

I called Arthur Ryan from the kitchen phone and told him the bad news. He was shocked. He hadn't even heard that Brady was in the hospital, but he said he'd get out Brady's will and get things moving before he left for the day.

I called Sue Kaminski down at the *Sun-Times* next, ready to ask my first favor.

''Kaminski, it's Ward,'' I said when she answered. ''Do you know anyone down in the coroner's office from your days doing obits?''

''Well, yes,'' she said slowly, reluctant to admit it.

''Barnes is dead. About an hour or two ago. The hospital is calling it a heart attack, but they have to do an autopsy.''

''So, what does that have to do with me?'' There was a little more interest in her voice, but she was still suspicious.

''I'm not convinced he died of natural causes.''

''Of course not. He was shot, you idiot.''

''No, no, that's not what I mean.''

''You think whoever shot him finished off the job?''

''I'd sure like to find out.''

The line was silent for a minute. ''I know a medical examiner down there. I might be able to get him to tell me the results before the autopsy's released.''

''I need a little more than that, Kaminski. Can you talk to him, see if he can get himself assigned to the case?''

''You know they don't work that way.''

''Tell him this one's hot. Tell him you've got a source who thinks he was murdered.''

She was silent again. "It might work. But it's going to cost. He'll want something in return."

"Anything. Whatever you have to bargain for, I'll pay the freight."

"Murder, huh? Okay, I'll do it. I don't like it, but I'll do it."

"Kaminski, if you can hook this guy, tell him not to look for the obvious. Challenge him. Tell him to look for things that would make Barnes' death seem natural."

"I think you're reaching."

"Maybe." I *was* reaching, but I hadn't felt good about any of this since Puppy's first phone call.

"Twenty says my friend doesn't find a thing. If there's a story in all this, it'll be worth that much."

"You're on."

I hung up with a small smile, and went to check on Kitty. She was still sitting on the couch looking numb. I told her that Ryan would handle things on his end. She nodded halfheartedly.

"Is there anything I can get you? Anything I can do for you?"

"No, thanks, Emerson. I'm not sure there's anything anyone can do."

"Do you want me to stay? You probably shouldn't be alone."

"I think I'll call my friend Diane and see if she can spend the night."

"That sounds like a good idea. You'll call me if there's anything you want?"

"I promise." She tried a small smile, biting back tears, and suddenly held up her arms. I knelt down and gave her a big hug, holding her for a long moment.

There are an incredibly large number of inane programs on television, and I managed to see a lot of them over the weekend. I'd never realized how mindless the medium is, but it was a pretty good prescription for the contemplative mood I found myself in. I wasn't particularly depressed. Brady's death saddened me because it had seemed premature. He'd been taken out of the game in mid-stride, leaving unfinished business. I would miss him, his booming laughter and larger-than-life presence, but his absence would affect me less than others he'd left behind. No, it was more a case of self-evaluation as I sat vegetating in front of the blue glow of the tube. I pondered my own life, wondering if I'd made a difference, if I'd had any positive effect on the lives of others. I wondered if I'd done enough, or if I'd wasted myself in pursuit of lusty ladies and a lazy life of semi-retirement.

I left the house only twice to walk up the street to check on Kitty and see how she was coping. She was holding up well, and it was her steely resolve to keep on living and not let herself die with Brady that brought me out of my reflective shell. Brady's death naturally reminded me of my own mortality. A little meditation was good for the soul, but I was not some character in a Frank Capra movie. Trying to envision what life for my friends would be like without me was selfish and silly. With that simple conclusion, I slept like a child Sunday night.

First thing Monday morning, I finished up a draft copy for the annual report and took it into Jayne's office. She was surprised I'd gotten it done so quickly, and said she'd walk it over to the client that afternoon. I promised her captions for the spreads by Tuesday, and went back to my office with a smug, self-satisfied smile. Peggy came in a minute later.

"What are you grinning about?"

"Just gloating a little. I don't think Jayne expected me to be as good as you made me out to be."

"You better have delivered. I have my reputation to think about, too, you know. When you're done with a job you just move on, but I have to work with these people." She smiled and paused. "Say, where were you Friday? You missed all the fireworks."

"What happened?"

"A memo went out announcing Tom Bruce's promotion to account manager, consumer products, and Jack rescinded it." She looked amused.

"I don't get it."

"Tom reports to Jim Bailey, the senior VP and manager of the Chicago office. Jim gave him a promotion without clearing it with Jack, and when Jack got the memo, he told Jim he had no right to give Tom the promotion. Jack didn't know the memo had been circulated to everyone in the office."

"Is he nuts? If Bailey runs the office and supervises Tom, why would Jack object to the promotion?"

"It's Jack's sandbox."

"Interesting. Is Tom in today?"

"He's here. Listen, I came in to see if you'd like to go to lunch today. I heard about Brady Barnes and thought I'd try to cheer Nell up."

"Sure. I'd like that. Let me know when you're ready to go." I'd avoided the studio that morning, not wanting to be the bearer of bad news, and reluctant to be there when the staff found out about Brady. I'd asked Arthur Ryan to handle it instead.

With time to kill before lunch, I went looking for Tom Bruce. His office was on the far side of the floor from mine, and he sat at his desk, obviously still upset.

"I heard the news," I said, poking my head in his door. "That's really a bitch."

He looked up. "Oh, it's you. Yeah, I'm so pissed I

could spit." He sounded disgusted. "Who'd you hear it from, anyway?" He looked at me suspiciously.

"Peggy."

"No one's supposed to know. I already feel like an ass. I deserved that promotion. At least Jack agreed that I could use the title unofficially in the office, the son of a bitch."

"Why'd he do it?"

"I don't know. Because he's Jack Thane. He said the promotion was too big to let Jim make alone. He said I need to get down to Evansville more often, get to know the account people there before I can be manager of all the consumer business. Shit, they only have one or two consumer accounts down there. Most of their accounts are business-to-business."

"You don't sound as if you like him much."

He shrugged. "Jack's okay. He just doesn't know how to let go, let other people help run his business. I don't think when a business gets this big that one person can, or should, be so hands-on. He's limiting himself. He's limiting the business."

"He seems to have done all right for himself."

"Jack Thane doesn't know shit about advertising." He said it a little too loudly, and caught himself, glancing nervously at the door behind me. "He's a graphic designer, for chrissake," he went on in a low voice. "He's done one thing right, and that's figure out how to convince bright people to work for him."

"Why are you here, then?"

Bruce looked at me curiously, as if suddenly realizing what he'd been telling me. He continued after a pause, apparently deciding I was no threat. "Because I can go farther, faster here than anywhere else. If Jack doesn't stand in my way, that is. From here, I can either write my ticket at a big agency, or start my own shop. I haven't decided which.''

He would have to be politically astute to survive. His ego was too big to last long in the same company as Jack Thane. Especially since the company belonged to Jack.

''How are things going on the photo shoot?'' I asked, changing the subject.

''I don't know. I suppose you heard that Barnes dropped dead. That's the last fucking thing I need to go wrong now. The studio called this morning to say the staff was taking the morning off out of respect. I told them they'd damn well better be there after lunch because we're coming in.'' He paused, seeing something in my expression I hadn't concealed.

''Sorry. I guess he was your friend. I didn't mean to talk bad about him, but I hope Marty can pull this thing off. Otherwise, without Barnes, I'm dead meat.''

''Maybe I'll come by this afternoon and see how things are going.''

''Fine with me, but just stay out of the way, will you? Irv will have my ass if this shoot doesn't start going right.''

There was a pall over the studio when I arrived after lunch. Brady's absence was even more pronounced now that it was permanent, and the shock of losing him was evident among the staff. Nick stalked the studio nervously, aimlessly moving from bay to bay, barking orders at random, making Sarah and Nancy jump from one task to another, leaving each half finished. Nancy appeared to be close to tears, and Sarah moved slowly and more sullenly than usual. Nell hovered, not sure whether to intercede on the girls' behalf or mind her own business, and finally disappeared, going back to her desk in the reception area. Marty seemed to be the only one in control, quietly and methodically working on his set, adjusting lights and props to his liking.

Irv Steinmetz and Tom Bruce were in the kitchen bay as promised, drinking fresh coffee and waiting for the magic to begin on Marty's set. Nick apparently had another shoot scheduled because a home economist and a food stylist were busy in the kitchen cooking and plating food. They worked quietly and spoke in hushed tones, affected by the somber mood pervading the studio. No other clients were in evidence, though, which meant Nick was probably setting up preliminary test shots in advance of a real session.

I found a quiet corner and watched, wondering if the studio would hold together after the initial shock wore off and Nick took charge. From what I saw, it didn't look as if Nick was capable of running the studio, but perhaps Nell was mother hen enough to keep things going. She would have to assert herself, something I sensed she wasn't comfortable doing. She'd been very effective working quietly and unobtrusively in Brady's shadow, with his authority. I couldn't imagine Nick giving her the same rein.

Marty called Irv and Tom over to the set when he was ready. Despite my curiosity, I stayed in the kitchen and poured myself some coffee. I wanted to see how Marty had solved the lighting problem, but Bruce had been right. It was better to stay out of the way. I waited fifteen minutes, listening to the low murmur of voices, then couldn't contain my curiosity any longer. I stole over to Marty's set and stood well behind the camera just beyond the periphery of light spilling out of the bay. Long-legged directors chairs were set up on either side of the camera for observers. Bruce sat sprawled in one, looking bored.

Steinmetz was on the set itself with Marty, scrutinizing and adjusting.

As I watched, I began to appreciate the painstaking detail Marty had gone to. He'd put a sheet of Plexiglas up on sawhorses, then used Plexiglas boxes to give the set dimension and height. A large swatch of rich royal blue velvet was draped over the boxes. The precious gems were carefully arranged on the velvet, and Marty had cut an undetectable hole in the cloth under each stone. On the floor beneath the set, he'd placed pin spots beneath each gem, so that the stones would be lit from below, appearing to give off their own internal light. In the center of the set piece, of course, was a cut crystal rocks glass that would hold the client's product when it was time to shoot. A jewel among gems. If it worked, it would be beautiful when the lights were on.

"Jesus Christ," Irv suddenly muttered, bringing me back to attention.

"What is it?" Marty asked.

"One of the stones is missing."

"What?"

"One of the damn stones is missing!" he repeated loudly.

The studio was dead silent for a long moment. Tom Bruce straightened in his chair, looking startled and incredulous as if he hadn't heard correctly. Then Nick scurried over from another bay.

"What the hell are you talking about, Irv?" he growled.

"I'm telling you, one of the stones is gone! It isn't here. I counted them!"

"That can't be," Marty said quietly. "I brought them all out. They were all in the box in the safe."

"Someone stole one of the goddamn gems!" Steinmetz roared.

The commotion had attracted everyone in the studio like a magnet, and they'd slowly converged on the set, standing on the periphery like me. Even the two ladies in the kitchen had come to see what the fuss was about.

"Calm down, calm down," Marty said quietly. "I'm sure it's just been misplaced."

"Well, find it, damn it!"

For a moment, no one moved. Then as if on some silent cue, everyone started moving. Someone turned on the overhead fixtures, bathing the whole studio in light. Marty got down on all fours to look on the floor around the set. Nick stalked off toward the safe with a worried look on his face, and everyone else started roaming the studio, eyes downcast, poking in shadowy nooks and crannies. The noise had brought Nell out of reception, and she came up beside me.

"What's going on?" she murmured.

"The shit has hit the fan," I said out of the corner of my mouth. "Just watch. Not a word, remember?"

I wandered away from her onto the set, pretending to help Marty look, but watching people instead, trying to read expressions. Bruce stood looking a little bewildered and worried, half-heartedly shuffling around the perimeter of the set, eyes on the floor. Not finding anything in the safe, Nick moved around the studio, directing other searchers, telling them where to look, snapping orders. His worried look held fear, too, I thought. Irv simply looked angry. He stood on the set, hands on his hips and mouth set grimly, watching everyone else search. Marty seemed calm, wearing only a quizzical expression, as if the whole matter was a puzzle that needed solving.

The search lasted for a good twenty minutes, and one by one people gravitated back to the set with shrugs of the shoulders, some looking puzzled, others defeated.

"That's it," Steinmetz said with disgust when everyone was assembled again. "I'm calling the police."

"Come on, Irv," Nick pleaded. "It's got to be around here someplace."

"Sure," Marty chimed in brightly. "No one would steal just one jewel. That would be silly. It's got to be here."

"Well, it didn't just walk off by itself. Someone took the goddamn thing!"

"What about you?" Nick said, whirling toward me. "You were here late Thursday night. After everyone else left. Maybe you took it."

I was startled as all eyes turned to me, and thought furiously. Of course Rosa would have told Nick about the stranger in the studio. "I came to get some files for Brady. Besides, Marty worked with the gems again on Friday. You didn't notice anything then, did you Marty?"

"Noo," he replied slowly. "But I never thought to count them. I just got them out of the safe, and locked them up when I was through."

"This is ridiculous," Steinmetz said angrily. "I'm calling the police."

"No," said a small voice from the back of the crowd. "Please don't. I did it." Nancy took a small step forward and burst into tears.

"What?!" Nick turned on her, grabbed her shoulders and shook her. "What have you done?" he said furiously.

"Brady made me promise not to tell," she wailed. "Please don't call the police."

It was Marty who finally calmed her down, gently pushing Nick aside and putting an arm around her shoulder, stroking her hair. The story came out then between sobs, just as Brady had told me, about how she'd tripped on the set, knocking over a studio light, smashing the stone.

"Jesus, this is incredible," Irv said when she was done. "What did Brady do with it?"

"I don't know," Nancy said, about to cry again.

"All right, no police. But I have to call the damn insurance company about this. Nick, look through Brady's office. I can't imagine he'd throw away the pieces. I don't know how that son of a bitch thought he was going to get away without telling me about it."

"Maybe he just never got the chance," I said.

"Maybe." He looked at me thoughtfully. "All right, let's get back to work. Marty, let's work with what we've got. It looks good. I want to see some chromes first thing in the morning. I'm going to go make the call. Jesus."

He walked away muttering, and the staff slowly dispersed, quietly going back to their tasks. Marty spoke to Nancy in low, reassuring tones, and she went back to work hesitantly, but looking a little brighter. Nell looked at me questioningly. I gave her a small nod. She seemed to accept that everything was okay, walking away wordlessly.

I breathed an inward sigh of relief. It hadn't all fallen apart yet. I had a little more time to try to figure out what was going on, but I silently cursed Brady for getting me into this.

A MESSENGER HAND-DELIVERED an envelope from Ryan's office mid-morning on Tuesday. There was a note typed on the law firm's stationery inside, a formal request to attend the reading of the last will and testament of Brady Hilliard Barnes. Half an hour after I got it, Arthur Ryan called.

"You received my note?" he asked after we exchanged pleasantries.

"Yes. It was quite a surprise." I couldn't imagine why I'd been invited.

"I'd like you to be there a little early," he said, ignoring the opening. "I have something to discuss. Twenty minutes should do it."

"But why—"

"Tomorrow," he said firmly, cutting me off. "I'll expect you."

The reading was scheduled for 12:30 on Wednesday at the Ritz Carlton Hotel. Just past noon, I rode an elevator up to the lobby and walked down the hall to a meeting room overlooking the old Chicago Water Tower. Ryan was already there, and I was surprised to see Brandt standing by the windows looking down at the little park. The room was large, with comfortable seating areas just inside the door and along the wall opposite the windows. There was a service door set in the wall behind a folding screen. A bar was built into the far wall of the room, but it was unstaffed. A lone rectangular table stood in the center of the room looking small in the space. It was elegantly set for lunch. I counted ten place settings.

"Ah, Emerson. Good of you to come." Ryan strode to meet me halfway into the room with an outstretched hand. "It's been a long time. Let's sit down."

Tall and elegant, with silver hair and craggy features, Ryan was a partner in a smallish Loop law firm that had been around for more than a hundred years. The firm still bore the name of one of the founders, though none of the founding partners' descendants worked there anymore. Ryan was now one of the old guard in the firm who did a little corporate work for some long-time clients and a lot of estate planning for a host of wealthy North Shore country club types, leaving the job of hustling new business to keep the staid firm alive to the young Turks. He'd been Brandt's lawyer and friend for years.

Brandt walked over to join us. I glanced at him, but he just gave me a small shrug and sat in a chair next to a coffee table. I took the chair opposite him, and Ryan sat between us on a couch.

"I'll get right to it," he began. "You're both wondering why you're here. As you know, Brady had a somewhat warped sense of humor. But he also considered both of you friends. Unfortunately, neither of you is about to come into any money. You're here as witnesses."

"To what?" Brandt asked.

"Frankly, I'm not sure. I believe Brady thought you would be amused. First of all, this 'reading' is unnecessary. Will readings aren't done anymore. Brady made a special request that I do this. As I said, for amusement, I think. Second, the issue of transferring the estate was resolved some time ago. Brady implemented a living trust many years ago, and transferred all his property into the trust over the years. His heirs already have what they're going to get."

"Who knows about this?" It was my turn to ask a question.

"No one that I'm aware of, but Brady certainly could have told whomever he chose. This little gathering was an idea Brady had a few years ago. I didn't think it was a good one, but I couldn't dissuade him. He said he wanted to accomplish a couple of things. He wanted to see the look on people's faces when they found out what he'd done. Obviously difficult under the circumstances, but perhaps he's here in spirit. And he told me at the time that if something happened to him, he wanted you here, Emerson, to keep an eye on his family. He didn't trust anyone except Katherine, but he didn't tell her anything about his estate planning because he wanted her to be able to claim innocence. He didn't want anyone else to accuse her of scheming to get his money.''

"The family's that bad?''

"They didn't approve of his marriage to Katherine.''

I'd heard that, of course, but Kitty had simply accepted that as part of marrying Brady, and she'd never complained. I'd never even heard her mention Brady's family, and I'd never met any of them.

"Why am I here?'' Brandt asked softly.

"To watch out for Katherine's interests. Brady wanted Emerson to see to her physical well-being. You're to look after her financial well-being.''

"What the hell's going on?'' I muttered. "Has Kitty been threatened or something? I'm a writer, not a bodyguard.''

"I honestly don't know. All I can tell you is that when Brady came up with this idea, he thought you'd both get some perverse enjoyment out of it. But I could tell he was concerned, too. He wanted friends around to help Katherine through this difficult time, and he told me that you two were the best qualified.''

"We're honored,'' Brandt said, smiling at his old friend.

"I'm just confused,'' I said. "It doesn't make any sense. When did Brady decide to do this?''

"About two years ago. But as I told you, he had me set up the trust shortly after he married Katherine.''

"So, what do we do now?''

"Watch, listen, drink a toast to Brady's memory. It should be a very interesting lunch.''

"Who's coming?''

"Katherine, of course, Brady's two children, his ex-wife and her son, and Nick Fratelli.''

An interesting lunch, indeed.

Kitty was the first to arrive, appropriately attired in widow's weeds, a relatively modest black cotton suit with a slim, knee-length pull-on skirt and a cropped jacket. Ryan greeted her gently, murmuring condolences and words of comfort. She smiled faintly when she saw Brandt and me, and said she was glad we'd come. I poured her a glass of wine from the bar, and decided that was as good a vantage point as any. Brandt could do the socializing. He was much better at it than I.

Next to arrive was a man about my own age with a full beard dressed in slacks and a sport coat, but no tie. Shorter than me, but husky, he bore a small resemblance to Brady. He stopped inside the door and his dark eyes searched the room. He strolled over to Kitty, took her hand and brushed cheeks, earnestly murmuring something to her. He didn't linger long, quickly making his way back to the bar.

"What'll it be?"

"Jack Daniels, rocks." He looked me up and down while I fixed his drink. "You're not staff. Friend of Kitty's?"

"Brady's. And Kitty's."

"Ron Barnes," he said, sticking out a hand.

"Emerson Ward." His paw was big like his father's, and callused from some kind of manual work, but his grip wasn't as firm as Brady's.

"Sure. Dad mentioned you a couple of times. You were there when he was shot, right?"

"Yes. I'm really sorry about what happened. Your dad was a hell of a guy. I really thought he'd pull through."

He shrugged. "So did I. He was a tough old bird. Now I feel bad I didn't visit him in the hospital."

He said it so matter-of-factly that it seemed obvious his sense of guilt didn't run very deep. In fact, it was curious that Brady's children hadn't come to visit, at least that I knew of.

A pair of newcomers showed up before I could ask him why he hadn't gone to the hospital. First through the door was a large woman in a billowy black silk dress and floppy-brimmed black hat. The veil draped over the hat helped conceal an aging face that attempted to look youthful with a thick layer of makeup and garish lipstick. Bleached hair fell in a bob to her shoulders. Half a step behind her, holding on to her elbow was a long-faced thin man in his late thirties or early forties sharply dressed in a dark double-breasted suit. Neatly trimmed sandy hair was brushed straight back from a receding hairline.

"Oh, this is terrible," the woman wailed as she entered. Her voice was loud and shrill. She immediately headed for Ryan with arms held open. "Arthur, how *could* this have happened?"

Ryan accepted her embrace and brushed cheeks as well as he could with the veil in the way, then held her at arm's length and murmured something.

"It's just awful!" she said loudly. "Stephen, darling, I don't think I can cope with this without a drink. Would you be a dear?" She lifted the hem of her dress with a dramatic swish and planted herself heavily on a couch.

"Yes, Mother." The man who'd been at her elbow spun on his heel and made his way toward the bar with a look of distaste.

"A double gin martini and a vodka-tonic," he snapped as he approached. "Hello, Ronald." Both the voice and his mannerisms were condescending and effeminate enough to suggest he was gay.

"Hello, Stephen." Barnes grinned disarmingly, obviously amused.

I fixed the drinks and watched him take them back to

the woman on the couch. Even from across the room, I could hear her now complaining about the weather.

"Brady's ex-wife?" I guessed.

"Yes, Jennifer Clifford Barnes, my former step-mother," Barnes said with a trace of sarcasm, the smile still on his face. "A real witch. Stephen is her son."

"How long were they married?"

"Fifteen long, loud, angry years. I think it was relief to everyone when they got divorced. Except Jennifer, of course. She always felt she deserved better. Better treatment when they were married and a bigger settlement when they were divorced."

"How old were you when they split up?"

"About nineteen or twenty."

"I don't know her, obviously, but I can't imagine Brady with her."

"Oh, she was attractive enough in her day, and charming when she wanted to be. She could be very convincing. She had a way of sweet-talking her way into getting what she wanted. I think it was having children that did her in. She wanted Dad, but she never wanted us. She wanted something more glamorous than the role of homemaker."

I caught movement out of the corner of my eye and turned to see Nick Fratelli hurry in then stop and take stock. After glancing around the room, he headed straight for us.

"Jesus Christ, Ward, is there any place you're not invited these days? Give me a Scotch and water." He nodded at Ron.

"Nice to see you, too, Nick," Ron said.

I poured his drink and handed it to him.

"Excuse me if I don't stand around and chat," he said, taking a quick gulp, "but I've got to pay my respects to the widow."

As he ambled over to the assembled group, my eyes strayed to an attractive brunette walking in the door. It was the same woman I'd seen at Greg Edwards' house the week before, and I felt an immediate twinge of guilt. She didn't bother to look around, heading straight for people she recognized.

"What's she doing here?" I asked, startled.

"She's my sister," Ron said, looking at me curiously.

"Sorry," I stammered. "She was introduced to me at a party last week as Ms. Meriwether. I didn't know she was Brady's daughter."

"Glynnis. Meriwether's her married name. Excuse me for a minute, will you?"

He turned and walked toward her. I watched as she first greeted Kitty and Arthur Ryan formally, with a simple handshake. She barely acknowledged Jennifer's presence on the couch. Stephen Clifford approached her to give her a kiss on the cheek, but she didn't seem to respond in kind. Arthur took her elbow and introduced her to Brandt, but the only person she seemed to greet warmly was Ron. When she turned and saw him they hugged, then stood for a moment with their arms around each other's waist as they made polite conversation with the others.

Finally she broke away and came toward the bar. Recognition, then a brief look of disgust flashed across her face as she approached. I suddenly felt small and stupid, and just a little bit humble. I may have prejudged her correctly at Greg's party, but I'd had no right to throw it in her face.

"What are you doing here?" The cold facade was back in place.

"I was a friend of your father. Art Ryan asked me to come."

"So you can poke your nose in our business and insult the whole family, too?"

"I feel terrible about what happened to your dad. I know how hard it must be to lose him."

"I didn't think you had any feelings."

"Look, I'm sorry about what happened the other night. It was rude and uncalled for. I don't even have a good excuse for my behavior. I was an ass, and I apologize."

She looked at me coolly.

"White wine, please," she said finally.

It was probably as close to acceptance of the apology as I was going to get, but I took one last shot.

"I'm not always an ass. I didn't know who you were. I'd like to start over, pretend we never met."

"Why? Because you found out I'm Brady Barnes' daughter?"

"No, because I never should have treated you that way in the first place. I'm Emerson Ward."

"Good for you." She picked up her glass and walked away.

I sighed. At least I'd tried.

It wasn't long before Arthur Ryan gently herded everyone to the table for lunch. He tried to get people seated according to some arrangement he had in mind, but Jennifer Clifford immediately pushed her way into the seat to the left of the head of the table, presumably where Ryan would sit. He was gracious, quickly adjusting his seating plan, suggesting where everyone else sit. Stephen, Ron and I ended up lined up to Jennifer's left. Kitty, Brandt, Glynnis, and Nick were seated in order on the opposite side. The table was big, with enough room between place settings. I was further gladdened by the fact that I was seated on the end where I could flap my left elbow without knocking over someone's water glass. Despite nu-

merous childhood attempts, I'd never learned to eat with
my right hand.

There was some small talk about table partners as wait-
ers began to ferry in the first course. Brandt leaned over
slightly to charm Glynnis and Ryan spoke with both Kitty
and Jennifer. I overheard Ron and Stephen exchange a
few questions about how things were going, then they
quickly ran out of things to say. It was Nick who suddenly
piped up, attracting everyone's attention.

"Who's the empty chair for?"

All eyes turned to the empty place at the foot of the
table next to me.

"Brady," Ryan said quietly. "You all, for better or
worse, are his family, and he wanted to be here with you,
in spirit at least."

"Oh, God, that's sick," Jennifer said in a disgusted
tone. "It's so like that presumptuous bastard to believe he
could come back from the grave."

"Shut up! Just shut up!" Kitty said loudly. She clutched
a water glass so tightly her knuckles were white. I'd never
seen her so angry.

"We may not like each other," she continued fiercely,
"but we're here out of respect for a man we all loved in
some way. If any of you can't think of anything decent
to say about him or behave yourselves for a few minutes
over a simple lunch, then please leave now."

The table was dead silent. Jennifer was taken aback for
a moment, opened her mouth to say something, then
thought better of it.

"A toast, then, to Brady," Ryan said quietly. He raised
his glass. "May his memory live on."

There was a murmuring of "here-heres," and Ryan
managed to prevent any further mishaps during lunch by
regaling us with stories of law office politics and court-

room derring-do. When dessert and coffee had been served, Ryan pulled a piece of paper out of his inside coat pocket, unfolded it, and donned a pair of reading glasses.

"In addition to honoring Brady's memory, this is one of the reasons you've all been invited here. As you know, this gathering is at his request, and what I'm about to read are his bequests, written in his own hand. Obviously, the will itself is more complicated and lengthy, but this will give you the gist of it. I'll ask that you let me read it through before you comment or ask any questions. Agreed?"

There was solemn nodding around most of the table, Jennifer's floppy hat bobbing the hardest, and Nick looking the least convinced.

"All right, then. He skipped the 'being of sound mind' part." Ryan smiled faintly, pausing for an instant. "So we begin. 'To Jennifer Clifford Barnes, my former wife, and to Stephen Clifford, her son for whom I provided food, shelter, an education, and the best fatherly advice and guidance in my ability, I leave the sum of fifty thousand dollars. A sum which should adequately compensate you, Jennifer, for cab fare and the dress you undoubtedly bought for this occasion.'"

There were both nasty and flabbergasted looks around the table, but I had to raise my napkin to my lips to hide my smile. Brady was getting the last laugh.

"'To my children, Ronald and Glynnis Barnes, I leave twenty-five thousand dollars each and any and all personal effects you may attach sentimental value to. Specifically, to you Glynnis, I leave your mother Victoria's jewelry, and the telephone stand conversation seat you so adored when you were a child. To you, Ronald, I leave my collection of miniature antique car models, and hope you get as much enjoyment out of simply admiring them as I did.

I hope you accept these gifts as a small token of my enduring love for each of you. I never told either of you often enough, but I hope you understand.' ''

Ryan took a breath, looked around the table briefly over the rims of his glasses, then continued.

'''To my wife, Katherine Ferguson Barnes, I leave the bulk of my estate, including our house on North Dearborn Street and all its furnishings, any cash, stocks, or other holdings I may own at the time of my death, and my business, Barnes Photography Studios, Inc.

'''To Nick Fratelli, my long time partner and companion, I simply leave this admonition: run the business as you would your own while it belongs to Kitty, or I'll surely come back to haunt you.' ''

Ryan carefully folded the paper and put his reading glasses in his pocket. The table was quiet for a long time, as if everyone expected something more.

SEVEN

"IS THAT IT?" IT WAS NICK who finally broke the silence.

"That's it," Ryan replied. "Short and sweet."

"Then if you'll excuse me, I've got work to do. I've got to go make some money for Missus Barnes." His voice dripped with sarcasm as he pushed himself away from the table abruptly and stalked out.

"This is an insult!" Jennifer wailed. "Fifty thousand for all the miserable years I spent with that bastard! I raised his children as if they were my own. I kept a model home. I wasted the best years of my life on that man!" With each successive complaint, her voice got louder and more shrill.

"Get over it, Mother," Stephen said disgustedly.

"I will not! How dare he leave everything to you?" She looked menacingly at Kitty. "You're nothing but a glorified waitress in the sky, you little tramp. You got into his pants and led him around by his dick, just like all the others."

"Mother, shut up! You're drunk," Clifford pleaded.

"Arthur, you must *do* something." She turned to Ryan, ignoring her son.

"It's already done, my dear," he said gently. "Your money is already in trust, and the transfer of property was done some time ago."

"I'll contest it."

"You can't. It's a *fait accompli*. What's done is done. Besides, you divorced Brady years ago. You're no longer related. Litigation would be a waste of time and money. He did this out of generosity, not some lingering sense of guilt, dear lady. Take the money and be happy."

"Oh, to hell with all of you!" She rose awkwardly, then regained her balance and wagged a finger in Ryan's face. "You haven't heard the last of this, Arthur. Stephen, take me home."

Clifford wearily got up and followed his mother as she imperiously swished out of the room. There was another moment of silence after she left.

"Any questions, you two?" Ryan asked softly, looking down the table at Ron and Glynnis. They both shook their heads. "Good. You know you can call on me if you ever have any problems. You're welcome to stay a while if you'd like. The bar's still open. I think I'll have another."

He rose from the table, and those of us still there followed suit. Glynnis and Ron followed him to the bar, but Kitty pulled Brandt and me aside.

"I don't want a wake," she said softly. "I think you can see why. Brandt, would you dedicate this year's party to Brady?"

"Of course. A Brady bash. A Barnes-storm." He smiled.

She laughed and squeezed his arm. "Thank you. Thank you both for being here. You're just what I needed." She took my arm, too, and walked us both to the bar.

Later, Brandt and I hitched a ride north in Kitty's cream-colored Mercedes 190. A present from Brady on her forty-fifth birthday, she told us. She drove it aggressively, and it was obvious that the little car delighted her. On the way up, Brandt suggested that we throw our own private wake. It sounded like a pretty good idea since the afternoon was shot anyway, and I didn't think it would hurt Kitty to have a little company. She said it was a wonderful suggestion, so we wheeled into the garage behind the big house on Dearborn, trooped in the back door laughing like kids over one of Brandt's bad jokes, and made a party.

I raided the refrigerator and found things to make a plate of munchies. I was still hungry even though we'd eaten only an hour before, and I bet that Kitty at least hadn't eaten much at lunch given the unappetizing nature of the company around the table. Kitty made drinks. And Brandt went to put music on the stereo. When we were ready with a tray, we found Brandt in the den browsing, perusing books and photos, swaying gently in time to the strains of Gershwin.

"So," he said, coming to get his drink, "have you thought about what you're going to do with your new-found wealth?"

"No." She looked a little startled. "I mean, I didn't expect it. I guess I always knew Brady would take care of me somehow, but I didn't think he'd leave everything to me. I thought most of it would go to Glynnis and Ron. The studio, at least, and maybe some cash, some kind of trust. I guess I don't know what I thought. Brady never talked about it." Her expression turned bewildered.

"Well, you don't need to think about it right away," Brandt said gently. "Once we see what's there, we can help you decide how to invest it and make it work for you."

"But I don't know anything about running Brady's business. He kept me away from all that. He spoiled me, really. He took care of all the bills except groceries, and gave me a very generous monthly allowance for food, decorating and anything I wanted to spend on myself."

"I'm sure Nick's capable of heading up the studio until you decide what you want to do. You have a lot of options. You can get involved in running it, you can simply sit back and take a percentage of the profit, or you can sell it. Nick might even want to take it off your hands. After all, he's been there almost since the beginning."

"I hate to throw a damper on the party," I said slowly, "but I'm not sure Nick *can* run the business. Nell's the one who really takes care of day-to-day operations. And I don't think she and Nick get along that well. She's always had Brady as a buffer."

"So we sweeten the pot for Nell, give her an incentive to stay on. Nick's smart enough to see that she's needed."

"Maybe. But the studio has bigger problems than that right now."

"Emerson, you promised you'd tell me last week what was going on," Kitty said accusingly.

"You had other things on your mind. It wasn't the right time."

"What *is* going on?" Brandt asked sharply.

I decided to tell them since they would probably find out anyway in time. I gave them Brady's version of what had happened, told them how Nancy had corroborated the story, and let them know what I'd been doing to try to find out who was responsible.

"What do you think?" Brandt asked when I was done.

"I don't know what to think. Tom Bruce didn't take them. I'm convinced of that. Jack Thane had motive, but I don't think he would have done it himself, and I don't know who he could have convinced to do it for him if it wasn't Bruce. I haven't gotten a handle on Steinmetz yet, but I don't think it was him. Which still leaves the studio staff. I trust Nell, but I haven't decided about the rest of them. And there's the possibility it was a former employee.''

"At least you've narrowed it down.''

"Maybe. Maybe not. Today might have put a new wrinkle on things. What if someone around that table knew about Brady's living trust, knew that they weren't going to get part of the estate? That might be incentive enough for one of them to steal the jewel collection to make up for it. They all could have had access to the studio. The locks and the alarm code haven't been changed for years. I mean, weren't you a little surprised that Ron and Glynnis took the news so well? They didn't get that much, really, and they didn't object at all.''

"True.'' Brandt rubbed his chin. "That is curious.''

"Do you get along with them all right, Kitty?''

"As well as can be expected, I guess. Ron's okay. He's been over a few times when he knew Brady wouldn't be around. Just to say hi, you know. He's been pretty friendly. Glynnis doesn't like me at all. I took Brady away from her. After he divorced Jennifer, Glynnis took it upon herself to sort of mother him. She wasn't happy when I stepped into the picture. I certainly can't be her mother—lord knows I wouldn't want to—and she won't let me be her friend.''

"I would have thought they'd be a lot more unhappy than they seemed about the fact that Brady left it all to you.''

She didn't say anything.

"Something else we can't forget,'' I said after a pause, "is that Puppy was killed. Someone wanted him dead, and whoever it was succeeded. A week late, and maybe not as planned, but the effect is the same. I don't know if it has anything to do with the jewels being stolen or

not. Whoever took them could have believed Brady suspected.''

Kitty shivered as if touched by a cold draft. ''Will you
find out?''

''I don't know. Maybe, if I poke around long enough.''

There was an uneasy silence, and Brandt finally managed to lighten the mood by launching into a story about
Brady that first had us smiling, then chuckling, then hoot-
ing with laughter because it was so typical of the man
who'd shared some of his best with us. Kitty brought out
picture albums then, and went through them page by page,
with Brandt and me looking over her shoulder, sharing
memories and reliving new ones through her. Brandt even
found some old high school yearbooks on the shelves and
brought them back. I sat cross-legged at Kitty's feet, and
Brandt pulled up a chair next to us and pored through
them, looking for pictures of Brady in his youth. When
he'd find one, he'd show it to us, so we could hoot some
more at the old-fashioned clothes and the freshly scrubbed
looks of innocence on the faces of his classmates. We
played a game, trying to guess the present occupation and
lifestyle of each, laughing at our own outlandish sugges-
tions.

It amazed me that for as long as I'd been Brady's friend
and as many times as I'd been to his house, I'd never
really known him at all. I knew little about where he'd
come from, his family, his compatriots. I'd never even
met his children until lunch that day, and they were my
own contemporaries. But perhaps that was why we'd been
friends. I'd accepted Brady just as he was. I hadn't wanted
anything from him, and after meeting his family, I could
imagine that he might have found that refreshing. Now,
looking through old pictures, I felt a little guilty, as though

I was prying into a private side of Puppy that he'd been reluctant to share.

The caption under one photo finally sobered me, and I stared at it curiously for so long that Brandt noticed and nudged me.

"Anyone still in there?"

"Sorry. Just wondering about something, that's all."

"What?"

"Coincidence." I shrugged. "Guy in the photo here with Brady is listed as 'S. Wroblewski.'"

Brandt took the book out of my hands and peered at the photo of two young men in old-time football jerseys smiling at the camera with their arms around each other's shoulders.

"So?"

"I heard the name Stanley Wroblewski recently. A district court judge, I think. I was just curious."

"Does it mean something?" Kitty asked seriously, perking up.

"Probably not."

"It shouldn't be too tough to find out if it's the same person," Brandt said, looking up from the book.

"I wouldn't worry about it." The curt tone in my voice surprised even me.

They both stared at me for a moment. "It's no problem," Brandt said softly.

"Okay," I said, a little chagrined. "See what you can find out. It's no big deal." I was grasping at straws, and I was embarrassed that they thought I'd found something worth pursuing. I shrugged off the feeling and turned to pick up a photo album, slowly thumbing through the pages until I could no longer feel their stares on the back of my neck.

I STARTED the family inquiries with Stephen Clifford. He managed a high-priced men's clothing store up on Clark

Street just north of LaSalle Drive. It was mid-morning and there was a parking place right out front, so I wheeled the Alfa around in an illegal U-turn and took it. There was a look of sour surprise on his face when he saw me come through the door. I browsed through the racks of fashionable suits while he waited on a customer, amused and thankful when I saw the price tags that I already had a closet full of suits I hardly wore anyway. Unlike women's clothes, men's suits are rarely out of style. A store like this could bankrupt a guy pretty quickly.

Clifford found me almost ten minutes later. "What do *you* want?" he hissed as he sidled up.

"A chat. Do you have an office?"

He looked around the shop. There were only two other clerks in the store, both trying to look busy arranging merchandise for lack of customers.

"All right. Five minutes. Come on."

He led me to the back and into a cramped space littered with boxes and papers and lifted a stack of dress shirts off the one chair before circling around the desk to sit down. I perched on the edge of the chair. He looked at me haughtily, as though I'd denigrated the store by showing up in simple white cotton slacks and an Izod sport shirt.

"Who are you, anyway?"

"Just a friend of the family."

"It's a little too soon to be moving in on the widow, isn't it?"

"My, my, aren't we bitchy this morning." I smiled.

His nostrils flared and his face turned red all the way up to the roots of his thinning hair, but he held himself in check.

"Let's try again," I said coolly. "A week ago, some-body took a shot at Brady. Now he's dead. I'm trying to find out who wanted to kill him and why."

"You think one of us killed him for his money?" He snorted derisively. "You heard how he divvied up the estate. If anyone was after his money, it was Kitty. Go talk to her."

"She had no idea he was leaving everything to her," I said softly.

He looked at me, surprised for an instant, then the con-descending look was back. "Brady Barnes got what he deserved."

"What do you mean?"

"Brady was a bastard. He treated me shabbily, and he treated my mother even worse. I'm not about to start feel-ing sorry for him now, much less forgive him."

"Tell me about it."

He shrugged. "He just wasn't much of a father, or a husband. Growing up in that house was a little like grow-ing up in hell. Brady expected perfection from everyone but himself. Talk about negative reinforcement. We never heard anything out of his mouth except how stupid we were and why couldn't we do anything right. Everything we did was a reflection on him, on his reputation, the artist, the humanitarian." He looked as if he wanted to spit. "He was kinder to dogs than he was to us."

"And when he found out you're gay he couldn't accept you."

Clifford looked at me sharply with new awareness in his eyes, then sighed. "The double whammy. I wasn't his kid. He could never accept me as his son. Being gay just iced it."

"It might have been worse if you *had* been his real son." I paused. "How did he find out?"

He looked at me again, then shrugged. "He caught me. I must have been about fourteen. A friend from school and I were fooling around in my room upstairs. We didn't really know what we were doing, but I remember it was the first time I realized I was different, that I felt different. Ronald used to talk about girls all the time back then, about how he'd seen a tit on one when she bent over, or a glimpse of the panties on another. He must have been sixteen. I never understood why it got him so excited. I figured it out that day. Brady came home from the studio early and found my friend and me naked. He knew, too. He knew it wasn't just adolescents fooling around. Life was real hell after that. Boarding school—which wasn't too bad, actually. I had my first affair there. But he shut me out completely after that."

"And your mother?"

"He treated her like dirt." He said it contemptuously. "I'll be the first to admit that Jennifer's a difficult woman. But she had a lot going for her back then. Looks, grace, charm. Brady just wore her down. She wasn't taking good enough care of his kids, or the house didn't look good enough. It was always something."

"What did she mean about Kitty being just like all the others?"

Incredulity spread across his face for a moment, then he laughed. "You didn't know Brady very well, did you? Hell, he screwed just about every model that walked through the door of the studio. I'll say one thing for him. At least he was reasonably discreet about it, but it was no big secret. And he had the balls to judge *my* lifestyle." His voice was bitter.

I was startled. I somehow hadn't expected this revelation.

"Did your mother know?"

"She knew. She could never prove it, but that's what half the arguments were about." He paused, then saw what I was driving at. "Look, she could have killed him back then and probably gotten off with justifiable homicide. She was very bitter about the divorce, even though she knew there was no way to save the marriage. It was all Brady's fault, but she wouldn't wait this long to get revenge. Mother's done all right for herself anyway, despite that bastard."

"She never remarried?"

He laughed again. "And make that mistake again? Oh, she remarried all right, but she got smart third time around. In the divorce, she got a big enough settlement to hold her for a few years, and Brady agreed to finish paying for my education. I think she realized she didn't have that many years left before gravity started to take over, so she used the settlement to buy a new wardrobe and wine and dine her way into the arms of a lot of wealthy men. I think that was partly her own way of getting back at Brady. For a couple of years she spread her legs for every old geezer with money. She finally found one who would marry her. John Tyler. I think Mother fucked him to death. He was dead inside a year, and he left her very well off."

He was not painting a pretty picture of his family, and I wondered, briefly, why he hadn't unloaded all this baggage on a shrink years ago. He probably had. The events that shape our childhood years tend to stay with us a long time no matter how we try to exorcise them.

"Do you know of anyone who would have wanted Brady dead?" I asked, changing the subject.

"Besides us?" The question brought him up short, and he looked thoughtful for a moment. "Probably lots of people. Like I said, Brady was a bastard, but he was a lot

more charitable to other people than he was to his family.
I can't think of anyone specifically who would try to kill
him.''

He frowned, as though uncomfortable with the idea of
not being able to come up with a name.

"Well, my five minutes are probably about up." I got
up from the chair. "Thanks for your time. Enjoy your
inheritance."

"Yeah, right," he said sarcastically.

I left him sitting there, and walked back out into the
heat and bright sunshine, trying to shake off the chill
of the store's air-conditioning and Stephen Clifford's
venom. Our conversation didn't make me eager to talk to
anyone else in Brady's family, but it did make me realize
there was a side to Brady I'd never seen, a side that didn't
sound like the person I'd known at all.

I left the car at the meter and walked over to a flower
shop on Wells to buy a bouquet of cut flowers before
making my next stop. I wasn't even sure the flowers
would help, but I had to make the effort.

Glynnis Meriwether lived in a coach house on one of
the little tree-lined side streets behind Wells in Old Town.
I stepped through the walkway between two houses into
a small, bricked courtyard that led to the front door of the
coach house. It looked comfortable and cozy, like a two-
flat in miniature. I pressed the bell outside the screen door
and waited a long minute before pressing it again. I was
about to give up when the inside door opened, revealing
Glynnis through the screen.

"You?! Go away!" She started to close the door.

"Wait. Please." I held out the flowers, and she hesitated. "Truce. I need to talk to you."

"What about?"

"Your father."

She stood indecisively for a moment, then swung the inner door all the way open and unlocked the screen door.

"Come on in."

She took the flowers out of my hand and led me through the living-dining room into a huge open airy kitchen with a dramatic two-story cathedral ceiling. A spiral staircase in an inside corner of the room wound up to the second floor. Someone had put a lot of money into rehabbing the building, and most of it had gone into the kitchen. The appliances were all top of the line Gaggenau equipment, and there was a commercial size stainless refrigerator-freezer combination on one wall built into the custom cabinetry. There was ample workspace, including an island, most of which was covered with food ingredients, mixing bowls and utensils. Two small stockpots simmered on the stove, filling the kitchen with enticing smells. It was warm in the kitchen despite the audible whir of both exhaust fan and central air-conditioning vents.

Glynnis put the flowers in a vase, then walked straight to a counter, pushing a strand of hair out of her face with a slender forearm, and went to work as though I wasn't there. Her dark hair was pulled back into a short ponytail, and she wore knee-length shorts and a cotton blouse that were both covered with a large white, food-spattered apron. There were thongs on her graceful feet, and when her toes curled to grip them, her calves stood out in relief, the kind of long, well-turned gams that make my insides go all fluttery. Her face was damp with perspiration from the heat, and even without makeup I realized how beautiful she was. I walked to the stove and lifted a lid with a potholder. I put my head over the pot and sniffed, then reached for a nearby spoon. Glynnis turned to look at me.

"May I?"

"Help yourself." She shrugged, then watched as I ladled some into the spoon and tasted. "Too little salt?" she asked, trying to read my expression.

"Lentil soup?"

"Mixed bean," she corrected me.

"No, the salt's okay. You might try a little more lime juice and some cilantro. If it were me, I'd add some chopped jalapeño, too. I like a little bite."

She looked at me with a touch of annoyance, then walked over to take the spoon out of my hand.

"What's all this for, anyway? Throwing a party?"

She blew on a spoonful of broth to cool it and tasted, ignoring the question. She frowned, and then her expression lightened.

"Maybe you're right," she murmured.

She found cilantro and a lime in the refrigerator, spent a moment at a counter chopping, and then added the ingredients to the pot. She stirred and tasted again.

"It is better. Try it." She handed the spoon back to me and walked across the kitchen to a table, sat down and made notes on a sheet of lined paper.

"You can cook," she said suddenly, turning around in her chair.

"So can you. This is good." I'd tried a taste of the contents in the second stockpot.

"Seafood bisque. *I* do this for a living, Mr. Ward. It always surprises me to run across a man who has even the faintest notion of what to do in a kitchen."

"Call me Emerson, please. You cook for a living? Catering?"

"I write cookbooks. I'm working on a soup cookbook. That's what all this is for."

"Now there's a coincidence. You cook for a living, and you can write. I write for a living, and I can cook." I said it good-naturedly.

She softened a little, and I thought I detected a small smile.

"Would you like some coffee?"

"Yes, please. With milk and sugar if you have it."

She got up to fix cups for both of us. "You said you wanted to talk about Daddy?"

"I'm surprised you didn't visit him in the hospital. Brady never mentioned seeing you."

She looked startled and a little guilty. "I *did* go. Twice. I went at night when I thought I wouldn't run into Kitty. Daddy was always asleep when I got there. I never had the heart to wake him, so I just sat with him a while. And I called the hospital every day to check on how he was doing. Is that enough?" Her expression turned belligerent.

"Sorry. You don't have to get defensive. Ron said he didn't bother visiting, and since I didn't see you there, I thought maybe you hadn't either."

"Ron and Daddy weren't the best of friends. I'm not surprised he didn't visit."

"What's with you and Kitty, anyway? Why do you feel like you have to avoid her? She doesn't have anything against you, you know."

"I'm just not that fond of her. It's easier to avoid her. I think she took advantage of my father, and I don't think she was right for him. I don't know what he saw in her. What is your interest in all this, anyway, Emerson?" She put emphasis on my name, as if saying it was distasteful. "Did she hire you to protect her interests or something?"

"Kitty and Brady are my friends. Or Brady was. I introduced them."

"And now you want to make sure the little widow gets what she thinks she should have coming?"

"Why shouldn't she?"

"I told you. I don't particularly like her, and I sure

don't know what she did to deserve everything Daddy worked for. She wormed her way into his life, took advantage of an older, lonely man, and now she thinks she should get it all.''

''How would you know? You've never even given her a chance. If you tried, you might even get to like her a little. Besides, you didn't object much when you found out how Brady divided up the estate. Or did you already know?''

''It's not the money. I don't care about the damned money! It's the fact that she's taken over the house, my mother's house. How dare she presume to lay claim on all the things I grew up with, all the memories she was never even a part of?''

She trembled with anger and emotion, on the verge of tears.

''I'm sorry,'' I said gently. ''I know how hard it is to lose someone close to you. I understand why you feel you have a greater claim on Brady. You're his daughter. But you have to know that Kitty loved him, too. She didn't want to come between you and your father. But she did want to share him with you. She didn't marry him for money, or status. She married him because she was in love with him, and like it or not, because your father was in love with her. That fact doesn't diminish the relationship you had with your father. It was just different. And if there are things, memories in that house you want, I really don't think Kitty will stand in your way. She knows she's an outsider here, despite the time she put in with Brady. Just give her a chance, will you? She's hurting, too.''

She stood silently, looking unconvinced, but some of her anger had faded. Her body had stopped trembling. She finally turned and walked over to a far counter, picked up a chef's knife and started chopping vegetables. I let her stew a minute, taking out her remaining emotion on the vegetables, not me.

"Why didn't you care about the money?" I said finally.

The chopping stopped, and she turned to face me. "None of this is any of your business, you know."

"Brady made it my business. He asked me to do him a favor, and when he got shot I couldn't just sit around and not wonder who would want to kill him."

"What favor?"

"That's none of *your* business." Stalemate. I paused, then tried another tack, guilt. "Aren't you just a little curious about who shot your father? Don't you care why?"

"Of course I care. But that's a matter for the police. What do you have to do with it?"

"I seem to have a propensity for these things." I shrugged. "But I need your help. I didn't know Brady as well as I thought, but he was my friend. It's too late in one sense, but I want to get to know him better. I have to. You loved him, lived with him. You can help me."

She looked at me, brows furrowed, and finally sighed, then took her coffee cup and walked across the kitchen to sit at the table. She stared into space for a moment, then started speaking in a low tone.

"Daddy was an only child. My grandparents were well off. Not rich, but well off. We didn't see them much when Daddy was married to Jennifer because they couldn't stand her. But after they moved to Florida, Ron and I would try to get down to visit them, like during spring vacation in college. They were nice people, fun to be with, and they let us do whatever we wanted when we stayed there.

"They died several years ago. Nana was the first to go.

Pop didn't last much more than six months without her, he was so broken-hearted. Anyway, they left everything to us, Ron and me. The way the will was set up though, the principal went into trust, and the interest went to Dad for as long as he lived. But Daddy decided he didn't need the money. The studio was doing pretty well, so he disclaimed the estate, meaning the principal came directly to us.''

"All at once?"

"No, in thirds. One-third when we turned thirty, another at thirty-five, the last third on our fortieth birthday."

"How much was it?"

"Almost six hundred thousand apiece."

"Why do you even bother working?" I muttered facetiously.

"It's a lot of money, but it's not enough to retire on," she retorted defensively.

"Surely with what your husband makes—"

"*Ex*-husband," she cut me off. "Even when we were married he never made enough to support us. We were always borrowing, getting behind." Her voice was bitter.

"I'm sorry. I just assumed..."

She shrugged. "I never bothered to change my name back. It all seemed like such a hassle, getting a new driver's license, new credit cards. I just wanted to put those nightmare years behind me."

She stared at the table, lost in thought, then slowly started talking again, almost to herself, not to me.

"'Chad the Cad,' Daddy used to call him. What a jerk I was to fall for him. He was an investment banker with big dreams and schemes and a lifestyle that exceeded his income. We had a condo in Lake Point Towers, expensive cars, nice furniture, and partied five nights a week. On top of it all, Chad had a coke habit that I never knew about. It all got old real fast. Daddy made sure I was well rid of him, divorce papers signed and delivered before he disclaimed Nana's and Pop's inheritance. He wanted to make sure that Chad couldn't get his hands on any of it.''

"I'm sorry," I said again. I didn't know what else to say. It brought her out of her reverie, and she looked at me with a touch of defiance.

"So, that's why I didn't care about Daddy's money. Well, I do care. I still don't think Kitty should get everything. But I guess Daddy knew Ron and I were taken care of, so what he gave us was just that—a token. I suppose it doesn't mean he loved us any less.''

"No, I don't suppose so," I said softly. "And if I know Kitty, she'll probably leave it all to you and Ron when she dies, or to your children if you ever have any.''

"You really think so?" She looked suspicious. "Maybe I have misjudged her.''

"Tell me about Brady. What was he like?''

"I miss him so much already. I haven't been able to stop thinking about him the last few days. I have so many good memories. When we were little, Daddy used to do things like come home at lunchtime and take us to the zoo or to the park for a picnic. When we started going to school, I remember him making time to come to all the school plays, the piano recitals, Ron's games, stuff like that. It was the little things he did that made him so special. He was always there for us, and I remember we all tried so hard to please him, to make him proud of us.

"I used to collect strays and orphans. You know, like baby birds that had fallen out of their nests, or lost kittens. Once I even found a baby squirrel with a broken leg. Daddy always let me keep them, and helped me to take care of them until they were well enough to go back out into the world.''

She paused, a dreamy look on her face.

"Christmas was the best, though. It was a wonderful time of year. Cold, crisp days. Roaring fires in the fireplace. Hot cocoa before bed at night. And decorations galore. It must have taken two weeks every year to get them all up in preparation for the big day. We always had a big tree, and every Christmas Eve Daddy actually dressed up like Santa Claus to put our presents under the tree just in case any of us woke up and went downstairs to peek. I think I must have been eleven or twelve before I finally figured it out. If there was snow, Daddy would take us all up to Montrose Harbor to go sledding, and if it was a cold enough winter, we'd go ice skating in the park."

"Jennifer too?"

Her eyes focused on me, and the dreamy smile was replaced by a frown of displeasure.

"She'd come and watch. She wasn't very athletic, and she always worried so about Stephen. Jennifer tried hard. She was pretty and smart, and she really tried to be a good mother, but she never really fit in. It was all right at first. Daddy must have married her when I was two or three, so I didn't really know the difference. I was excited, really, to have a mother. Ron and I never remembered our own mother. Well, Ron maybe a little. She died giving birth to me.

"As we grew up, though, it was pretty obvious that Daddy had made a mistake marrying Jennifer. They fought more and more. I think she was more interested in being Daddy's wife than being our mother, and Daddy just needed to have a woman in his life. I don't think he would have married Jennifer if he hadn't met her so soon after my mother died. It just got so ugly. I was relieved when Daddy finally decided to divorce her. It was as if things suddenly went back to the way they were supposed to be after all those years. I moved back into the house after college and looked after him.''

She was silent for a moment. ''Stephen's the one I really feel sorry for. He got caught in the middle. Jennifer was overprotective. It made us jealous at first. And Daddy never warmed up to Stephen. I'm sure it must have been awful for him growing up in that house. Ron thought he was a sissy. I tried to be his friend, but he was always a little standoffish. He never trusted us.''

Glynnis took a sip of her coffee. It had gotten cold, and she made a small face, then looked at me.

''Well, there you have it. The family history in a nutshell.''

''And now?'' I raised my eyebrows.

''I go on with my life. It hasn't been easy, you know. First, I helped Jennifer take care of my brothers. Then I took care of Daddy after the divorce, and tried to take care of Chad after that. When I was finally free from Chad, I didn't know what to do. I'd never really taken care of myself before. I had to figure out what *I* wanted out of life. I had the money from Nana and Pop, and I knew how to cook, having done it for so many years. I had a college education. So I decided to write cookbooks. I bought this place and borrowed the money to rehab it, and here I am.''

''I'm impressed.''

She looked at me sharply, trying to decide if I was being patronizing. I was sincere. What she'd told me changed a lot of the preconceived notions I'd had about her. There was still a wall there, an immense steel and concrete fortress containing and protecting her emotions, but now I had a sense of why it was there, why her subconscious had constructed it. Suddenly, I felt challenged.

She was as much an Everest in a different way as her
father had been, and some foolish macho impulse suddenly made me want to take her on.

"Would you like to have lunch, or dinner sometime?"
The words were out of my mouth before I could even
think.

Her mouth opened in surprise, then she shut it and her
eyes narrowed in suspicion.

"Not a date or anything," I said hastily, stumbling a
little over my own tongue. "I just feel I still owe you an
apology, and I'd like to buy you dinner. I mean, I know
you like food, and eating is one of the things I do best."

She smiled and put up a hand. "All right, all right. I
hate people who beg."

"Next week sometime?"

"Fine. Give me a call."

"I will. Listen, I appreciate all your time. I'd better let
you get back to work. I can find my way out."

I got up and started for the door, trying to make a dig-
nified exit before I did something even more stupid like
drool, but her voice stopped me on the way out.

"Emerson?"

I turned around reluctantly, hoping she hadn't changed
her mind about dinner. Her expression softened for a moment.

"Thanks for the flowers."

EIGHT

I DECIDED I NEEDED a major cholesterol fix, so I walked over to Nookie's on Wells Street for lunch and ordered a patty melt dripping with mounds of sautéed onions. It came, of course, with hot, greasy steak fries covering most of the rest of the large plate. As small acknowledgment to another food group, a thin slice of tomato on top of a limp piece of lettuce and a kosher dill pickle spear took up a small corner. Just what the doctor ordered.

I mulled the morning's conversations while I chewed. Given what I was learning about Brady's family, it shouldn't have surprised me that Stephen and Glynnis had painted such different pictures of Brady's familial abilities. But there had been an underlying current to Glynnis' comments that suggested her relationship with Brady had not been all sweet and light. A certain competitiveness, I sensed. They all had it—Jennifer, Stephen, Glynnis, Nick, even Nell to a degree. Maybe not so much competitiveness as a need to please Brady. Had he been that hard a taskmaster? Kitty seemed to be the only one who had been truly comfortable with Brady just as he was, as if perhaps she saw through the bullshit, or just wouldn't put up with it. Brady had had them all scared of something, but the picture wasn't complete yet.

I retrieved my car after lunch. There was a ticket on the windshield because I hadn't fed the meter. I put it in a conspicuous place so I wouldn't forget it. The city was seriously cracking down on parking violators, and I didn't want to risk getting "booted." Ryan had given me a work address for Ron Barnes that was in the River North area. I found it in less than ten minutes, but wasn't sure Ryan had given me the right number. The building at the address was a small showroom and repair shop for exotic imported cars. I pulled up to the curb right out front. Through the showroom window I could see a Lamborghini Testarosa and a Lotus Esprit parked on the floor. A person could buy a small townhouse in a decent neighborhood for what those cars cost.

I got out of my car and looked at it sadly. The old red Alfa coupe paled in comparison to the shiny, sleek beasts squatting on the other side of the window. I shrugged and pushed open the showroom door, then stood motionless for a moment, blinking, letting my eyes adjust to the relative dimness. A young man strolled casually in my direction, trying hard not to appear too eager. He was darkly handsome, with an expanse of white teeth and perfectly groomed hair. No suits and ties here. He wore baggy black silk pants, a loose pale yellow silk shirt open at the collar, and Italian leather loafers. He clasped his hands in front of him as he approached.

"Can I help you?"

"Yeah, I'm looking for Ron Barnes. Does he work here?"

His face fell even though the smile remained in place. "Sure. He's out back. Just go right through that door there."

The door he pointed to led to the garage. I spotted Ron leaning over the open hood of a new Jaguar XK8 painted in traditional British racing green. He wore jeans and a blue work shirt with his name embroidered inside an oval over the breast pocket. Another surprise.

"Hey, Ron," I called, walking toward him.

He turned his head and saw me, then straightened up and wiped his hands on a rag.

"Emerson, right? What brings you by?" He flashed a friendly smile.

"Wondered if you could spare some time to chat."

He glanced at his watch. "Sure." Then he turned and called over to the service desk. "Hey, Eddie, I'm knocking off for lunch, okay?"

The service manager waved without looking up. Ron made me wait a minute while he went to wash his hands and get a brown paper bag that sat on top of his tool chest.

"Come on, let's go outside and get some fresh air," he said when he rejoined me. "You want a soda or something?"

I shook my head and followed him out a side door into the sunshine. He looked around, squinting, and took a deep breath. He suddenly noticed the Alfa.

"Hey, is this yours?" He walked up to it and caressed a fender with the palm of his hand. "What is it, a seventy-five, seventy-six?"

"Seventy-four," I told him.

"Jesus! And it still runs?" He walked all the way around the car, appraising it.

"Reasonably well. It gives me some trouble now and then, but it gets me where I want to go."

"How many miles you got on it?"

"A little over a hundred twenty thousand."

"No wonder. You must baby it."

"Not exactly," I said wryly. "I don't need it much in the city, and I try to service it regularly."

"Yeah, now I see. Had some fender work done here, huh?"

"A couple of years ago. I got pissed off and tried to run a Jeep off the road."

"Not a very good job. Paint doesn't quite match." He shook his head. "Should have come to us. We got the best body man in the city." He cupped his hand against the passenger window and peered inside. "You know, we could restore this thing for you. Rebuild the engine, reupholster the interior and replace the glass, fix the dings, and give it a new paint job. It would be better than new. It was a good little car in its day, and it looks in pretty good shape."

Pretty good shape, he said. "How much?"

"I dunno. Five, six thousand, maybe. It'd be a hell of a lot cheaper than buying a new one."

"I'll think about it." The idea was appealing. I'd considered buying a new car for years, but hadn't been able to bear the thought of abandoning the Alfa. It was a classic. I perched on the hood of the car, putting my feet on the bumper. "What got you into cars, anyway?"

"It's a long story." He sat down on the curb in front of me, pulled a sandwich out of the paper sack and took a bite. "I always liked cars. I was always tinkering with my friends' family cars when I was in high school. I'd dreamed of being a race-car driver when I was a kid. Dad wouldn't hear of it, of course. So I kind of forgot about it.

"I did a two-year stint at Yale, pre-law, and hated it. So I dropped out and kicked around Europe for a year, and spent the summer following the Grand Prix circuit, sneaking into the pits whenever I had the chance, picking up jobs as a grease monkey when I could. When I finally came home, I went back to school. After I graduated, I got a job as a runner down at the CBOE. I hated that, too. Then I tried insurance. Same thing.''

He chewed while he talked, taking big bites out of the sandwich, occasionally pausing to wash it all down with a gulp of soda.

''I finally realized that all I wanted to do was work on cars, and to hell with what Dad thought. Of course, he never really forgave me. He thought I was throwing my life away. We weren't on very good terms after that, but hell, I like what I'm doing. I'm happy, been happy for years.''

''You aren't sore about Brady's will?''

''Naw, why should I be? I do all right here. You know, I was a fuck-up in Dad's eyes. I couldn't do anything right, and I was never good enough. My grades weren't good enough, my aspirations weren't good enough, I didn't win enough trophies. He was good and pissed when I dropped out of Yale. He ranted and raved about throwing away good money on my education when all I wanted to do was goof off. But I never asked him for a dime after I finally graduated. I made it just fine on my own. I didn't need his money. Despite our differences, I think the old man really did care about me—all of us—but I'm not surprised he left everything to his wife. Besides, Kitty deserves it.''

''Glynnis doesn't think so.''

''You talked to Glynnis?'' He looked at me sharply. I nodded, and he looked away for a moment. ''Glynnie thinks Kitty took advantage of Dad, that she moved in on him. I thought so too at first. I mean, she's not much older than me. It seemed a little weird. I didn't see Dad very often. We didn't have much to talk about, but it didn't take me long to see that Kitty was good for him. So I started dropping by every so often to see her, try to get to know her. I like her. Kitty's good people.''

Ron stuffed the empty sandwich wrappings back into the paper bag and dusted off his hands.

"Anyway, Glynnie probably told you about the inheritance we got from our grandparents." He saw me nod. "It was Dad's way of making sure we had something to fall back on in case we really fucked up. I think we disappointed him."

"What do you mean?"

"I'm sure he thought we'd blow it all as soon as we got it. We didn't. He probably thought I'd spend my share on a Formula One car or something."

"What *did* you do with it?"

"Put it into CDs, some tax-free municipals, a no-load equity fund. I'm not as stupid as he thought. I'm averaging better than thirteen percent a year, enough to splurge on a few toys once in a while. But I don't need much."

"Glynnis seems to be doing okay, too."

"Yeah, finally. She's been through a rough time. It's good to see her back on her feet. Getting rid of that husband of hers was the best thing that ever happened to her."

"Chad?"

"Yeah, you know him?" I shook my head. "Big, handsome guy, but a real asshole. All sizzle, no steak. I never liked him. He liked to live the fast life and brag about it. All just a cocaine rap if you ask me. Glynnie was just another trophy to him, and she drove him nuts because he couldn't really have her."

"In what way?"

He looked uncomfortable suddenly. "Aw, I shouldn't really tell you. It would just piss Glynnie off."

I waited expectantly. He shifted nervously.

"Look, all I'll say is that Chad thought he was a real ladies' man before they got married. I don't think things were that great after the wedding."

I began to catch his drift.

"You gotta understand, we grew up in a pretty messed up family. Our mother died when we were just babies. Did Glynnie tell you that? Yeah, well, then we were raised by a witch of a stepmother. Real fairy tale stuff. Our step-brother turns out to be queer. I was a little wild myself when I was younger. And all the time, it turns out Dad's screwing just about everything in a skirt. It's no wonder we both ended up a little screwed up."

"Did she know about Brady's affairs?"

He frowned. "I don't think so. It took *me* a while to figure it out. Even if she did suspect, she's the type that would never believe it. She'd choose not to see it. She worshipped Dad."

Ron wadded up the paper bag he'd been holding and rolled it between his hands, gazing down at the pavement. After a moment he looked up again.

"Not that I mind sitting around shooting the shit, but what's your interest, Emerson? What's so fascinating about my family?"

"I liked your dad. He was a friend, and he helped me out on a few occasions. I owed him a favor. When he asked one, of course I said yes. He died before I could deliver. I want to find out why. It's the least I can do."

"Fair enough. Has any of this helped?"

"Yes and no. I'm finding out Brady wasn't the saint I thought he was."

"He's always been nicer to outsiders than his family."

"So I've heard. What about you? Any ideas who might want him dead?"

"Hell, I would have taken a shot at him if I was mad enough. But I decided a long time ago not to let him get under my skin anymore. Anyway, I thought he was shot by a mugger."

"The guy was waiting for him in the bushes."

"Could be he was a burglar, and you and Dad surprised him before he could break in. He could have panicked and shot at you to scare you so he could get away."

"Maybe." It was a theory I hadn't considered.

"I gotta get back to work." He slowly got to his feet and stretched. "Listen, if you need any help, give me a call. Dad and I weren't that friendly, but if someone killed him, I'd like to know. And let me know if you want us to work on that car."

"Sure. I'll do that."

He strolled back in the side door, leaving me sitting on the hood of my car.

Kitty had asked me if I would go clean out Brady's files at the studio, so when I finished up at the agency that afternoon, I got my car out of the lot and headed west across town again. It was rush hour, and the traffic on Ontario was bumper to bumper, drivers beeping impatiently at lights and hanging out their windows in the heat. It took fifteen minutes just to go eight blocks, and I was thankful I wasn't getting on the expressway with all those people. Mercifully, I found a parking place on the street near the studio.

Sarah and Nancy were on their way out just as I came up to the street entrance. They barely acknowledged me when I wished them a good evening. When I stepped off the elevator, Nick was in the reception area saying something to Nell before he left. He gave me a gruff "goodnight" as he brushed past me into the elevator. Nell gave me a big, but tired smile, and caught me up on what had been happening in the studio in the past few days. Steinmetz was happy with the way the shots were turning out, and Marty was continuing to fine-tune the lighting and the set, giving him a few different things to look at. Nick had been moodier than ever, with big swings from cheery scout leader to morose grouch. And the girls had just walked around like zombies, still in shock over Brady's death.

I patted her shoulder, and told her I was sure she was doing the best job anyone could to keep it all together. It was just a period of adjustment, I said, and when things settled down, everything would be a lot better. She nodded, sighed, and smiled again, putting on a brave but disbelieving face. I told her why I'd come by, and asked if she could help me find some boxes for Brady's stuff. She led me back into the studio where Marty was wrapping things up for the night, and showed me where to look. When I thought I had enough of them, I suggested she go home and take a long bath and put her feet up. I said I'd lock up, and with small murmurs of protest, she let me gently push her out the door and on her way.

I heard some faint "goodnights" on my way down the hall to Brady's office, the closing of doors, and finally silence when the studio was empty. The summer sun still hung high over the horizon, blazing through Brady's windows, making the office bright and cheery. As I looked around wondering where to start, it was as if I was seeing a part of Brady for the first time. I'd never really noticed the antique car models, but they were everywhere, on the bookshelves, the desk, on top of the filing cabinets. Their bright colors and chrome gleamed in the light. I boxed them up first, admiring each one before carefully putting it away, then used a marker to write Ron's name on the box.

As I moved around the room I looked at the prints and photos on the walls, noticing for the first time a pretty set of watercolors with scenes of the Irish countryside. I never knew Brady had any interest in Ireland, but maybe he'd just liked the paintings. They would all have to wait, anyway. There wasn't enough room in my car.

I started in on the desk, boxing just personal items, leaving everything that appeared to be necessary to the business. The desk set went in a box, along with a personal checkbook, knick-knacks, executive toys, and small framed pictures of Kitty, Ron, and Glynnis. His former wives and his stepson were notably absent. I smiled wryly as I picked up one small picture frame from the desktop. It held a piece of parchment covered with beautiful calligraphy that read, "The road of life is littered underfoot with stones." That seemed so like Brady to keep a reality check on his desk to make sure he kept things in perspective.

The file cabinets were next. I went through each drawer quickly shuffling through the folders, leaving those pertinent to the business, weeding out those that were of a personal nature. The folders in a couple of drawers all held photographs, labeled in pencil by subject. Almost all were in black and white, the medium Brady had preferred. There were pictures of people, both strangers and friends, cityscapes, landscapes, every kind of photo imaginable. Looking through a couple of the folders was like thumbing through old issues of *Life* magazine. They all showed strength and character, demonstrating Brady's artistic side. But he'd never taken himself seriously when it came to photographs like these. He'd always considered them snapshots, not art. He'd been wrong. Kitty had the makings of a wonderful retrospective, a thick coffee table book, if she chose to memorialize him that way.

I decided to pull them all out and stack them neatly in boxes so they wouldn't get out of order. I emptied three file drawers full, a compendium of life through Brady's eyes and the lens of his camera, and as I was closing the last drawer, a flash of white caught my eye. In the back, on the bottom of the drawer was a five-by-seven print, its corner caught in a flange, as if someone had meant to put the photo back, but had slipped it between folders by mistake. I worked it free and took it out to look at it.

It was a picture of three men sitting on a park bench. At first glance, it looked innocuous, a common scene of friends who had stopped to chat in the park. But one of the faces looked vaguely familiar, and as I looked more closely, I could see that the man who looked familiar was taking something out of the hand of one of the others, an envelope perhaps. I sat back and closed my eyes, trying to remember where I'd seen the face. At Kitty's, looking through old yearbooks.

I bent over the folders I'd just boxed up and ruffled through the tabs quickly, reading off the subjects. And there, staring me in the face was that name again—Stan Wroblewski. I yanked the folder out of the box and opened it on the desk. All the prints in the folder were slightly yellowed with age. They were old photos, pictures of Stan Wroblewski in his youth. He'd obviously been Brady's friend. Most of the pictures were of Stan and other boys, clowning around in different settings. A few included Brady, the shutter snapped by someone else. They all appeared to have been taken around the same time period.

There were other pictures of Wroblewski in the file, too, taken over the years. Some were almost snapshots, a picture of him with his arm around an attractive woman, both dressed for a night out, another of him standing on a dock holding up a large salmon by its gills. Others were more formal, like portraits, that could even have been used for campaign posters.

I held the photo of the three men next to a photo of Stan by himself. It was the same face. I stared at the shot of the three men.

I had to think. Suspicions were starting to scuttle through my head like cockroaches. When I turned to look at them, they were gone, leaving me with only impressions. Brady's family all thought he was a bastard, except Kitty, of course. But had he been a big enough bastard to stoop to blackmail? I needed to find out who the other two men in the picture were. I stuffed the photo in the file and put the folder in the box.

As I started piling all the boxes up by the office door, I thought I heard noises in the studio. I stopped and cocked my head, but didn't hear anything more, so I went back to work labeling and taping the boxes shut. As I bent over to pick up one box, a sharp voice spoke behind me, nearly giving me a heart attack.

"What are-a you doin' in-a Mister Brady's office?"

I whirled around to see Rosa standing in the doorway, dressed in what looked like the same clothes I'd seen her in before and a scarf tied around her graying hair.

"You nearly scared me to death, Rosa. I didn't think anyone else was here."

"What are-a you doin'-a here?" she repeated sternly.

"Brady's wife asked me to bring home his personal things, so I'm cleaning out his office."

"I don't think-a you should-a be here."

In the light of day, I could see that her brown eyes were clear and bright, not the rheumy eyes of an old person. She was obviously still very sharp.

"It's okay, Rosa. Nell and Nick know I'm here. They

said it was all right." Maybe she hadn't heard for some reason. "Mr. Barnes is dead, you know."

"I know." Her mouth was set grimly, but I thought I detected a note of satisfaction in her voice, as if to say her son was *finally* going to be head of the studio, after all.

"Look, if you want, I'll make a list of everything I'm taking. You can even go through it with me. Then you can check to make sure I take everything on the list to Mrs. Barnes."

"No, that's okay. You just-a make sure you hurry up and-a get outta here."

"I'm just about done now. In fact, if you'll hold the elevator, I can probably load all these boxes on at once."

Tough old bird, but it was probably good she was suspicious. It made me wonder, though, how anyone had gotten by her to take the Winton collection out of the safe. She seemed to live here when the staff was gone. She called the elevator for me and pushed the hold button so she could go to work. I noticed her watching me, though, as I lugged boxes down the hall. She seemed anxious to see me go. When the last of them was on the elevator, I pulled out the stop button and waved to her as the doors closed. She didn't wave back.

KAMINSKI CALLED ME after a morning run up through the park to Diversey and back. I'd finally ceded to my guilty conscience that I was badly in need of a workout despite my personal feelings toward physical fitness nuts. It left me breathing hard and sweating profusely. Kaminski was concerned for my health when I answered the phone, which I found touching.

"What the hell's wrong with you?"

"Nothing," I gasped. "I just had to run to catch the phone. What's up?"

"I should have some answers for you today. Pick me up at the office after work. About five-fifteen outside the Wabash Street entrance. And dress nice."

"You can't tell me over the phone?"

"You owe me, Ward. Just be there." She hung up without further explanation.

I spent the day catching up on mail and correspondence I'd neglected since the day Brady got shot. There was a stack of bills that needed to get paid, editors who needed follow-up information on some stories I'd done, and a few clients that wanted to know my availability for projects over the next few weeks. I tackled it all conscientiously, and slowly worked my way through both the stack of mail and the long to-do list, but it was late afternoon when I finished. I jumped in the shower and rinsed off quickly, then dressed "nice" in dark wool slacks, a dress shirt and sport coat, but no tie.

Kaminski was waiting on the curb outside the *Sun-Times* building when I drove up, and she quickly climbed in the passenger door. Her hair still couldn't hold a curl, but she'd put on a little makeup, and looked more feminine than the few times I'd seen her.

"Where to?" I asked, pulling away from the curb.

"Swing back around to Wacker and take that to Madison."

I did as I was told, and we drove in silence. Kaminski looked out the passenger window, and from her demeanor, she didn't seem to want any pleasant chitchat. She directed me west on Madison, and after another mile, she finally broke the silence.

"Okay, here's the scoop." She turned to look at me. "The guy I know down at the coroner's office is kind of sweet on me, so I had to promise him dinner. Don't laugh.'' She looked at me severely. ''I'm not too thrilled about it, so not only are you going to buy dinner, you're going to come with us. I don't want to be left alone with this guy.''

''Dinner,'' I agreed. ''After that you're on your own. You're a big girl, Kaminski. I'm sure you can take care of yourself.''

''We'll see,'' she muttered.

In another five or six minutes, we found the big cement block of a building on Harrison that served as the county morgue and pulled up to the entrance marked ''Deliveries Only.'' A young guy with dark hair and Asian features stood outside waiting. Kaminski rolled down her window and waved. When he came up to the car, she opened her door and pulled her seat back forward.

''Come on, get in.'' She made introductions as he climbed in the back seat. ''Kent Fujikawa, Emerson Ward. Emerson's buying, so treat him nice, Kent.''

Kaminski gave me instructions to drive back east to Greek Town. Apparently the choice of restaurant had been prearranged. I listened to the two of them make small talk about their jobs on the way, and eventually found a metered spot on Halsted. We all climbed out and walked a block to the restaurant. Kent took hold of Kaminski's elbow firmly, ignoring her attempt to shake him off, and they led the way a few steps in front of me.

It wasn't until after we'd gotten drinks that Fujikawa finally turned his attention to me. I could see it was an effort for him to drag his eyes away from Sue.

''Sue tells me the stiff was a friend of yours?''

I nodded, a little taken aback by the choice of words.

''Sorry.'' He smiled. ''Goes with the job. We don't really think of them as people once they come through the door. Actually, I should be grateful to you for getting Sue to call me. It's a pretty interesting case. What do you know about pathology?''

''Practically nothing.''

He nodded. ''Okay, I'll go slow and try to put it in layman's terms. Sue said you thought this guy might have been killed. If it had been anybody else that called—a relative or something—I wouldn't have asked for the case. If it was assigned to me, fine. But Sue sweet-talked me into it. It sounded intriguing. We finished up today, and if the coroner signs it, the report will go to Violent Crimes tonight or tomorrow. You're getting a special preview.

''First thing we do, see, is make a physical inspection of the body. Other than the bullet wound and the surgeon's incisions, I couldn't find a mark on it that you could call recent. Since he came from Northwestern, I figure the easiest thing to do is run a 'tox' screen and see if anything unusual turns up. That didn't turn up anything except normal concentrations of painkiller and sedative. With me so far?

''Okay, so Sue says you think I shouldn't look for the obvious, but we're thorough, so we open him up and see the damage from the myocardial infarction. Sorry, heart failure. It looks pretty straightforward. The trauma from the gunshot wound along with the surgery—added to the fact that this guy is in his sixties and has plugged arteries—are pretty good reasons to suggest that his heart just gave out. But something bothered me. I might not have looked if Sue hadn't planted the idea in my head that the guy was murdered.''

Seeing he had me hooked and on the edge of my seat, he took a sip of ouzo and chased it with a big swallow of beer. He wiped his mouth on his sleeve, and smiled at my look of impatience.

"When they brought him in, he had a small fleck of dried blood in the corner of his right eye. I put that down in the notes, of course, but when I wiped it away, there was no evidence it was his, no sign of a wound. It could have come from the hospital somehow, but it bothered me. So I decided to open up his skull and take a look. Could have been real trouble for me if I hadn't found anything. From everything we could see, there was no reason to look inside his head. And our caseload is pretty heavy down there."

I couldn't contain myself. "What did you find?"

"Scrambled eggs, man. His brains were scrambled." He grinned, and I notice that Kaminski looked a little green around the gills.

"I don't get it." I frowned.

"Okay, you know what the medulla oblongata is? It's a small piece at the base of your brain that controls respiration, heart function, and stuff. The way I figure it? Someone used a sharp instrument—a length of stiff piano wire, or an ice pick more likely—and shoved it into the corner of his eye. It slid right past the eyeball, that's why there was only the one drop of blood. But whoever did it aimed down toward the base of the brain and then twisted it around some. The result is scrambled eggs, and almost instantaneous death. Respiratory failure, heart failure, everything shuts down."

"Jesus Christ!" I couldn't hold it in.

Kaminski mumbled something, excusing herself and hurried away from the table.

"He probably didn't feel much of anything," Kent went on, oblivious to Sue's exit. "Judging from the drugs in his system, he was pretty well doped up. He was probably asleep when it happened, really out of it. Pretty easy for someone to sneak up on him, thumb open an eyelid and shove in the ice pick. It was good, clean work, too. Someone thought it out. I hate to admit it, but we probably wouldn't have caught it if it weren't for you.''

''You're sure about this?''

''Of course. Guy was definitely murdered. He might have survived the gunshot wound. I don't know how many years he would have had given the shape of his arteries, but his heart looked strong enough. Pretty ballsy move though to kill him in broad daylight. Whoever did it must have looked like they belonged there.''

''You think it was a pro?''

''Pro? You mean like in 'hitman'? Mafia? No, everyone knows that nine times out of ten they use a bullet to the head and stuff their victims in car trunks. This was cold, calculated. Someone who had a lot of balls, a lot of rage. Maybe a psycho. Maybe all three. But anyone with a little knowledge of anatomy could have done it, not just a professional killer. Why?''

A little numbed, I sat back and drained my drink in silence, ignoring his question. Kaminski rejoined us after a few moments.

''You guys done yet?''

''I think so.'' Kent grinned again. ''We done?''

I nodded. ''Let's order and eat before anymore war stories. Okay, Kent?''

''Sure,'' he laughed.

With enough ouzo, dinner was kind of fun. Kent was an interesting guy, and despite her protestations, to the contrary, I could see that Kaminski liked him. Towards the end of dinner, Kent excused himself to go to the men's room, and I took the opportunity to talk to Sue.

''Hey, thanks for the favor. Dinner was worth it.''

''No problem. Any ideas who did Barnes in? I'd still like a story out of this.''

"Not yet. I'm still in shock. I didn't really believe he was murdered until now."

"You got me into this on a *hunch?*"

"Yeah, well, just wait. I need another favor."

"No way, Ward. Not until I get something out of this."

"You might. Take a look at this." I pulled the photo I'd found in Brady's office out of my coat pocket.

She peered at it closely in the dim light. "Judge Wroblewski. It's not that recent, though. He looks younger here."

"I thought so. Who are the other two?"

"Guy on the right is Ted Grettel, ward alderman. I don't recognize the other one."

"Could you find out?"

"Is this what I think it is?"

"What do you think it is?"

"A payoff."

"That's what it looked like to me, too."

"Where'd you get this?"

"Barnes' office."

"Jesus, this could be the scoop of the year!" The excitement was evident in her face.

"We need more."

"*I* know that."

"Will you help?"

"What do you think I am? Crazy? Of course I'll help. This is Pulitzer material. What are *you* going to do?"

"Keep digging. Look, Sue, you've got to keep this very quiet. If this is what we think it is, we could both end up dead. I don't want to stir up a hornet's nest until I've got a big can of bug spray. You know what I mean?"

"I'm not stupid, Ward. I know how to do my job. Can I keep this?" She held up the photo.

"Guard it with your life."

"Sure." She slipped it into her purse just as Kent returned to the table.

"By the way, you owe me a twenty," I told Kaminski with a grin.

"What for?" Kent asked.

"She bet me you wouldn't find anything in the autopsy."

"All right, all right," Sue said indignantly. "I was wrong." She dug in her purse, pulled out a bill and smacked it on the table.

"Thanks." I took the twenty and excused myself to go find our waitress. I settled our tab, gave her a generous tip, then gave her Sue's twenty and told her to buy Sue and Kent a couple of rounds on me. Then I went back to the table, thanked Kent for his cooperation and said goodnight. I didn't want to intrude any further on the lovebirds.

On the way home, I turned over the possibilities in my mind. I'd found a suspicious photograph of a circuit court judge, a city alderman, and an unknown third party in Brady's office. Brady had been shot with a gun that had been conveniently stolen from an old fart who just happened to live across the street from the judge. It smelled like blackmail to me, and the victim had gotten tired of being squeezed. So he'd hired some punk to take Brady out. But who had shoved an ice pick into his brain? That question still haunted me as I fell into an uneasy sleep.

SATURDAY PRESENTED even more problems. Kitty called with consternation in her voice and asked if I could come over when I had a chance. Since I'm not usually likely to be doing much of anything on a Saturday except puttering around the house, I told her I'd be there after I'd had some coffee. The effects of the ouzo still lingered, giving me a dull headache and a fuzzy tongue. I don't know why I'd drunk so much of the stuff. I don't even like the taste of licorice.

A hot shower, half a pot of coffee and some food helped, but I still felt a little out of sorts when I started walking up to Kitty's. I was stiff and sore from the run the day before, and I shouldn't have been. It was time to get off my lazy ass and tone up a little. I suddenly realized that age was creeping up on me. It was getting harder to keep everything in shape. Body parts I'd taken for granted in my twenties and early thirties were now reminding me of their presence in unpleasant ways. My knees had never been in very good shape. I'd banged them up too much in college ball. I'd learned to ignore the little pains that were always with me, and now I realized I'd been ignoring other pains in the process. It was time to listen to what they were telling me.

Kitty met me at the door in shorts and a sleeveless silk blouse, then took me out to the back yard and offered me orange juice and coffee. I declined, already feeling like I was going to float away on all the coffee I'd drunk.

"I tried to reach you last night, but I guess you were out," she said when I sat down on a patio chair. "Art Ryan called me yesterday. To ask me why Brady had cleaned out all his accounts. I told him I didn't know."

"When was this?" I asked sharply, my headache suddenly forgotten.

"I don't know. All I know is that Brady was broke." She looked about ready to cry. "There was some money in the studio checking account, and some in our joint checking account. But most everything else is gone. Even the trustee accounts he set up for me."

"Glynnis's and Ron's too?"

"No, they weren't touched. Emerson, what am I going

to do?'' She sniffed, and I reached out to take her hand, giving it a reassuring squeeze.

"First thing we're going to do is call Nell and see if she had any idea what was going on."

I used the portable phone on the patio table, got her number from information and dialed it. She was surprised to hear from me at home.

"I'm at Kitty's," I said after we exchanged hellos. "She says Art Ryan called to tell her Brady's accounts were cleaned out. You know anything about it?"

"Goodness, Emerson, all *hell* broke out at the studio yesterday." Her voice was agitated, and I could tell from her use of a swear word that she was very upset. "A small army of accountants swooped down on us, demanding to see the books. They think *I* had something to do with all this. I don't have the faintest idea what's going on. I told you last week I was concerned about the low balance in the money market account, but I don't know anything about those other accounts. Brady took care of those himself."

"Okay, Nell, I believe you," I said gently, trying to calm her down. "We need to start somewhere, though. Can you bring the books over so we can try to see what Brady might have been up to?"

"That's what I'm trying to tell you, Emerson. They confiscated the books. They're trying to find out if *I* embezzled the money."

I sensed she, too, was close to tears. "That's ridiculous. Of course you didn't. Tell you what. Why don't you come over here and have a glass of wine, and we'll see if we can figure out what's happened. Can you jump in a cab? I'll meet you out front."

"I guess so. All right. Give me fifteen or twenty minutes."

It was closer to twenty, and I was standing impatiently out on Dearborn, shifting my weight from one foot to the other when the cab pulled up. I stuck my head in the open passenger window to read the meter and gave the driver some bills before Nell had a chance to open her purse. Then I helped her out and gave her a hug before leading her inside. She was obviously distraught, and my reassurance seemed to help a little.

Kitty greeted Nell warmly. She seemed to be genuinely fond of her, and she, too, gave her a quick embrace, as if commiserating. We had to twist Nell's arm to get her to have a glass of wine. She thought it was too early in the day, but I thought it would help calm her down. She finally acquiesced, and I decided to join her. A Bloody Mary sounded good, and might just take the edge off my hangover.

"Has anything unusual been going on at the studio, Nell?" I asked when we got settled.

"Gracious, yes. You know how crazy it's been lately." Her eyes flashed at the stupidity of the question.

"No, I mean was Brady acting strangely? Was business okay?"

"Business has been fine. We're almost always booked. I can't think of the last time we were slow. It's been years. As for Brady, I can't say that he was any different. Maybe a little moodier the past few years than he used to be. I chalked it up to his age. Men don't accept aging gracefully. No offense." She was still indignant.

"Kitty?" I looked at her for corroboration.

"Yes, he's been different, was different," she said quietly. "Maybe it *was* the fact that he was getting older. I don't know."

"Nell, you say you don't know how Brady handled his

money, but you did keep the books. Was he spending money on new equipment or anything like that?"

"The studio account usually had enough to handle purchases like that. As I told you last week, if there wasn't enough money in the checking account, we'd just transfer funds over from the money market account. Those are the only two accounts I ever pay any attention to."

"If business was good, then there's no reason Brady should have been broke, right?"

"I can't say," Nell said hesitantly. "I'm not that familiar with how he lived." She glanced at Kitty.

"It's okay, Nell," Kitty said softly. "I won't be offended by anything you have to say. But I can tell you that I don't think we were extravagant. Comfortable, yes, but not extravagant."

"How much are we talking about here?" I asked.

"A lot," Nell replied. "Even without the books, I can give you a pretty good idea. Hmm, let's see." She closed her eyes and moved her lips silently. "Okay, here's approximately how it works out. Salaries, bonuses and benefits are about five hundred sixty thousand. Lease cost and expenses are about a hundred eighty thousand a year. So total operating expenses are around seven hundred fifty thousand in round numbers. Last year we took in about eight hundred fifty thousand in revenue, so we had a gross profit of about a hundred thousand. No, I take that back. Take out payroll taxes, so the gross is less. Brady paid himself a hundred fifty thousand a year plus bonus. I know. I wrote the payroll checks."

"Does that sound right, Kitty?"

"It certainly should have been enough. We really didn't have any big expenses."

"The house was paid off," Nell volunteered. "I remember the mortgage burning party about nine or ten years ago.''

"He could have taken out a home equity loan. This place is worth a lot more than he paid for it forty years ago. He probably could have borrowed as much as half a million on this place, and he might have drained all the accounts to meet a balloon payment.''

"But why would he need to borrow money?'' Kitty asked. "I don't understand. We had everything we needed.''

A light suddenly clicked on. "His personal checkbook, Kitty. It's in one of the boxes I brought from the office.''

"They're still in the den where you put them. I haven't gone through them yet.''

I went into the house and rummaged through the boxes until I found what I was looking for. Brady had saved everything, including check registers, and had filed it all as neatly as his collection of photographs. I brought out the checkbook and two of the more recent check registers. I handed one to each of the two women and told them to look for big withdrawals or large deposits. Within half an hour we'd found a pattern. About every three months for almost the past four years, a flurry of small deposits had been made to Brady's personal account, sometimes five or six thousand, once as much as fifteen thousand, but usually about ten thousand. Then a few weeks after the deposits, Brady had drawn a large check for cash against the deposits, from thirty to eighty thousand. The checks for cash almost always added up to the amount of the deposits themselves.

Kitty looked at me balefully, shocked by the discovery. Nell looked frightened.

"What does it mean, Emerson?''

"I'm not sure.''

It was only half the truth.

NINE

ON FRIDAY, I'd thought Brady was blackmailing a circuit court judge. On Saturday, I hadn't known what to think. On Sunday, I tried not to think at all.

Kitty and Nell had assured me that they'd seen no evidence that Brady was into drugs, gambling, or anything else that would soak up large amounts of cash. For a fleeting instant I'd wondered if Brady, as trustee, had been siphoning money off from the business and salting it away in a numbered account in the Cayman Islands. But why steal from himself? And why wouldn't he want Kitty to get the money? I was convinced they really had been in love, and I abandoned that line of thought as too far-fetched and complex anyway.

So, after waking up early, I did mindless stuff like stretch and work out with the thirty-five pound weights before it got too hot, clean the kitchen floor before things started growing in the corners, and do a couple loads of laundry before I ran out of socks and underwear. I have a woman who comes in every other week to help do a thorough cleaning, but she refuses to pick up dirty laundry. Knowing she's coming in motivates me to keep things reasonably tidy. I don't want her to think I'm a complete slob.

When I thought it was late enough, I called Brandt to see if he wanted to come over for coffee, and maybe

brunch if I felt like cooking. I knew he'd bring the Sunday
Tribune, which would give me more mindless things to
do like read the funnies and do the crossword puzzle.
He'd showered, but hadn't had coffee yet, and said he
thought having some of mine sounded like a good idea.

A front had moved through during the night, spreading
rain in the southern suburbs and from Waukegan north,
but leaving the city dry as every front had for the past
several weeks. In its wake however, was cooler, less hu-
mid air, not the heat I'd expected. We took coffee out on
my patio, and sat silently, each engrossed in our own
pieces of the paper, the arts section for me, and the business section for Brandt. We sat like two old men, glad of
each other's company, but absorbed in our own worlds
and our own problems.

I asked Brandt how my portfolio was doing since he
had me invested in all sorts of things I knew little about.
He grunted, looked at some stock quotations and said I
was doing fine and didn't I read my quarterly dividend
statements?

He tried to involve me in his dilemma again, explaining
how he'd found out that both charitable organizations he
was considering for grants had tried to conceal some skel-
etons. The chairman of the children's charity, apparently,
had once been arrested, but not convicted, for indecent
exposure. The school's board of directors, whether
through ignorance or willfulness, had misrepresented its
financial position to the banks that had agreed to lend
money for purchase and construction of the new school
building. I only half listened, grunting now and then to
feign interest.

When he was done, I launched into a rambling tale of
life amongst the Barnes clan, blithering stream-of-
consciousness impressions and half-baked suspicions.

Brandt kept his nose stuck in his paper, not even giving me the courtesy of pretending to be interested. So we sat silently for an even longer time, each stubbornly refusing to swallow our pride and concede that we could both use a little consolation and friendly advice. Eventually, I cooked up some Irish sausage, black pudding and eggs, and toasted some sourdough bread. We switched from coffee to Bloody Marys. And eventually, we grudgingly found a neutral topic of conversation that got us back on speaking terms. When he left for home sometime around mid-afternoon, we were almost friends again.

I called Glynnis to make a date for lunch on Monday. She agreed to a time and place, filling me with anticipation. When I started wandering around the empty house with a head full of licentious fantasies, I realized it was time for a walk to rid myself of such notions. I strolled up to North Avenue and over to the beach, spending the rest of the afternoon people watching, losing myself in the ebb and flow of the crowds of summer fun-seekers. There's nothing like a public beach for amusement.

MONDAY CAME SOON ENOUGH. I picked up Glynnis at her house and drove down to Hat Dance. She glanced at me a couple of times with a peculiar expression when I opened doors for her, or helped her out of the car. I wasn't being patronizing. That's just the way I am, a bit of a throw back to a time when that sort of behavior was called good manners, not chauvinism. Things got off to an awkward start between us, she still harboring some reservations about me after our first encounter, and me a little unsure of my own motives toward her. But we found we had more in common than we thought we would, and were soon more at ease.

We weren't that far apart in age, it turned out. I'd

thought she was much younger when I first glimpsed her at Greg's party, but we found we were almost contemporaries when we started talking about our college days. She'd attended Skidmore in upstate New York, not far from where I'd gone to school, and we traded stories about experimental curriculum and campus shenanigans. Brady had expected her to go to college and get a good education, I found out, but hadn't expected her to do anything with her degree. He'd had the old-fashioned notion that being well educated would land her an intelligent and moneyed husband, not necessarily provide her with an interesting and potentially lucrative career.

With a degree in English, a major in American literature, and no idea of what she wanted to be when she grew up, she found that she was well on her way to fulfilling Brady's expectations. I sensed resentment in the way she told it, as though she might have chosen to save the world if she'd only been given the encouragement that she could do anything she put her mind to. When Brady and Jennifer broke up, she decided to look after Brady when she graduated rather than risk striking out on her own. It was sad, in a sense, that it had taken her so long to grow up and out of Brady's shadow, but I could see she took great pride in who she was and what she did now.

"Why was Stephen the only one of the three of you to go to boarding school?" I asked at one point in our conversation about school. "Was it just because Brady found out he was gay?"

"Who told you that?"

I told her about my conversation with Clifford.

"Stephen is still very resentful towards Daddy," she said wryly. "Maybe justifiably so, but it tends to give him a distorted perspective about things. He was probably more like thirteen when Dad found out. I think I knew

Stephen was gay before he did, even though I didn't really
understand what it meant to be gay at the time. Anyway,
it was more than that, really. Daddy wanted all of us out
of the house. Ron was starting his first year at Yale. I only
had another year or so at the Latin School before I went
off to college, and I think Daddy knew that he wasn't
going to stay with Jennifer much longer. In his own way,
I think he wanted us out on our own for a bit, to get a
taste of independence before he divorced Jennifer so it
wouldn't be so hard on us.''

Despite the competitiveness she obviously felt, the subconscious resentment towards Brady, it was surprising
how protective she was of him, justifying his motives and
his actions. Ron was right. She'd concocted a John Wayne
image of Brady and put it up on a Cinemax screen to
admire and adore. In one way or another, maybe all of us
who'd known him had.

We talked and laughed about a lot of things over lunch,
and though she remained reserved and always in control,
I found myself liking her more and more. There was no
way she was cracking open the steel door even an inch,
but she was letting me close enough to see that there was
a whole person there somewhere. A little messed up, but
perhaps not unsalvageable. There was warmth somewhere
behind the facade. I got the best glimpse of it when we
somehow ended up on the subject of animals, and her
expression lightened when she spoke of them. People,
she'd learned to distrust, but she could still show affection
for animals.

She started telling a story of a pregnant neighborhood
cat that had recently chosen a quiet dim corner of her yard
to have its kittens. When she'd discovered the cat in labor
and saw that it already had dropped two kittens, she'd
rushed to find a laundry basket, line it with an old sheet,

and get the mother into it to deliver the rest of a litter of eight. She told it with joy and fierce pride, as if she'd delivered them herself. Suddenly her face turned sad.

"It reminds me of Harry," she said, staring into space.

I looked at her, puzzled. She slowly focused on me again.

"Sorry. Harry was my cat."

"What happened to him?"

"It's funny, I don't really know." She frowned. "A few years ago, when I was having a lot of work done on the house, I had to get rid of Harry for a while. The workmen, the dust, the noise were all driving him crazy. He was spooked all the time. so I gave him to Ron to keep until the work was done. It was fine with Ron. He liked Harry, and Harry was never much trouble to take care of.

"One day, Ron came home from work and found Harry dead on his kitchen floor. There wasn't a mark on him. I cried and cried for weeks. Poor Ron felt terrible about it. We never did find out what happened, but Ron figures that Harry must have caught a mouse that had gotten into poison or something."

"I'm sorry," I said softly. "It sounds like you can have your pick of this new litter, though."

"Oh, yes." A smile came to her lips. "I have just the one all picked out. Fortunately, most of the litter is spoken for. My neighbors have been great, helping feed the mother and offering to take kittens when they're old enough."

"That's really great." I said it with sincerity. Those little balls of fluff obviously meant as much to her as anything in her life just then.

When we finished lunch, I drove her back to the coach house, and even walked her to her door. She got it unlocked, then turned and solemnly shook my hand.

"Thank you for lunch. I guess I should thank you, too, for helping take care of all the arrangements for Daddy. I'm not sure I could have dealt with it. I suppose I should give Kitty a little credit."

"That would be nice. Maybe you could drop her a sympathy card. She'd really appreciate it."

"I might do that." She started to go in, then paused briefly. "You know, you might have been right about yourself. I haven't quite decided." She pursed her lips, then vanished into the dim interior of the house.

After some indecision, I made up my mind to swing by the studio and check in. I didn't know what I could do other than lend Nell moral support, but that was better than nothing.

When I arrived, things were in their usual state of affairs, barely controlled chaos. Nell was at her desk wearing a worried and frightened look. When she saw me, she glanced nervously over her shoulder. Two uniformed police officers stood a ways behind her conferring with a third man in a suit. He had a jowly, red face with a pug nose and small, wide-set eyes.

"Now what?" I asked in a low voice, stepping over to Nell's desk.

"More trouble," she whispered. "They found out the jewel collection was fake. What are we going to do, Emerson?" She was shaken.

"You don't know a thing, so don't worry."

Bulldog-face spotted me and came over to the desk.

"Who are you?" he demanded.

"Emerson Ward."

"What're you doin' here?" His voice matched the face, low and gruff.

"Friend of the family. Brady Barnes asked me to keep an eye on things here when he went into the hospital."

"What do you know about all this?"

"All what?" I feigned innocence.

"The Winton collection."

"Who's asking?"

He looked at me, stuck an unlit cigar butt in his mouth and worked it around for a minute. "Joe Butler, Great Midwestern Property and Casualty," he said finally. "You folks got a real problem here."

"Gee, what could that be?"

His expression turned pained. "Seems one of the people here switched fake stones for the real thing. I don't suppose you'd know anything about that?"

"Nope. First time I heard about it, Mr. Butler. Last I knew, one of the girls admitted to knocking one of the jewels off a set and accidentally smashing it. A week or so ago it was, I guess."

He looked at me hard, chewing the cigar butt. I noticed that Nell had dropped her eyes to the desk, as if pretending not to hear.

"Well, you can take your turn telling it to the detectives. As long as you're here, why don't you just park yourself in the kitchen back in the studio with the rest of them."

"Sure." I shrugged. "Anything I can do to cooperate."

I gave Nell a reassuring pat on the shoulder on my way past the desk and wandered into the studio. The whole staff except Marty was in the kitchen bay, sitting around with expressions ranging from fear to anger to depression. Nick was ranting, as usual.

"Jesus, Irv! None of this is our fault! It's that bastard Brady. Who knew he was going to up and die before telling us what really happened? He's the one who ripped them off, if you ask me. Why the hell do we have to drag the cops into this?"

Steinmetz sat quietly through the tirade, but suddenly pounded the table with his fist.

"Because it's my job if we don't recover those stones, you ass!" he roared. "I *have* to report it to the police. And unless you have any better ideas, they're probably the only people around here smart enough to find them!"

Nick lapsed into sullen silence, but started muttering aloud a moment later. "I don't know why we have to have the fucking cops around here. They're not going to find what isn't here. This is fucking absurd. We've got work to do."

No one paid him any attention. Nancy cowered in a corner, and Sarah thumbed absentmindedly through a magazine. Irv finally looked up at me, bleary-eyed, then looked away without acknowledging my presence. Two plainclothes detectives appeared a moment later, looking a little disinterested in the whole affair. Marty walked in a step behind them, calm but a bit befuddled. One of the detectives motioned to Nancy, and she walked away with them, head bent and shoulders stooped.

One by one, the detectives came and got us, and the little group dwindled. As each returned from being questioned, he or she would wander off to some other part of the studio, presumably to work. Those of us left tried studiously not to look at each other, as if afraid of revealing or discovering a source of guilt. It was an hour before the detectives finally got around to me. One of them recognized that they didn't have my name down on their list and asked me who I was and what connection I had with the studio. I told them why I was there, and suggested I couldn't add much to what they'd already been told, but he said I might as well tell them what little I did know. I shrugged and followed them back into the hall. They'd chosen Brady's office for their interrogations.

I made myself comfortable on the couch and launched into the story of how Brady had been shot, how I'd gotten him to the hospital, and how he'd asked me to stop by once in a while to see how the staff was getting along without him. Then I told them about the day Steinmetz had noticed a missing gem on the set, how we'd searched high and low for it before Nancy had finally broken down and admitted what had happened. None of us had suspected at the time that the collection had been stolen, switched for fakes, I said. Steinmetz had been understandably upset, but hadn't felt the situation warranted a call to the police. They let me go, trying to hide huge yawns, and said they'd be in touch if they had any more questions.

I went to find Nell to see how she was doing. They'd taken away the books, they'd brought in the cops, and the studio had been turned upside down by Brady's death and the discovery of the theft, but Nell had gotten back to business as usual. She was in the studio making sure everyone knew about upcoming projects and their assignments on each. I had a few words with her before I left, telling her to call me if she needed me for anything.

On my way out, I ran into Butler again. We'd taken an instant dislike to each other, but I tried to be civil. He'd obviously never learned any manners, and had probably lost his sense of humor sometime during his early childhood.

''I unnerstand you been asking a few questions of your own about the jewels, Ward.'' He grabbed my arm above the elbow and squeezed hard. His grip was strong, but he looked a little out of shape otherwise, with a belly that rolled over his belt. He appeared to be several pounds heavier than me even though the top of his butch haircut came only to the tip of my nose.

"I offered to help out. Like I said, anything I can do to cooperate."

He stuck his face close to mine, breathing the smell of stale tobacco. "This is my investigation now. Whatever you think about this case, you keep to yourself. And stay out of my way."

"Sure. Anything you say."

He nodded and released his grip. "So long as we unnerstand each other, we'll get along fine."

Anger didn't wash over me until after I stepped on the elevator, and I descended to the street in a black mood. It was close to 5:00 already, so I walked a few blocks over to the garage where Ron Barnes worked and waited out on the street, pacing with the first cigarette I'd had in days. He emerged shortly after quitting time with a wave over his shoulder and shouted good-byes to co-workers. He came up short when he saw me, then smiled.

"Didn't expect to see you again so soon."

I fell in step with him. "Wondered if we could go get a beer somewhere."

"Sure. I'm not doing anything."

He led me to a bar not far away, and I bought us a round and took it to a corner table.

"I'm stymied," I said, not sure how to begin. "I'm not having much luck, and I wondered if you'd thought of anything that might help me."

"I'm not sure what you mean."

"Look, I don't know if you've been following what's going on, so maybe I should fill you in. First off, Brady was definitely murdered. Someone stuck an ice pick in his brain at the hospital to make sure he didn't recover from the gunshot wound. I'm surprised the police haven't been around asking you questions yet."

"Jesus, I didn't know. When did you find out?"

"I found out Friday, which means the cops have had a few days to work on the file, but maybe no one looked at it over the weekend. Anyway, second thing is that your dad was broke. The money for you and Glynnis and the Cliffords wasn't touched, but every other account was cleaned out, leaving Kitty with nothing except the house and the studio. Now it could be that someone didn't want Kitty to get anything, so they forced Brady to move the money somewhere else. Or maybe something else is going on that we don't know about."

He looked surprised and concerned. "I don't get it. I can't see anyone holding that big a grudge against Kitty. Okay, so Glynnie doesn't like her that much, but she wouldn't do a thing like that. And I can't see anyone, not even Jennifer, forcing Dad to do anything he didn't want to. It's gotta be something else."

"Okay, so, what? Has anything unusual happened that might point me in the right direction? Think. Go back a few years if you have to."

Ron looked at me blankly. "Nothing comes to mind. I told you, Dad and I weren't close. I didn't pay much attention to what was going on in his life."

"What about the cat? Glynnis told me something happened to her cat."

"Oh, that." He was startled, then thoughtful. "You know, there was something peculiar about that." He told me basically the same story Glynnis had told. "The thing that was strange was that I didn't have any bait out for mice. I left the cat in the apartment, and the apartment was locked. It couldn't have gotten out into the alley or anywhere there might have been poison that I can think of. The other thing I didn't want to tell Glynnie was that the cat had some blood on the back of its neck, at the base of the head. Not much, and I couldn't find any kind of wound, so I didn't mention it. I didn't want her to freak out. I just sort of forgot about it until now."

"What else? Have any other strange things happened?"

He leaned back and thought. I waved the waitress over and ordered another round while he pondered. He drained his glass, looking out the window, then sat up slowly.

"Maybe there is something else. When Kitty got that little Mercedes, I told her to call me if she ever needed work. I told her I'd be happy to do it in my spare time, no charge. Well, she called me one day not too long after she got it. She couldn't get it started. I came up to take a look. The car was out in the garage, and sure enough, it wouldn't start. I checked it out totally, and I couldn't find anything wrong. I was about to give up, thinking there must be a loose wire that I was missing. I figured I could have it towed down to the shop and run diagnostics on it to find the problem. Just for the hell of it, I took one more look, going over every inch, even sliding under the car again to see if I could spot anything. I did.

"Someone had jammed a potato in her tailpipe. I never would have thought to look. Go figure. The garage was locked. Someone went to an awful lot of trouble to play a practical joke."

"Brady?"

"No way." He shook his head. "Dad had a pretty bizarre sense of humor sometimes, but he wouldn't do that to Kitty. Especially not to that car. She loves it too much. That kind of joke is almost downright mean. If she'd called a garage, they probably would have charged her a fortune before finding the problem, and then would have been too embarrassed to tell her the truth. *I* was embarrassed. Hell, it took me almost two hours to find that potato."

A dead cat and a dead car. Ron and Kitty.

"What about Glynnis?" I said suddenly. "Has anything happened to her?"

"Other than her cat dying in my apartment?" He shook his head again. "I can't think of anything. You'll have to ask her."

"I guess I will," I murmured.

TUESDAY WAS HOT AGAIN. I dressed for it—shorts and a sport shirt—especially since I was leaving the car at home and taking public transportation. I walked over to the Clark Street subway station and took the first train downtown. It was cooler down in the subway, but dank. The El cars, though, had the air-conditioning cranked up to high, so the transition back to the heat in the Loop was even more pronounced. It was only a two-block walk from the subway to the Mahler's Building on Wabash, but my shirt was damp by the time I got there.

Dave Kliewer had a jewelry shop on the seventh floor of the building. Elevator operators still ran the open-caged cars manually from floor to floor, and I squeezed on with a crowd of people who had been waiting some time for an empty car. Getting out was difficult without jostling elbows and almost stepping on toes, but I managed to ease my large frame through the crowded bodies without injuring anyone. There were a lot of jewelers in the building, and I had to look at the numbers on the shop doors to find Kliewer's.

Like the rest of the stores and offices on the floor, the shop had a plate glass window in front from waist-high up and a glass pane in the door with the shop name painted on it. There were display cases behind the glass window with collections of watches, necklaces and rings. I peered through the window and saw more display cases on both side walls of the store and a glass-covered coun-

tertop toward the back of the store. When I opened the
door, a small bell tinkled above my head.

The man sitting behind the glass case in the shop was
small, with dark wavy hair that didn't know which way
to be combed. He looked to be in his forties, and wore
dark slacks and a white shirt buttoned all the way up to
the collar. He was bent over a broach on the counter when
I entered, and I saw he wore an embroidered yarmulke on
the top of his head. He looked up and smiled as I walked
across the worn linoleum floor to the counter.

"Can I help you with anything?" His voice was pleasant.

"Mr. Kliewer?"

"Yes?"

"My name is Emerson Ward. I'm a friend of Brady
Barnes. He told me he consulted you a few weeks ago,
and I wondered if you could answer some questions for
me."

His face still smiled, but he'd tensed when I'd mentioned Brady's name, and now seemed uncomfortable.

"The Winton collection," he sighed.

"Yes. Brady said you told him the entire collection was
fake two weeks ago."

"He knew—" He started to say something, but caught
himself. "Yes, I examined a few of the stones quite
closely. They were imitations. After looking at the rest of
them, I surmised that none of them were real."

"You may not have heard. Mr. Barnes is dead, and the
fake gems have been discovered."

He started, and there was a flash of fear on his face. "I
assure you, I had nothing to do with the switch."

"I'm not suggesting you did. Brady said he trusted you.
I'm asking you to trust me. The police know about the
switch, as does the insurance company, including a par-

ticularly nasty investigator named Butler. Brady told me about you, but I haven't told anyone else. I don't think anyone else will come asking you questions.''

His thin shoulders seemed to sag in relief, but he looked at me suspiciously for a moment before letting down his guard anymore.

"How did Mr. Barnes die?"

"He was murdered. I don't know if it had anything to do with what has happened to the Winton jewels or not. I'm trying to find out."

"Why?"

"Because he was my friend. His wife, Kitty, is still my friend. She deserves to find out who killed her husband.''

"What can I do for you?"

"The fakes were good?"

"Very good. The right color, the right size and cut. It would take a seasoned eye to tell. In the case of those particular stones, however, I'm sure that the real ones had been tagged with laser identification numbers. These had no such numbers.''

"Is there any other way to tell?"

"Two. One is the hardness of the stones themselves. In the case of diamonds, the fakes will obviously not be as hard as real gems. Other precious gems aren't as hard as diamonds, so a material like cubic zirconia may approximate them. But every diamond has its own peculiar atomic structure which can be identified by x-ray. You could tell fakes from the real thing that way, too.''

"There were about thirty stones in the collection. How long would it take a good faceter to duplicate the collection if he had the right materials?"

He shrugged. "Hard to say. To make duplicates good enough to fool a trained eye would take some time. Months, probably, for the whole collection. One stone can take a week or more to cut just right if it's a large one and the faceter wants to get the most out of what he's working with."

"It couldn't have been done in less time?"

"I doubt it. Why?" The questions seemed to make him nervous.

"Someone would have to have had the gems for some time," I murmured. "Long enough to be able to copy them."

"I suppose so." He was hesitant, and his eyes blinked rapidly. Something was bothering him, but perhaps it was just fear of being associated with the theft.

I looked at him for a moment, but decided not to push it. "Well, thanks for your time." I started to turn.

"Uh, Mr. Ward, is it? I'd like to avoid any trouble, if I could."

"I won't mention it."

He nodded and swallowed. I'd gotten what I came for, and it wasn't until much later that I realized I hadn't asked the right questions.

With nothing to do, I was at loose ends, so I figured I'd call my answering machine from a pay phone to see if I had any messages. There was one, from Sue Kaminski. I walked slowly up Wabash and across the river to the *Sun-Times* building, trying not to break a sweat in the heat. Despite the breeze, it wasn't possible. My shirt still clung to me in spots.

Kaminski was in her cubicle, and she looked up, startled, when I rapped on a partition with a knuckle.

"Oh, it's you. That was fast."

"I was in the neighborhood."

"I've got something for you. Come on."

She pushed away from her desk and stood up to lead me to a small conference room. She shooed me in and left me there alone for a few minutes. When she returned, she had an older man in tow, and she shut the door behind them both.

"Emerson Ward, Bob Goldsmith," she said, coming to the table.

The man extended his hand silently, and I gave Kaminski a sideways glance as I matched his flaccid grip.

"He's okay, Ward," she said. "I need him on this one, and it's a way to cover my cute little tush. Bob's been working the political beat for years."

"All right. What have you got?"

Kaminski produced the photo I'd given her and laid it on the table. Goldsmith pointed to it and started talking in a soft, low voice.

"The third man in the picture is Phillip Acardo. Acardo has long been thought to play a key role in organized crime in Chicago. He started out years ago as muscle, and worked his way up. In the Seventies, Acardo was head of mob gambling operations in the western suburbs, and moved up again. The feds now think he's the number two or three man in Chicago.

"For years, they've also been trying to build a case tying Ward Alderman Grettel to the mob. There's never been enough evidence, though there's been talk recently of a federal witness, a mole, with taped conversations between Acardo and Grettel. But there hasn't been any grand jury investigation yet, so we don't know what kind of case the feds have.

"This, however, is pretty damning evidence." He tapped the photo with a finger. "Something big must have been going on to bring them out into the open like this. Hard to believe they would have risked being seen together. Judging from the age of this photo, it appears to have been taken when Wroblewski was still with the D.A.'s office, before he was elected to the circuit court. If Grettel was arranging mob payoffs back then, you can bet that they haven't stopped now, not with Wroblewski on the bench. That would be just what they'd want."

He looked up at me with the smugness of a reporter who knows something no one else does.

"What do you know about Wroblewski?"

"General background stuff. Spent a number of years in the P.D.'s office before he got sick of it and switched sides. Went to work for the District Attorney and worked his way up. Divorced, two grown kids somewhere. That sort of thing. We're checking him out now."

I pulled on my mustache, thinking. "So, how do you prove all this?"

"We go through court records," Kaminski piped up. "We look up all the cases Wroblewski has been involved with for the past fifteen years, and see what the disposition was on each. We try to find cases that might have been mob-related. We look for a thread that will support what the photo suggests."

"How did this guy Barnes happen to have this photo?" Goldsmith asked. There were some things reporters didn't know.

I glanced at Kaminski. She hadn't clued him in. "My guess is that he took it himself. He and Wroblewski went to high school together. He probably saw his old friend in the park and snapped a picture without even thinking about it. He may not even have known what he had." And then again, he might have.

Goldsmith excused himself, saying he had to get back to a story. I talked with Sue for a few more minutes. She gave me back the photo, saying she'd had a copy made for her files, assuring me it was under lock and key.

"What's going on anyway, Ward?" she asked as I rose to leave.

"What do you think?"

"Barnes is dead, killed. He and Wroblewski knew each other. You find a photo in Barnes' office that incriminates Wroblewski. Blackmail?"

"I promised you a story about Barnes. I gave you something bigger. Be happy with it because I don't know any more than you do."

She shrugged and smiled sweetly. "Okay."

The bigger story would keep her busy for a while. I still wanted to know who killed Brady, and I was tired of the indirect route. I took a cab home, got out my phone book, and after three calls got the direct number for Wroblewski's chambers. A woman with a deep voice answered after four rings.

"Circuit court."

"Is Judge Wroblewski in chambers?"

"No, honey, the Judge is on vacation."

"Well, I hope he's gone some place cool," I chuckled. "This heat is really something, isn't it?"

"You said it, honey. Almost makes me glad I'm working today. At least the office is cool. I think the Judge is home sweating in his garden. Least he didn't tell me he was going anywhere this summer. I'll bet he wishes he had."

"Well, thanks."

"Any message?"

"No, thanks. I'll try him when he gets back."

I hung up and went out the back door to get the car out of the garage, making sure the photo was secure in my back pocket. It was time to take a poke at the hornet's nest and see what came flying out. I was itching for a good fight, anyway, anxious to flush something out so I could take a look at what I was dealing with. Bumbling around asking questions hadn't gotten me anywhere so far.

I drove the little red car angrily, revving it hard through the gears. The evidence was hard to ignore. I was mad at Brady for hiding the truth. I was mad at the thought of tax dollars going to waste on a system that was corrupt. I was mad at getting sucked into all this on the basis of a friendship with a man I obviously hadn't known well, or had misjudged.

I was still angry when I punched the bell of the house in Ukrainian Village. The windows were dark, and after I got no response, I leaned over the porch rail and cupped my hand against the one nearest the door to see if there was any sign of life inside. I rang the bell again, and waited, turning to look up and down the street. There wasn't a soul in sight. It was high noon on a lazy hot summer day, and all the smart people were at the lake or indoors where it was cooler. Gardening, the secretary had said, so I stepped down to the sidewalk, hopped the low iron picket fence, and walked through the side yard to the back of the house. The shrubs and flowerbeds by the side of the house were all well tended, but dry, as if no one had watered for a few days.

The backyard was empty, too, but I hadn't driven over for nothing, so I went up the back porch to try the bell at the back. I stabbed at it with a forefinger, then noticed that though the screen door was closed, the inside door was open a crack. Someone had to be home. I pushed the button again and heard the bell ring somewhere inside the house. Still no one came.

I opened the screen door and pushed on the inside door to shout a hello. When the smell hit me, I froze. I knew instantly what it was, and it yanked me back for a moment to summer days as a boy on a farm. Every so often, a dog would turn on one of the sheep, or one would up and die of old age, and eventually we'd find it out in the fields. The smell had been the same. It was the smell of death.

TEN

I TOOK A SLOW STEP INSIDE, heart pounding from a sudden rush of adrenaline, breathing through my mouth to avoid smelling the stench. The house was quiet. The kitchen blinds were drawn, and my eyes slowly adjusted to the dimness. I didn't have to look far. A man's body was slumped over the kitchen table, and it had been there for a while. I snapped on the kitchen lights and looked at his face. The sightless eyes of Judge Stanley A. Wroblewski stared back at me. He sat in a chair, his left cheek resting on the table with an arm thrown over his head. The other arm dangled at his side. The hand that protruded from the sleeve of his shirt was bright red, as was the side of his face that touched the table. Lividity, I guessed.

The body was bloated with gas, and I knew I didn't want to be there when they tried to move him. The body would probably start to fall apart from decomposing in the heat, and the smell would be ten times worse. We used to bury a sheep by digging a big hole, then scooping up the carcass with the hydraulic bucket on the front of the tractor. A couple of times, though, the bucket had torn through their hides, popping them with a hiss like a falling soufflé. The smell wasn't easy to forget.

I walked around him carefully, trying not to disturb him. There was a dark spot on the white hair just above his shirt collar. I bent closer to look at it. It was a small patch of dried, matted blood that ended in a short, rust-colored trickle along the hairline. A couple of big, black houseflies buzzed around his head, and a wave of nausea suddenly washed over me. The smell was getting to me. I pinched off my nose and took a few quick steps out to the back porch to gulp some fresh air. Smog never tasted so good.

I'd seen enough. I walked back around the house and pulled out my cell phone to dial 9-1-1. For good measure, I called Lanahan and told him he'd better meet me at the address across the street.

I sat on Wroblewski's front steps and watched as two blue-and-whites pulled onto the side street and up to the house in minutes. Their blue lights continued to flash, but the short squawks of their sirens faded quickly. There were three uniforms in the two cars, and they all got out and strolled over, hitching up their pants and donning their caps in exactly the same way as if they'd been taught the move at the academy.

"You the one that called in a body?" one of them asked.

I nodded. "In the kitchen. Back door is open, but try not to disturb anything. He was a judge, and it looks like murder to me."

Two of them walked around the side of the house, and the one who looked the most senior stayed with me. He started asking me my name and address. I obliged, but told him to save the rest of it until Lanahan got there.

"Don't know him," he said, taking out a notepad and a pencil.

"He's not in your district," I explained.

The other two came back around the corner of the house looking slightly green.

"Been dead a couple days, I'd say," one of them

called. He used the walkie-talkie on his shoulder to call it in to dispatch. And we all stood around smiling politely at each other until Lanahan pulled up ten minutes later.

"What's the story?" he said quietly, flashing his shield at the uniforms as he walked up to us.

"Guy here says the body inside is a judge," one of the cops replied, gesturing at me. "Body's been there a while."

"Homicide?"

"Could be. There's a spot of what looks like blood on the back of his head, Lieutenant."

"Who's been inside?"

"Me and Bobby, and the guy who found him."

"Start roping it off until the lab guys get here. I'll take a look in a minute. Well, Ward?" He turned to me.

"Stanley Wroblewski," I said wearily.

He looked at the house, then back at me. "How did you just happen by to discover the body?"

"I came to see him. I wanted to talk to him."

"Why?"

"Let's go to your car, okay?"

He looked at me sharply, then shrugged. As we walked to his car, a meat wagon pulled up, followed by a forensics team. Lanahan stopped to give them instructions, then turned and told me to get in. I climbed in the passenger door and left it open to get some air.

"What the hell is going on?" he said loudly as he climbed in.

"Take a look at this." I handed him the photo, and saw his eyes widen. "That's Wroblewski and Phil Acardo—"

"And Ted Grettel, I know," he said, finishing my sentence. He frowned, taking a close look at the picture. "Where did you get this?"

"At the studio, in Brady Barnes' office. Put it together, John. The gun that was used to shoot Barnes was stolen from an old guy right across the street there. The old guy turns out to do odd jobs for Judge Wroblewski. Barnes and Wroblewski went to school together. When I found this photo in Brady's office, I started thinking maybe Brady was blackmailing the judge, and maybe the judge got tired of being squeezed and hired somebody to take Brady out. I didn't want to think Brady was capable of blackmail. It takes a lot of greed or spite or desperation to get into that game. I still can't believe Brady was any of those things, but it sure looks that way. I came over to ask the judge in person, just to see his reaction."

"Not very smart."

"Maybe not, but the papers are onto this already. I showed this to a reporter at the *Sun-Times*. If Wroblewski was dirty, you may be reading about it in tomorrow's morning edition. Anyway, I figured I didn't have much to lose."

He looked at me, and I could see the wheels turning in his head. "But if it happened the way you say, then who killed the judge?"

"Exactly. And, who finished off Brady in the hospital? The judge's man? Or someone else?"

"Who told you about Barnes?" he asked sharply.

"I can't tell you that, Lieutenant." I matched his stare, and he finally looked out the windshield at the flurry of activity around the house. Yellow plastic tape had already been strung around the perimeter, and a crowd of curious neighbors was beginning to gather, drawn like moths to the flashing blue lights.

"Christ, Ward, you're a pain in the ass. A circuit court judge. I'm beginning to dread the sight of you." He paused a moment. "All right, get out of here. Meet me back at the station in an hour. I'll pull a stenographer and get your statement then. The photo stays with me.''

"Sure, but don't show it to the media if you don't have to, Lieutenant. I promised my friend an exclusive on this story." I didn't have any further use for it. I climbed out of the car, walked back to my own and drove slowly home.

Before meeting Lanahan, I called Kaminski to tell her what had happened. She was furious with me for going to see Wroblewski, accusing me of trying to sabotage her story. She finally calmed down when I reminded her that my decision to confront the judge, foolhardy or not, hadn't made a damn bit of difference. He was already dead. I also reminded her that even though Wroblewski's death would probably make it on the local evening newscasts, she could still break the story of his possible mob connections. She'd just have to dig a little harder, a little faster, and run with what she had. She was mollified, but only a little.

Lanahan had some curious news for me after I finished relating my statement to a stenographer in the small interrogation room at the station.

"I took a look at the body," he told me. "After seeing that photo you gave me, it looked like a mob hit to me. Bang, one shot, small caliber in the back of the head. Pathologist says it ain't so. He says the wound is too small, more like somebody stuck him with something sharp."

"Like an ice pick?" I hesitated to ask.

"Yeah, like an ice pick. Which suggests the killer was someone he knew, or someone he thought was harmless." He sighed. "This is starting to get messy. You ought to consider backing off, you know."

"I know."

"You won't, though, will you?"

"No."

He sighed again. "Try not to keep any secrets, will you? Just tell me what you find out and let us handle it, okay?"

I PICKED UP A BOTTLE of good red wine and dropped in on Glynnis around 7:00. She was surprised to see me but didn't seem to mind the company. She led me back to the kitchen, graciously accepted the wine, and went to a counter to get an opener and two glasses. I parked on a stool at the center island. It was easy to see why she was most comfortable in the kitchen. It was not only her work-space, where she could keep things on a professional not personal level, but it was also the place in which she was at her best, where she was most complete. It was homey, too, despite the high tech, Eurostyle look, with just enough personal touches, from the choice of wallpaper to the country kitchen potholders, to give it warmth.

Glynnis came and sat on a stool across the island from me, and handed me the glasses and corkscrew. I opened the bottle and poured a glass for each of us, then raised mine.

"To your dad." She took a sip silently. "You know, through all this I've never really told you how sorry I am about Brady's death. We had some good times. I enjoyed his company, and I'm sorry he's gone."

"Me, too. I miss him. He'd call me at least once a week, you know, just to check up on me, say hi, see how things were going. I miss just hearing his voice."

"I think I know how you felt about your father, and I want you to know how much I admired and respected him. But in the past week or so I've also found out that he sometimes wasn't as nice a person as we'd like to believe. He alienated a lot of people.''

"Daddy made enemies just by being himself, Emerson. I know that. Some people were jealous of his talent. Some people were jealous of what he had—a family, a nice house, a business. I never paid much attention to those kind of people because they never took the time to get to know my father.''

"He alienated his own family, too,'' I reminded her. "I wouldn't exactly call your family close.''

"What family doesn't have its problems? Daddy did the best he could. His wife *died,* remember, and he was left on his own with two babies. I think she was the love of his life. When Jennifer came along, I think he married her out of necessity as much as anything else. He needed a woman in his life. He needed a mother for his children. Oh, I know he cared for her, but it wasn't the same, and it wasn't easy bringing the two families together. Of course we have our problems. Why wouldn't we?''

"It's more than that. Brady made some *real* enemies, people he ticked off so badly they wanted to hurt him, hurt his family.''

She shook her head. "No, a lot of people like to challenge him, to see if they could beat him at some game, but hurt him, hurt us? I don't believe it.''

"He was killed, Glynnis.'' I said it gently, but firmly.

"By some awful punk kid who wanted to rob him.''

"No, by someone who wanted to silence him. He wasn't accidentally killed by some scared punk. He was deliberately murdered by a cold-blooded killer.''

I told her about the autopsy report, and she listened with wide eyes, disbelief on her face at first, then horror.

"Oh, my God,'' she murmured. "I feel sick.''

I quickly went to the sink and got her a glass of water, then gave her a moment to collect herself.

"You all right?" I asked as I sat down on the stool again. She nodded. "I'm sorry to dump this on you all at once like this, but better you hear it from me than the police. And they will get around to you eventually. I'm surprised, actually, they haven't been here yet. They're going to ask you a lot of hard questions about you, your family, looking for a motive."

"But that's absurd to think any of us would want to kill him, let alone have the courage to actually stick something through his eye. Oh, God, I can't even think about it." She shivered violently, with a look of distaste that screwed up her pretty face as if she'd sucked on a lemon.

"*Somebody* wanted to hurt him. It takes an awful lot of hate to kill a person that way. I need your help, Glynnis. Who hated Brady enough to kill him?"

"I don't know. It's so awful. I really don't know."

"I think whoever it was may have been trying to hurt your family to get to Brady. Brady was worried, moody, for the last couple of years. Both Kitty and Nell noticed it. I think he was worried that something might happen to you, or Kitty, or Ron. I want you to think hard, try to remember anything strange that's happened to you in the past few years."

"What kind of thing?"

"Anything unusual. Something you thought was weird at the time. Something you couldn't explain."

She pursed her heart-shaped mouth and stared into her wine glass, brows knitted in concentration. She said nothing for a long time, then slowly her expression changed.

"There might be something. I don't know if it's what you're looking for or not." She paused and looked up at me.

"Go on."

"It was a while ago. Maybe a year and a half, two years. Let me think. It was spring, April maybe, so it was almost two years ago. Ron had a package delivered to his house, a box of candy with a note from someone saying how much they'd appreciated his work on their car. The note wasn't signed. Anyway, Ron doesn't like candy that much, so the next time he saw me, he gave the box to me. He knows I can't resist every now and then. I can't afford to eat sweets, but every once in a while I get an incredible craving for chocolates, and this was a nice box of chocolates, the kind with gooey centers. You know, each one is different, and you have to guess what they have inside, mint, cherry, nougat, apricot, that sort of thing.

"I put them in the refrigerator and tried to ignore them. But one day I was in just the right mood. You know, when you're a little blue and you don't know why, and you don't have any energy or will power? When I feel like that I indulge myself. I go shopping and buy myself something, or I pig out on junk food. I always feel guilty, but I feel better, too. You know what I mean?"

I nodded.

"Anyway," she went on, "I was just sitting here feeling depressed, and remembered the chocolates. I got such a craving that I knew I wouldn't be able to stop until I'd eaten at least half the box. So, I took them out of the refrigerator, opened them up and took my time deciding which one I wanted first, which to try second. They looked so wonderful. I picked a round one, I think, dark chocolate, but when I bit into it I got the surprise of my life. It was full of cayenne pepper, and I hopped around the house with my mouth on fire for twenty minutes!

"I was so darned mad, I called Ron up at the shop and

started yelling at him for playing such a nasty trick. He acted innocent, and that made me even madder, but when I calmed down enough to explain, he didn't know what I was talking about. He told me he didn't have anything to do with it. And then he started laughing because he figured that one of his buddies must have been trying to pull a gag on him, and the joke was on me.''

"What about the rest of the chocolates?''

"Oh, I checked them all right,'' she said with a grim smile. "I cut them all open. The whole top layer was doctored. The bottom layer was fine. What a waste of good chocolates.''

"They could have been poisoned.''

"It was a joke, that's all. I only mentioned it because you asked me to think of unusual things that had happened. And that was definitely weird.''

"Did Ron ever find out who sent them?''

"No. At least no one in the shop ever admitted it.''

"You could have been killed.''

"Not with cayenne pepper. Besides, the package was sent to Ron, not to me. Whoever sent it couldn't have known I was going to eat them.''

She was right, but the pattern was there—her cat, Kitty's car, and Ron's candy—and it was all suddenly coming clear.

"Did you tell Brady?''

"Of course. By then I could laugh about it, but he didn't think it was that funny.''

Brady wouldn't. Someone had been sending him a message, telling him how easy it would be to do something really malicious, like cut the brake lines on the little Mercedes, or wire a stick of dynamite to the ignition. How easy it would be to fill the chocolates with poison, not pepper. How easy it would be to break into a locked house and kill a person, not a cat. Brady would have done whatever that someone wanted, including even giving away his life savings.

I drained the last swallow of wine in my glass, thinking, feeling Glynnis' eyes on me. It was enough she had to deal with the news of Brady's murder. She wouldn't believe Brady had had secrets worth blackmailing him for. She wouldn't have any idea of who would go to the lengths of threatening his family to make sure he did as he was told. I raised my eyes to look at her. She'd let her hair down, and it softly framed the high cheekbones, the wide-set tawny-colored eyes, the square yet delicate jaw and the long thin nose.

"I called Kitty today," she said suddenly, dropping her eyes for a moment. "I wanted to talk with her about arranging a memorial service for Daddy. She told me how sorry she felt for me about losing Daddy. She asked me if there was anything she could do for me. I was surprised."

She paused, and squirmed a little on her stool, as if uncomfortable admitting she might have been wrong. "You told me, of course, but I didn't expect her to be so concerned. I thought she'd be wrapped up in herself, playing the grieving widow. You know. I guess I was wrong. She really seemed to care about how *I* felt, how I feel."

And looking at her in that moment, I saw the steel door open behind those eyes. I saw for an instant that she believed that maybe she *could* trust other people. I saw a little girl, vulnerable and alone, longing to reach out to someone for a little warmth, a little love, a little acceptance. It made me glad she'd taken a chance on calling Kitty.

Impulsively, I stood on the rung of the stool and awkwardly leaned across the island to kiss her gently on the lips. They were cool, soft and dry. She didn't recoil, but there was no response in her lips. I sat down quickly, embarrassed by my own impromptu display of emotion.

She looked at me curiously, her eyes narrowing. "What was that for?"

"Nothing."

"You bring me some flowers and a bottle of wine, and you think you can just hop in bed with me, is that it?" Her eyes smoldered now.

"No, not at all," I said quietly.

She ignored me, working up a head of steam. "I don't know what it is with men. You think all you have to do is pay a little attention to a woman and she'll fawn all over you, panting with lust. Chad used to think I should get goosebumps from kissing him, used to think I should be ready to go to bed with him just from the way he looked at me. I never understood what the big deal was. I don't know why you get so excited about it, why you think we're just dying for it."

"Look, I'm proud of you for calling Kitty. I'm glad that maybe you two might get to be friends. I think you could use each other about now. I'm happy for you as a friend, or as someone who would like to be your friend. I wanted to show you I care, that I'm glad you're reaching out a little, so I kissed you. I'm sorry I was so forward. It wasn't meant to be a big deal, and I don't expect anything from you."

"No, Emerson," she retorted quickly, still angry. "You're interested in more than a simple friendship, more than just consoling the family of one of your friends. I see the way men look at me. Some of them almost drool. I don't understand it, but you have some of that same look. I've seen it in your eyes. What is it you want from me? And why me? There must be hundreds of lonely women out there who would go out with you if you're looking for a date. Why did you pick me? I'm not just someone you can conquer to prove to your ego how macho you are. I don't want to be part of some male fantasy.''

I took it all in and thought for a long minute. "Maybe you're right." I stood up and paced the kitchen floor, trying to find a way to put it into words.

"I'm already past my fortieth birthday, and I'm still not married. It isn't for lack of dates or suitable mates. Yes, there are a lot of women out there, and yes, many of them would be happy to go out with me. Some of them would even consider trying to prod me down the aisle to a life of kids, and PTA and Cub Scout meetings, and a lawn to mow, and backyard picnics, and dinner with the neighbors every now and then, and an occasional vacation to Hawaii without the kids. And maybe someday I'll be ready for that. In the meantime, I live a life that's not conducive to permanent relationships. I'm not bound by traditional schedules, and I sometimes live a little too close to the edge for comfort. I've been shot at and clunked over the head a few too many times. I don't live up to a lot of women's expectations of how a potential husband should act or live his life. I'm too irresponsible.

"But the fact is that I love women. I like everything about them. I like the way they smell, the way they feel, the way they look, the way they dress, and especially the way they think. I like the way they look at the world, and the way they open themselves up to so many more possibilities than men do on an emotional level. It's not a male ego thing. I genuinely like women. I like their company.

"I didn't *pick* you. You're here. I'm here. You just appeared in my life. I acted like an ass when I first saw

you because it was so obvious that you've cut yourself
off, that you've shut out the world, and I think that's a
waste. I was angry, and I took it out on you. Now that
I've gotten to know you just a little, I think maybe I was
wrong. Maybe there is a real person in there somewhere,
but you've buried her. I think maybe she's trying to get
out. I get the feeling that you've lost a piece of yourself,
and if you could be convinced you wouldn't get hurt, you
might go looking for it.

"So, you're a challenge. Not a conquest, a challenge.
I don't have anything to prove to myself, and I'm not
some love therapist, or some shrink that thinks you need
to be saved from yourself. I *do* think you're worth getting
to know, and I'd like to get to know the real Glynnis. I'd
like to show you my world. I'd like to see you laugh and
take the same delight a child would in looking at life. I'd
like to try to open some doors for you and let you take a
peek at what you might be missing. I'd like to try to help
you find yourself by being your friend, by listening, really
listening to you, by being there for you. And if that leads
to something, that's fine, too. I don't expect anything from
you, and I'm willing to take you as you are, in little bits
and pieces of yourself, or all of you, however much you
want to share."

I stopped pacing and poured myself another glass of
wine. Glynnis sat quietly, a frown on her face.

"I suppose you know all about me." There was a trace
of sarcasm, even bitterness, in her voice.

"No, I know a little about you."

"Chad used to try so earnestly," she went on as if she
hadn't even heard me. "All that grunting, sweating effort.
Very straightforward at first, and I pretended to enjoy it.
I wanted so much for him to be pleased. But I just didn't
understand what all the fuss was about. No bells, no

fireworks. When he realized, when I couldn't hide it anymore, he tried even more earnestly. New positions, new
techniques. He bought manuals and books. His poor ego
was at stake. He even brought home another woman a
couple of times.''

Her voice held disgust. She swallowed some wine, then
looked at me suddenly with piercing eyes.

"Suppose we became lovers. What makes you so special? Why would you be any different?"

"We wouldn't become lovers unless you wanted it that
way." I paused. "Look, I won't kid you. I think sex is
one of the most wondrous, joyous, mystifyingly beautiful
things in the world when it's an act of sharing, of giving
and taking, of mutual respect between two people who
not only care deeply about each other, but like each other
and trust each other enough to laugh at themselves, at the
little things that they're embarrassed about. There *are*
bells and fireworks, but only if you like yourself enough
to let them happen. Maybe that's where you start, Glynnis,
by learning to like yourself a little.''

She sat silently again, and I couldn't tell what she was
thinking. I'd come this far, though, so I plunged ahead.

"Now, since we both like food, why don't we both
pretend we're restaurant critics for *The New York Times,*
pick some snooty restaurant in town, order the best they
have on the menu, and then cut it to ribbons?"

There was no reaction at first, and then slowly there
was the smallest beginning of a smile.

"I get to play Phyllis Richmond," she murmured.

"Done. I'll call you to set a date." I set down my
unfinished glass of wine and let myself out before she had
a chance to object.

I SENSED SOMETHING terribly wrong when I let myself in
the back door, but I couldn't quite put my finger on it. I

stood stock-still in the doorway, not even turning on the light until I could get a feel for what was bothering me. The smell of the rotting body in Ukrainian Village was still burned into my olfactory nerves, and it took me a while to realize that I smelled gas. The kitchen was thick with it, and when the realization came I could suddenly hear the faint hiss from the far side of the room.

I turned and took a deep breath of fresh air, held it, and fumbled my way in the dark to the stove, feeling all the knobs to see if any were on. One was off-center, and I turned it to close the valve. Then I went back to the patio door to get another lungful of air before opening all the windows in the kitchen and the back den. I stumbled back out on the patio and took great gasping breaths until my heart slowed a little, then took one more deep breath and plunged back into the house, through the hall into the living room this time. I let some air out of my lungs and sniffed cautiously. There was still an odor, but it was much fainter. I took a chance and turned the thermostat to low and the fan to high, hoping that the spark of a solenoid switch turning on the air-conditioning system wouldn't blow me sky high.

Air stirred in the room, and I felt a finger of cool breeze from the ceiling vent touch my cheek. No flash. No boom. I was still standing. I went back out to the patio before turning blue and fainting from lack of oxygen, and flopped in a deck chair in the dark.

I'm usually not careless or forgetful. Habits acquired from years of living alone are hard to break. But I suddenly couldn't remember if I'd forgotten to turn off the stove for some reason. And I somehow had the thought in my head that I'd left a kitchen window open a crack before leaving. The weatherman had predicted a cool eve-

ning, and I thought I'd opened it to let some fresh air in
the house before I left. But it had been closed tightly just
a moment ago.

It was either age creeping up on me, making me forget,
or someone had paid me a visit when I'd been out, leaving
a deadly calling card. Both thoughts made me feel a little
paranoid. I sat on the patio for nearly an hour, trying not
to think of who might have gotten in. After all, there
hadn't been any signs of a break-in that I'd seen. Instead,
I let my mind wander, hopping willy-nilly from one image
to another—Kitty, Brady, Nell, Wroblewski, Glynnis…

She hadn't even cried yet, I bet. She hadn't let herself
grieve for Brady. If only life had a soundtrack, we'd all
know how to act. Sad when the violins groan softly in a
minor key and a lone reed wails in gentle counterpoint.
Happy when the brass bleats out a snappy tune. Frightened when the cellos and basses play discordant, eerie
chords. Triumphant when the tympani pounds, the or-
chestra swells, and the sound of the French horns rises
above it all as crisp and clean as a blue spring sky over
the Canadian Rockies. The problem with Glynnis, I decided, was that she had no soundtrack.

I finally shook myself and climbed stiffly out of the
chair. I sniffed around all the corners of the kitchen. The
smell was gone. I closed and locked the windows and
doors in the dark, then double-checked them all just to
make sure. When I felt safe, I felt my way up the stairs,
undressed by the light that filtered through my bedroom
window from the street and tumbled naked into bed,
yawning hugely. I was asleep in seconds.

ELEVEN

I DRESSED PURPOSEFULLY, determined to spend some time at my desk. When I got to the kitchen, however, my attention was diverted to the window. It was louvered, and I'd taken off the screen months before because it had ripped. I saw no marks on the sill or the sash to indicate anyone had forced it, but an enterprising person could have gotten a hand far enough through the opening I'd left to turn the crank and open it wide. Wide enough to climb through from outside with the help of a stepstool or ladder. I walked outside onto the patio to look at the back of the house. There were no scuff marks on the wall, but that didn't mean much either. My fears from the night before looked a little silly in the light of day, and I went inside scratching my head and feeling foolish.

I made coffee and toasted an English muffin, then took both into the den to wade through the pile of mail that had accumulated for the past week. It was August already, and there were bills to pay and invoices to get out. Despite the fact that Brandt had me well invested, I still needed pocket money, and that meant I had to work now and then. I accomplished a lot, though, in just a few hours, and after lunch I decided to drop in on Kitty.

She'd given up her widow's weeds, answering the door in blue jeans and an oversized cotton work shirt with rolled up sleeves, but when she invited me inside I could see she hadn't stopped mourning. The house was dark, blinds and curtains drawn to shut out the world. Kitty wore a melancholy look, and she moved listlessly, almost as if drugged.

She tried a smile, but it turned into a sob, and she buried her face against my chest for a minute. "I just miss him so much," she said in a choked voice. "This place is so empty without him. He filled it, Emerson. He was so big, his presence was so big, he took up a lot of space, but I never knew how much space he took up in my life until these past few days."

"I know, I know." I gently turned her around and walked her into the living room to sit down. "It's like a piece of you dies, but you still feel it. You rattle around looking for it, trying to figure out why it still hurts if it isn't there anymore."

"Kind of. You're right."

"It's trite, of course, but we have to go on living, you know. Cry for him, mourn him, curse him, miss him, but don't shut yourself away, Kitty. Don't do this to yourself. I'm the king of self-pity. I know. It feels good at first, but it immobilizes you, cripples you. And then a piece of you *will* die, not just the part of you that shared Brady's life."

"We shared everything, Emerson," she said a little taken aback. "Don't you see? Brady *was* my life."

I shook my head. "No, Brady was a magnifying glass, or a prism, or a catalyst. He made part of your life better. He gave it a different perspective. He gave you someone to care for, and in turn, he cared for you. You still have that, you still have all the memories. More importantly, you still have yourself, the Kitty that brought him out of his shell in the first place."

"I'm scared, Emerson. Damn it, I'm scared." There was a note of anger in her voice, and she looked at me with both defiance and vulnerability in eyes that welled with tears. "I don't want to live alone. I don't want to be single again. God knows, I'm not even close to being ready to date again, but I'm not sure I could anymore. I can't face that again. Look at me. I'm fifty. I can't do the bar scene anymore. I can't do any of it. I couldn't face the rejection. And I can't stand being alone with myself."

"Time, Kitty. You've got to give it time. Of course you're lonely now, but you're not alone. You've got friends, and in time, you'll feel comfortable with yourself again. Don't even think about what happens down the road yet. Make friends with yourself again first. Find that person inside that did pretty well on her own before you met Brady. We'll help you. Use us. Call us up and talk to us. Ask us to come spend the night when the house feels too empty. Cry on our shoulders. But don't give up."

"I don't know what I'm going to do. I don't want to go back to work. I feel like I'm too old to go back to flying."

"Why would you have to?"

"There's nothing left, Emerson. There's Brady's life insurance policy. Prudently invested, as Brandt puts it, that will give me about forty thousand a year. That's not enough to keep up the house. The taxes alone will eat up a big chunk of it. I'll have to sell the house. What am I going to do?"

She sat curled on the couch, bare feet tucked under her, looking as small and vulnerable as a little girl.

"There's still the studio. I know it won't be the same without Brady, but it's still a good business. It should be able to make you a decent profit."

"I can't count on it, Emerson. I wish I could, but what if they lose all their clients because Brady's gone? Brady's reputation is the one that brought clients in the door, not Nick's or Marty's. Nell told me that a couple of clients have called already to cancel sessions, saying they need to 'reschedule.' What if they all walk away?''

She burst into tears. I put my arms around her, held her close and rocked her gently until the tears subsided. She was rattled, and I wasn't sure what I could do to bring her out of the funk except just be there. It was nearly five minutes before she raised her tear-streaked face to look at me and self-consciously snuffle, looking around for a tissue.

''I'm sorry, Emerson.''

''Nothing to be sorry about. Your life has been turned upside down. But try not to worry so much. Things will work out. You'll see.''

She fell silent, then rose abruptly and paced the living room, finally ending up in front of the grand piano that sat in the window bay. The top of the piano was covered, like almost every other square inch of space in the house, with framed photographs, maybe as many as thirty. She paused there, leaning against the piano, gazing at the pictures. She picked one up to look at it more closely, and her expression lightened.

''You know, I met Brady's parents before we got married,'' she said softly, still looking at the picture. ''We flew down to Florida for a short vacation, like a five-day weekend, and went and met them. Brady wanted to introduce me. They were very nice people. Sort of North Shore, but not in a bad way. Just very proper and, well, refined, but also down to earth in a way.

''It's funny, but no matter how old you are parents are still parents. Can you imagine Brady acting like someone's son? He was fifty-something when we went down there, but you would have thought he was a teenager asking his parents' permission to borrow the car.''

She gave a short laugh. ''He was so sweet. He wanted so much for them to like me. He was totally different around them, meek, quiet. You remember how your mother told you to act the first time you went to spend the night with a friend? That's how Brady was—polite, well mannered, accommodating. All the time I could see they were driving him nuts, like parents do. You know, was he taking care of himself, was he eating right, was business good enough, that sort of thing.

''I didn't understand why meeting his parents was so important to him. He lived his life his own way. Then I realized that he was really proud of me. So much of his personal life had been such a mess, particularly his marriage to Jennifer, he just wanted to show me off, show his parents he had the sense to find someone who could make him happy.''

I came up behind her and looked at the photograph she was holding. An attractive elderly couple stood on a sunny beach, arms around each other, smiling for the camera.

''You *did* make him happy.''

''I sure tried.'' She sighed and put the picture down, then turned and went back to sit on the couch. ''It wasn't always easy, but it was good most of the time. I think age mellowed him. I'm not sure *I* could have stayed married to him when he was younger. I mean, I see what he put Ron and Glynnis through, and I know what a perfectionist he was. But at this point in his life, we just seemed right for each other.''

''He was a wonderful man, yet he made a lot of people unhappy.''

''Yes, I guess he did.'' She was silent for a moment. ''Maybe because he was an only child. Brady was used to getting his own way. As generous as he was, he could be very selfish in a sense. Self-centered is a better word, maybe."

I leaned against the piano and folded my arms across my chest. "Did he cheat on you, Kitty?"

She didn't seem startled by the question, but it took her a while to answer. "I knew Brady's reputation when you introduced us," she said slowly. "When things started to get serious between us, I had to stop and ask myself if that mattered. A leopard doesn't change his spots, you know. I had to put a little distance between us for a while. I didn't know if he was sincere, if he truly loved me. But I was too far gone. I was too much in love with him. I decided it didn't matter as long as *I* was happy.

"I don't know if he cheated on me or not. I chose *not* to know. I think he probably did. It's just the way Brady was. It never seemed to affect our relationship, though." She looked at me curiously. "Why?"

"Someone was unhappy with Brady. Unhappy enough to kill him. A jilted lover maybe?" I shrugged. "I'm groping, trying to make sense of all this. Someone wanted to hurt him, to destroy him little by little. Somebody got to him by threatening his family."

"What do you mean? Nobody's threatened me."

"The potato in your tailpipe, Kitty. Ron told me."

"That? That was somebody's idea of a practical joke."

"By itself, maybe, but not when you look at it in combination with things that happened to Ron and to Glynnis." I told her about the cat and the candy, and she stared at me openmouthed.

"Whoever it was sent Brady a message, then milked him for all the cash he had. I don't think it would have stopped there. I think someone wanted to take everything he had, but something happened that made it necessary to kill him.''

"God, Emerson. What are you saying?''

"I'm asking you to think, to open up the blinds in here, and the ones you've had over your eyes all these years, and help me find out who killed him. If he was sleeping with someone, I want to know who. If he and someone in the family or someone on his staff had a falling out, I want to know why. Whoever it was may not stop with Brady. They may come after you next, or Glynnis, or even Ron. I don't want that to happen.''

"All right,'' she said quietly. "I'll think about it. I'll try to help.''

"Good.''

If nothing else, it might divert her attention, keep her from feeling so depressed. She fell silent, and I turned to look at all the photos on the piano for a minute. Pieces of Brady's several lives were chronicled there, pieces that were impossible to put into a complete picture without a guide. Every photo there was worth a thousand words, but I could only guess at the feelings, the motivations, the secrets behind the smiling faces. Of the thousand words I could choose, only one might be right.

"Emerson, I hate to ask, but could you do me a favor?''

"Shoot,'' I replied, still looking through the collection of pictures.

"Art Ryan is trying to make sure all Brady's accounts are cleared up, all his bills paid. I think he must have taken some to the studio. I can't find statements from a couple of credit card companies. Would you mind checking his office next time you're there? I'm not ready to go down there yet.''

"Sure. No problem. Say, who's this?'' I picked up a

small, ornate silver frame with a four-by-five snapshot in it. "It looks like Glynnis."

She came over to join me. There were four people in the photo: Brady, Nick, and two women, one of whom bore a strong resemblance to Glynnis. They posed as couples standing close, arms around each other as if they were good friends. The shot was a little fuzzy, and the color was faded.

"Well, Brady and Nick you know," Kitty said, looking at the picture. "This is Vicky." She pointed to the woman who stood next to Brady. "Victoria, Brady's first wife. And this is Candice, Nick's ex-wife."

I looked at the picture more closely, and realized that it was old. Both Brady and Nick looked young, full of exuberance. I hadn't noticed at first because my eyes had been drawn to the women. Kitty's finger rested on the young woman who looked like Glynnis.

"Are you sure? Isn't it the other way round?"

"No, that's right. That's Victoria, and that's Candice."

"What ever happened to her?"

"Candice? I don't know."

"Did she remarry? Did she move away?"

"Brady never told me. Maybe he didn't know, either."

Disjointed thoughts tumbled through my head, and I felt a glimmer of excitement. "Can I take this? Borrow it?"

"I guess so, sure." Kitty looked at me quizzically.

I took the photo out of its frame and after looking at it one more time, put it carefully in my shirt pocket. It revealed more secrets than all the other photos in the house, and I intended to find out what they were.

I STOPPED BY BRANDT'S HOUSE on my way home. Thankfully, he was there. I didn't want to have to try to track him down. He didn't appear that happy to see me.

"I'm a little busy right now, you know," he said as he led me upstairs to the den that served as his office. His cat Rocky slept curled comfortably on a pile of papers that were stacked on a leather chair.

"That's okay. I won't stay long. What you want, old friend, is to experience the thrill of wading in all the muck I usually find myself in. I try to spare you that indignity, but you insist, so I have a job for you. It will show you how glamorous my job is."

I pulled the photo out of my pocket, put it on the desk next to him and pointed to the woman next to Nick. "Candice Fratelli. Nick's ex-wife. I need to find her, talk to her. I don't know where she is, or what her name is now. You could start down at City Hall, maybe dig up her divorce papers, find out her maiden name, and go from there. I'll let you be inventive. Will you do it?"

His eyes gleamed. "A challenge. Yes, I'll do it. Give me a few days."

"Fine, but the sooner, the better."

Brandt just liked feeling he was an integral part of my life, and for a time he'd felt shut out. Giving him this chore was easier than throwing a bone to a dog. I would have done a lot more to make sure we stayed friends, but sometimes I'm stubborn and have to be nudged in the right direction.

Glynnis and I had a dinner date on Wednesday. I called her late in the afternoon to see if she minded being picked up early. I wanted to swing by the studio and see if I could find the bills Kitty had asked me to look for.

I had to talk Glynnis into coming up with me. She hadn't been there in years, she told me, and wasn't sure what sort of memories it might bring back. I suggested

they might be good memories, and what could it hurt to
see, anyway? The studio was still busy, even though it
was after 5:00. A few client types milled around the reception area talking. They were casually but artfully
dressed in a way that suggested they were in the enter-
tainment or fashion industry, not typical business. Nell
and Glynnis greeted each other cordially, and I waited
while they exchanged condolences and chitchat. Nell
threw me a curious look when Glynnis rejoined me and
took my arm as I started through the doorway into the
hall.

There was a buzz of activity coming from the studio,
and Glynnis paused for a moment to poke her head
through the double doors. I peered over her shoulder and
saw at least a dozen people moving around, talking
loudly. It looked like a fashion session, and it appeared
they were wrapping for the day. Some guys were busy
breaking down a set in the second bay. Two women were
busy hanging clothes on a rolling rack. A group of models
were talking amongst themselves as they packed makeup
and personal items in their nylon sports bags.

Glynnis turned away from it all with a dazed look and
a smile. "I'd forgotten how busy it gets," she murmured.

I took her arm and walked her down the hall to the
quiet of Brady's office. I opened the door and let her walk
in ahead of me. She took three or four steps, turned, then
gasped and went rigid. Her eyes glazed, and the blood
drained from her face, leaving the skin a pasty gray. I
took two great strides to her side, grabbing her shoulders,
afraid she might faint, and looked to see what had startled
her so.

A young model stood at the far end of the room by the
couch, wide-eyed with surprise and a touch of fright.
Straight red hair half hid a pale, freckled face with pretty,

aquiline features. She was naked, and she stood casually turned halfway toward Glynnis, one leg bent at the knee. Her skin was milky white except for freckles on her shoulders and forearms, and she had small pointed breasts tipped with soft pink nipples. Between the flat stomach and the long thin legs was a pubic patch a shade darker than the red of her hair. She held a filmy pair of silk panties in one hand. She didn't move for a moment, then, as if suddenly realizing she was naked, she began to dress hurriedly. She got the panties on, pulled on a pair of shorts and a blouse, then gathered up the rest of her things without bothering to button up the blouse.

"Sorry," she said, brushing past us. "They said I could use the office. There wasn't enough space in the dressing room."

Glynnis still stared with glazed eyes toward the couch, her body stiff. Without warning, she turned into me and her body went slack. I held her, afraid she might fall, then slowly sensed that something else was going on. Her body heated up, and all that warm weight pressed against me, the soft heavy breasts, the full hips. Her breathing came faster, and she pressed her face up into my neck. And suddenly, she was all motion, face nuzzling my neck and lips planting little kisses, searching for my earlobe, hips grinding gently against mine, hands caressing my chest, then moving down to rub the crotch of my pants. I could feel my own body respond.

Her breath was hot and moist, but she suddenly pulled away, took my hand in hers, and tugged me in the direction of the couch. She licked her lips lasciviously, and waggled her hips. I looked at her face, trying to read what was happening to her. Her eyes looked at me, but they didn't seem to be focused. They seemed to be seeing something far away. I frowned. She pursed her lips, trying to look seductive in an exaggerated parody of the expressions on a centerfold model.

"Come on, lover boy," she breathed. "I thought this is what you wanted. Little Glynnie, all primed and ready. Come on and get it." She let go of my hand and fell back onto the couch, opening her arms to me.

"No," I said softly. "This isn't what *you* want. Not this way. Not now."

She pouted and then mewled softly like a kitten. "Aww, come on, honey. I'm all ready for it now. Why do you tease me so?"

"Glynnis, stop it," I said more firmly. "You don't want this. It's not right."

She pouted for another moment in silence, her breathing slowly returning to normal. Suddenly her face changed, she came back into focus, and she looked at me with fear dawning in her eyes.

"Oh, my God, Emerson. What's happening? Did I just do what I think I did? What happened to me?"

I looked at her thoughtfully for a moment, then turned and paced the room.

"I'm going to tell you a story. It's a story about a beautiful little girl, a princess born in a happy kingdom of funny, friendly people with smiling faces. The king and queen of the land already had a son, an heir, but they wanted another child, and so the little girl was born. Unfortunately, her mother died when she was still a baby, leaving her alone with her father. The father was big and strong, good and kind, and the little girl grew up worshipping him, dedicating herself to pleasing him because he had sacrificed so much. She loved him, and wanted to take her mother's place in his eyes and in his heart.

"But the girl's father was lonely, and eventually he married another woman, the wicked stepmother in this fairy tale. The little girl was crushed, her fantasies of growing up at her father's side, of becoming just like her mother dashed. Eventually, she accepted the wicked step-mother because she knew her father needed a wife, and she would do anything to make her father happy.''

"A wonderful bedtime story," she interrupted sarcastically, "but I don't need your psychoanalysis of my childhood."

I looked at her and saw the steel doors shutting behind the eyes. "Just a minute, Glynnis. You're right, I'm not your shrink, but I have a pretty good idea of what just happened here, and I'll tell you if you want to know. If you don't, that's fine. We'll drop it."

"I'm sorry. I know you're trying to help. I just feel a little confused." She said it hesitantly, as if she wasn't sure she really wanted to hear what I had to say, but some of her defensiveness was gone. "Go on. What's your theory?"

"You loved Brady. So much so, that I think you tend to overlook his faults. He was always perfect in your eyes. At least you wanted him to be. Now, while you didn't care much for Jennifer, she *was* Brady's wife, and in your mind that meant all the trappings that go with marriage— love, honor, cherish, and so forth.

"It's not much of a secret that Brady was a ladies' man. He was big, boisterous, attractive, and he had an appetite for sex. You've never admitted it, but Ron knew, Stephen knew, Jennifer knew, even Kitty knows, for Christ's sake. Brady slept around. A lot.

"My guess? You came to the studio often when you were little, right? Brady used to take you on picnics at lunchtime, to the zoo, stuff like that. Sometimes you'd meet him here. I think that one of those times, when you were young, you interrupted him, right here in this office, on that couch. He was making love to a model, a girl that probably looked a lot like the one who was just here. He wasn't making love to your mother, or to Jennifer, who you could probably accept. No, he was doing the big It with a total stranger, violating his wedding vows, memories of your mother, and most importantly, violating your trust in him.

"You couldn't accept it, so you blocked it out, shut the memory away in some deep corner of your mind. And it cut off a piece of you somehow. It turned you off to sex, numbed your body as well as your mind. In your fairy tale world, sex became something nasty, something only bad people do. How could it be enjoyable if it was bad? Seeing that naked girl just unlocked the memory, that's all. Your body turned on because your subconscious remembers that Brady was probably turned on, and whoever he was making love to was turned on. They were enjoying it. Your body knows that's okay, even if your mind doesn't. Does that make any sense?"

"Yes, Dr. Freud. Thank you for curing me."

I let her sarcasm slide off me. After what had happened, she was probably feeling a little defensive. She turned her eyes away, and I watched her think. Her brows furrowed, and I could see something begin to nag at her.

"Why *didn't* you take advantage? Isn't that what you wanted? Didn't you find me attractive enough?"

"I find you incredibly attractive, Glynnis, and it took a whole lot of willpower not to jump your bones. But that's not what you want, and though it may surprise you, that's not what I want. You weren't all here. What happened gave you a glimpse of what's possible, but this isn't the time or the place. I told you, if we become lovers, it will be because we want to share something. And when it happens, all of you will be there, not just a piece of you.''

I fell silent, unable to think of anything else to say. Glynnis got a faraway look in her eyes and sat unmoving. I finally sat in a chair close to her and waited a little uncomfortably, trying to find something in the room to look at. When I finally glanced at Glynnis again, her eyes had filled with tears, and big salty drops rolled down her cheeks.

"Damn him," she said softly.

There was suddenly so much pain in her face I wanted to reach out, fold her in my arms and take away all the hurt, but I didn't dare. Not until she gave me a signal. She needed to work this out herself.

"Why did I let him do this to me?" she cried. "Everything I ever did, I did to please him. All I ever wanted was to have him tell me he was proud of me, to tell me he loved me."

"He loved you. He just wasn't the kind of man who found it easy to say. He tried to show you in a hundred ways—calling you up to check on you, taking you to lunch... He just couldn't put it into words. All the things he did wrong, he didn't intentionally do to hurt you. He was just Brady."

She cried for a long time, grieving, letting Brady go, and I imagined it was probably the first time she'd cried hard about anything since she was a child. I took her hand and held it, and let her get it out of her system. Slowly, her tears subsided.

"God, what a mess," she sniffed, reaching for a box of tissues on the table. "I must look like hell. I can't believe I'm crying like this in front of you. You just seem to, well, understand."

I shrugged and smiled.

"I was a virgin, you know, when I married Chad. You probably think that's strange. Maybe you don't."

I wasn't sure I wanted to hear this, but she seemed to want to tell it, so I didn't stop her.

"Anyway, I told you how much I wanted to make it work, how much I wanted to please him, too. I never understood why nothing ever happened for me. I mean, like you said, it is supposed to be bells and fireworks, but I just felt dead inside, numb. When nothing worked, Chad started to hit me. Not hard at first, but when it didn't get any better, he'd go out drinking sometimes and come home in a rage. He beat me pretty badly a couple of times. I lived with it for a long time, partly because I was embarrassed to admit what was happening, but more because Chad was dominating, charming, and totally convincing, like Daddy.

"When you're abused, you start feeling like it's your fault, that you've brought it on yourself, and I thought if I just tried a little harder to please Chad, he'd stop. He didn't. He came home one night drunk, told me that he'd lost thousands that day on the market, and then proceeded to beat me as if it was my fault. That was the last straw. I told Daddy. I didn't tell him why. I just told him that Chad hit me, and I wanted out. He helped me find a lawyer, and made sure that Chad couldn't get his hands on any of the trust fund money when we split.

"I was terrified of being on my own. I'd never done anything except take care of Daddy, then Chad. I didn't know what to do. A friend suggested I send some of my recipes to the newspaper. I couldn't for the longest time. I couldn't see why they'd want them. But I finally got up the courage, and they used them. Eventually, they asked me to write for them, and that led to cookbooks.

"I shut everything else out of my life—men, most of

my friends, even Daddy for a while, especially when he first married Kitty. I had my stove and my typewriter. That's all I needed. They were mine, nobody else's. I was doing something for myself for once in my life.''

She paused, and dabbed at her nose with a tissue, staring into space.

''I went to camp one summer when I was little,'' she went on quietly. ''There was a river not too far away, with an old wooden bridge across it. The kids used to go over there to go swimming, and the brave ones would climb up the banks to the bridge and jump off into the water. You weren't part of the club, part of the cool crowd until you'd jumped off the bridge. It was probably fifteen feet over the water, and I can't tell you how many times that summer I climbed up on the bridge only to chicken out. I was terrified of heights, but I couldn't tell anyone.

''One day, I finally did it. I just stepped out into space and fell. It was the most frightening thing I've ever done. I was sure I was going to die. I was going to plunge down, down into the river and never come up. It was exhilarating, though, too. The wind whistled in my ears, rushing past my face, and my stomach floated up into my throat. I hit the icy water and went down into the dark, the sudden quiet, and I didn't die. I just bobbed back up to the surface, and did it twice more.''

She turned to look at me, staring into my eyes. ''I feel like that now. I feel like I'm stepping off a bridge with you. I don't know what's going to happen, and I'm scared, but I think it's all right. I think I'll be okay. Can you understand that, Emerson?''

I nodded. ''I'll go with you one step at a time, Glynnis.''

She sighed and touched the back of my hand with her fingertips. ''I'm tired, all cried out. Would you mind if we didn't go to dinner tonight? I think I'd just like to go home.''

''That would be just fine, but only if you promise to spend the day with me tomorrow. No stove, no typewriter, no work.''

She smiled. ''Okay. I promise.''

TWELVE

I SPENT A LOT OF TIME with Glynnis the next week. I'd been right about her, but it was more than I could have hoped for. She blossomed, each day becoming more trusting, more comfortable, more carefree, more spontaneous. She took delight in everything we did, as if seeing it all for the first time.

We took a tour boat ride up the Chicago River, and she marveled at all the new buildings going up she'd never noticed before. We went to the botanical gardens in Lincoln Park and she quietly reveled in the beauty of the plants and flowers, then cavorted on the lawn out front, teasing me into a game of tag. We went to a Sox game in the new Comiskey Park, and sat in the steeply pitched upper deck, clutching each other in mock terror, laughing at our own fear of heights. We ate hot dogs and popcorn and cotton candy, and drank too much beer, and came away with satisfying stomachaches.

We dined elegantly, cheaply, at her house, and at mine. We traded recipes and good-naturedly critiqued each other's cooking. We changed clothes as if we owned stock in Dayton-Hudson, running from one activity to another, experiencing the city as if there were no tomorrows, only the delight of now, every delicious moment in each other's company. We saw a play that made us cry, stand-up comics that made us hold our sides to keep from her-

niating with laughter, and the city skyline by night from
a horse-drawn carriage that made us sit in silent wonder.
I used plastic for so many things that a representative from
the credit card company called me to ask if my card had
been stolen.

I couldn't take credit for her transformation. It wasn't
my usual dose of old-fangled chivalry, "Emerson Ward's
Elixir of Romance," that swayed her. I simply gave her
the opportunity to be herself, to come out of her shell.
She'd already decided, for whatever reason, to start living
again. Maybe it was because with Brady gone, she had
nothing to prove to anyone anymore, and no one to please
but herself. Whatever, I made no promises I couldn't
keep, and made no demands. I took her to places I thought
she would enjoy, and didn't give her a reason not to trust
me. I suppose I wished it was my charm and good looks
that turned the trick, but it didn't much matter. She was
fun to be with. More importantly, she found herself fun
to be with, and if I had anything to do with that, so much
the better. Maybe I would get some points for it in the
afterlife.

Every day, I checked in with Kitty and Nell, but they
seemed to be getting along fine without me. And despite
my best intentions to go out and solicit some new business, it was a lot more interesting spending time with
Glynnis than making phone calls. The projects I already
had on my calendar would keep.

Every day, I tried to follow the unfolding story of the
late Stanley Wroblewski's involvement with the seamier
side of Chicago politics. Sue had broken the story in the
paper the day after I found his body. She'd had to run
with bare bones facts and carefully worded innuendo, but
it had been a good poke at the hornet's nest. After her
initial story came regular updates—the announcement of

a grand jury investigation into allegations that Grettel had arranged payoffs and court case dispositions, the appointment of a special federal prosecutor to the case, the surprise revelation of the identity of a federal witness and the existence of taped conversations. It was all business as usual in Chicago.

And every day, I called Brandt to see how he was coming in his search for Nick's elusive ex. The easiest thing would have been to ask Nick himself, but the idea made me uneasy. I felt uncomfortable nosing into his personal life. I didn't want him to know I was rooting around in his past. I don't know why. He probably could have cared less about a woman he'd been divorced from for 35 years. But I warned Brandt off, nevertheless.

For the most part, I couldn't think of much else except Glynnis. She astounded me, fascinated and captivated me. My infatuation with her was growing deeper by the hour, and every so often I would catch myself wondering if she was the one, if maybe I'd found my romantic match, my significant other, my Rapunzel.

More than anything, we talked. Or, she talked and I listened. She told me about growing up with Brady, and worse, growing up with Jennifer.

"Jennifer was charming, almost charismatic in public," she told me after dinner one night, "but with family she was negative, critical, unbalanced. She was terrified of aging, of not being able to control her family. She was frustrated; she couldn't boss Daddy around, so she took it out on me. I had no role models but her. She criticized every woman I might have looked up to, and when no one else was home she would make me stand for an hour or so while she ranted and screamed at me, about what a horrible child I was, how I made everyone miserable. I tried just as hard to please her as I did Daddy, hoping she would stop, hoping *he* would see how hard I was trying and make her stop.

"I was a princess and I was shit. After a while, I didn't know what I was. It wasn't until after I left Chad that I began to heal myself, bought the house, and began to start over, recreate my life as I wanted it to be. It's been hard and painful, but it's *my* life now.

"For a long time, I've been trying to yank out the programming that's been put in my mind, so I pay a lot of attention to intuition. I make decisions based on what feels right, and after spending all this time with you, you feel right. I think maybe we were supposed to meet. Does that make any sense?"

"Yes," I replied a little breathlessly. "Despite our rocky beginning, I think you might be right." *Something* had attracted me to her that night at Greg's house, and if she wanted to call it fate, that was fine with me. I only knew that I was hooked.

IT WAS EIGHT DAYS before Brandt called me. He sounded pleased with himself, and I knew he had good news for me. I said I'd be right over. He was beaming when he met me at the door with a beer.

"Candice Fratelli is now Candice Carpenter," he told me, leading the way inside.

"How did you find out?"

"Sometimes you just get lucky," he chuckled. "I started digging through old records, like you suggested, but I also figured that if she was still in the area someone might know her. So, I started asking around. A society page editor I know recognized her from the picture you gave me. It seems Mrs. Carpenter is a generous, if modest, patron of charitable causes. She donates lots of her husband's money to different projects, but usually very quietly, almost always anonymously. My friend says she's met her, though, a few times at fundraisers. Mrs. Carpenter, apparently, was actively involved in raising money for the oceanarium down at the Shedd Aquarium. I'm surprised I didn't know her myself, but I may have met her and just don't remember.''

"Where does she live?"

"Up in Lake Bluff. She's lived there for quite some time.''

"You deserve a medal."

He beamed some more. "Why are you so interested in her, anyway?"

I didn't answer for a minute. "What do we really know about each other, Brandt?"

"What do you mean?" He frowned.

"We've been friends for years. We've been through a lot, you and I, but what do we really know about each other? Do you know who I had a crush on in fifth grade? Do I know who your best buddy was when you were six?"

"No," he said slowly, "but I suppose we know more about each other than almost anyone but our mothers. What difference does it make?"

"In our case, it doesn't. It's just curious that you can think you know someone, but not really know them. I've found out more about Brady, about the kind of man he was, in the last few weeks than I did in all the time I knew him. And I still don't know enough to understand him, understand what's going on in his family. There's something wrong, something nobody knows about, or nobody's talking about. I think Candice Fratelli, or Carpenter, knows what it is.''

He looked at me for a moment, then raised his beer bottle. "Well, then, here's to truth," he said quietly.

A HOUSEKEEPER ANSWERED when I called the number in Lake Bluff. She told me that Mrs. Carpenter was busy and couldn't come to the phone, and asked if I'd like to leave a message. I was insistent. I gave her my name, and told her that I had to speak with the lady of the house. There was silence on the line while she relayed my message, then she came back on.

"Sir? Mrs. Carpenter suggests you leave a number where you can be reached, and she'll call you back when she has a chance."

"I'd be happy to do that, but would you please try again. Tell her that I must speak to her about Brady Barnes."

I made her repeat the name. She sighed and told me to wait. There was a longer silence this time, and finally another voice came over the line.

"Mr. Ward, is it? I don't know what you want, but I'm sure I can't help you."

"Mrs. Carpenter, wait. I was a friend of Brady's, and there are things about him I need to know, things I believe you can tell me."

"Why would you think that? Why would I know anything about this Barnes person?"

The question threw me off for a moment, but Brady's name had brought her to the phone.

"Because you were his partner's wife. You were married to Nick Fratelli, weren't you?" The line was silent. "Brady's dead, Mrs. Carpenter. He was murdered."

"Yes, I know," she said softly.

"I'm trying to find out who killed him."

"I still don't see how I can help you. I haven't seen Brady for years, and I certainly don't know who killed him." The voice was more forceful this time.

"This has to do with more than just Brady. It involves his family. It involves Glynnis. I really need to see you."

There was a long silence this time, and for a moment I was afraid we'd been cut off.

"All right, Mr. Ward," she said finally. "Can you be here at four o'clock this afternoon?"

"That would be fine."

She gave me directions to the house, then hung up.

I got on the Kennedy just after three to give myself enough time, and found myself moving at a crawl all the way up to the Edens. Construction crews were out, and traffic on Chicago expressways never seemed to abate much anymore. It seemed that every hour of every day was rush hour. It was a hot day in mid-August, and the afternoon sun burned through the windows on my side of the car, making the air-conditioning work overtime to dissipate the heat.

I found the house without too much trouble, a small and stately colonial at the end of a cul-de-sac, shaded by large, old oaks and a few elms miraculously untouched by the ravages of disease that had swept through the area more than thirty years before. A small slender woman in her late fifties answered the bell. She was simply, but stylishly dressed in black silk pants and a billowy white silk, long-sleeved blouse. Her features, a little worn and wrinkled with age, were still pretty, and still reminiscent of the photo of the young woman I carried in my pocket.

"Mr. Ward? Come in." She opened the door for me, and after closing it behind me, turned to lead me into the house. Her dark hair, elegantly streaked with gray, was pulled into a tight chignon.

The house was larger than it appeared from the outside, and she led me through a maze of hallways and rooms to a sunroom at the back of the house. It was all glassed in, with big sliding doors that opened out into the yard. It was comfortably furnished and green with so many plants, it was almost like a jungle.

She stopped in front of a loveseat. "Please, sit down," she said with a gesture of her hand. "Would you like some iced tea?"

There was a pitcher and glasses on the table in front of her.

"Yes, thank you." I chose a large wicker chair next to the table, and sat when she did. "You have a lovely home."

"Thank you," she murmured. "It's a little cluttered, I'm afraid. After thirty years of collecting odds and ends, it becomes hard to find places to put things. You get so attached."

"I appreciate your taking the time to see me."

"Exactly who are you, Mr. Ward?" Her face turned serious.

"I'm a writer. Freelance. I'm very mercenary, so I write for lots of different types of clients. As I told you on the phone this morning, Brady was a friend of mine, as is Kitty Barnes, his wife. Brady had asked me to do him a favor when he was killed. I felt obligated to help Kitty find out who killed him."

"Isn't that a matter for the police?"

I shrugged. "Yes, it is, but I have a more personal interest in it than the police do."

"How did you find me? It couldn't have been through Nick. I don't even think he knows, or cares, where I am."

"I didn't. I asked a friend of mine, Brandt Williams, to try to locate you."

She tilted her head to look at me, then nodded. "I know who Mr. Williams is. He was on the board at Northwestern Memorial when I served on the Women's Auxiliary at Prentiss. You say he's a friend of yours?"

"Probably my closest."

Her eyebrows arched, and there was a hint of a smile on her face. "I'm not quite sure what to make of you, Mr. Ward. You have an interesting assortment of friends between Brady and Brandt Williams." She paused. "So, you're looking into Brady's death?"

"Yes. I thought you may know something that would make sense of what's happened."

"I really don't think I can help you. I haven't seen or talked to Brady Barnes in over thirty-five years. I agreed to see you because you were so insistent, but I'm sorry if you've wasted a trip out here."

"Mrs. Carpenter, please. I realize you probably don't know much about Brady's life since you last saw him, and you probably don't care. But I need to know about what happened when you did know Brady, when you were married to Nick. I must know."

"I left Nick Fratelli a long time ago, Mr. Ward. I started a new life. I fell in love with a kind and gentle man, a very successful man who has provided well for me, who has enabled me to raise two beautiful children, live in a lovely home, and contribute my time and energy as well as some of his money to worthwhile causes."

Her face remained impassive, but there was anger in her voice as she went on. "I've worked hard for what I have, and I have a lot. My husband loves me, I get along well with my children, I like the way I live, and I've asked nothing in return except to be left alone. We make donations anonymously to the causes we support so people don't see our names and ask us to get involved in things in which we have no interest. I spend most of my time shielding my husband from inquiries, sometimes from legitimate organizations, but mostly from con artists and hucksters who want a piece of his money. I'm still not sure you aren't one of them, trying to come at us from a very unusual angle. I don't like people poking their noses into my life, Mr. Ward."

"What *does* your husband do, Mrs. Carpenter?"

"He's retired, but he still has assets to manage, so he spends quite a bit of time in his office. Not that it's any of your business."

I let her anger cool a moment before I replied. "You're right, it's none of my business. I'm not interested in your money. I am interested in finding out who killed Brady Barnes and why someone threatened him, threatened his family, before he was murdered. I apologize for nosing into your life, but you have answers to questions. Answers I must have. I have no intention of trying to compromise you in any way. If you tell me what I need to know, I'll leave quietly and never bother you again, and no one will ever know we talked."

She shook her head. "It won't do any good to dredge up the past. I've spent all this time trying to forget the past. For my husband's sake, for my sake, don't ask me to do this."

"I have no choice, and I don't think you do, either."

"What do you mean?" She looked at me, startled.

I pulled the photograph out of my pocket and handed it to her. She took it hesitantly, then looked at it curiously. She put it down on the table in front of her and looked back at me.

"I assume you got this from Brady?"

I nodded, then placed a second photo on the table next to the first. It was a snapshot of Glynnis I'd taken the day we went on the boat tour, a tourist's shot of her standing on the sidewalk with the Wrigley Building in the background. Candice stared at it for a long time without speaking. When she finally looked up, her eyes were wet, and sadness and pain showed through cracks in the impassive face.

"Maybe no one else sees it, but there's a certain resemblance there. Tell me what happened," I said gently. "Please."

"I think you should leave now."

"No. I can't."

Her face darkened, and I was afraid she would call the housekeeper, or worse, the police, and have me thrown out. Finally, she heaved a sigh. She rose and walked to one of the sliding glass doors, looking out at the sunny day without speaking. When she turned to face me, she seemed to be in another world.

"I met Nick when he was selling photos to the newspapers. I was still a girl practically. I'd moved here from Indiana, a wide-eyed country girl in the big city. I had a job as a secretary at one of the papers, and that's how I knew Nick. He was young and handsome and exciting. And after a while, we started dating. He'd take me out to get a hot dog for lunch once in awhile, that sort of thing. It was fun, and he was very romantic. All that Italian blood, you know.

"When Brady offered him a job, he suddenly realized he had a steady income, and he started dating me seriously. It wasn't long before he asked me to marry him. There were no good jobs for women back then. I lived with friends, and we scraped by every month, trying to come up with enough money for rent and food. Nick was very dashing, and I was infatuated with him. I didn't see any future for myself on my own, so when he asked me to marry him, I said yes.

"We were very young, and convinced we could do anything, be anything, of course. Brady was already pretty well known, and for Nick to get a job with him was the start of something big as far as we were concerned. We got a little studio apartment, and we were happy. Everything was wonderful. We got to know Brady and Vicky well. They were very kind to us, and we became close friends. We did a lot together, went places, made dinner for each other, all the things friends do.

"Brady used to flirt with me. He was that kind of person. He'd joke with Nick and poke fun at him, and flirt with me, and lavish attention on Vicky, all at the same time. It was all in fun, and Brady was so big and warm and loving he wrapped us all up into a family. After a while, though, I realized that Brady's attention to me wasn't just platonic. He was never forward or overt, but I knew he wanted me. And Nick started to get jealous. Not often, but he'd get moody. It was a side of him I hadn't seen before, a side I didn't like.

"I was young and foolish, and when Nick tried to control me, tried to tell me how to behave, I rebelled. Who did he think he was? I was attracted to Brady, so I returned his attention, flirted with him just to provoke Nick. It wasn't serious. I mean, I wasn't as interested in Brady as I was in showing Nick that he couldn't tell me how I should act or who I should see.

"But I felt sorry for Brady, too. Vicky wasn't well. She was a very frail woman, and it was easy to see that her health was a strain on their marriage. Brady loved her, but he was miserable a lot of the time."

Candice turned and looked out the window, then started in again a moment later.

"We were involved in Vietnam by then. Before the protests started. You wouldn't remember. You're too young. After the Gulf of Tonkin, it became a real war.

Nick got caught up in it. He was itching to go. I don't know, maybe to prove something to Brady, or to himself, so he volunteered. Once he signed up we didn't have much time to figure out what it was going to do to our lives. He never thought about that. It all happened so fast. We had two weeks from the time he signed up to the time he shipped out to boot camp. Brady and Vicky offered to let me stay in the house while Nick was gone. It made sense. We couldn't afford the apartment unless I went back to work, and Nick didn't want me to. Brady even suggested that Nick's mother move in, too, to help Vicky with the house and with little Ronnie. It was a big house. There was plenty of room, so that's what we did.

"We packed up all our things and moved them into Brady's basement. We didn't have much, just a bed, a table, a few chairs. All of Nick's brothers and sisters were grown and gone, except his baby sister Maria, so Rosa brought her along and moved into the old servants quarters on the third floor. I moved into a bedroom on the second floor. The night before Nick shipped out, we had a farewell dinner at the house. Rosa cooked lots of Italian food, and we invited Nick's family and some of his friends over, and drank too much wine, and somewhere in the middle of it all, Brady and Vicky announced that Vicky was pregnant again.

"Vicky had diabetes. She shouldn't have gotten pregnant with Ron, but since she'd gotten through one pregnancy, she was determined to have the second child. From almost the very first day, she was in bed, and Brady was miserable."

She paused for a long time, and I wondered if I should give her a gentle nudge. Before I could speak, she finally turned to look at me again.

"You must understand, I fell in love with Brady. He'd

been so kind to us, and he was worried sick about Vicky. My heart just about broke for him, and I was lonely in the house without Nick. When he came into my room late one night after everyone was asleep, I knew I should turn him away, but I couldn't. I needed him as much as he needed me. I was a young woman. My husband was gone, and I didn't know if he was ever going to come back alive. And Brady was there. It just happened. I let him into my bed, and made love to him with a longing and a hunger I'd never known with Nick. And I got pregnant that very first time.

"I had to tell Nick. It was close enough to the time he left that I thought we might just get away with it. So I wrote to him and told him that we were going to have a baby, that I'd gotten pregnant the night of his farewell party. Brady and I couldn't stop seeing each other. We were in the same house, in rooms just steps away from each other. We were cautious. We were careful, but we didn't stop.

"Vicky got worse and worse as her pregnancy went on. She went into premature labor twice, but still held on to the baby. She was a fighter, and I felt even guiltier because of it. I liked Vicky. I couldn't stand the thought of making a fool of her in her own house, but I couldn't stay away from Brady. My own pregnancy seemed to be going fine, and I wrote Nick almost every day to tell him how things were, what the baby was doing, how it felt. God, it was awful. I'm still haunted by the guilt I felt. Can you understand that?"

She was crying now, tears rolling down the side of her nose, and I could do nothing but let her try to compose herself and tell it in her own way. She swiped at the tears with the back of her hand, and I looked around for a tissue. The only thing close was a linen cloth hanging on a tea cart nearby. I went to get it and handed it to her. She dabbed at her face, then looked at it and gave a short laugh between sniffles.

"I should have come equipped," I said softly.

"Do you always make women cry, Mr. Ward?" She smiled faintly.

"It seems so lately."

She took a deep breath and walked over to the loveseat to sit. "I suppose you want all of it?"

"You've come this far."

"Yes." She sighed and looked away for a moment. "Vicky held out until almost the end of her term. When she finally went into labor, it was horrible. I'll never forget that night. Everything that could go wrong did. It was April, April fourth, and there was a terrible thunderstorm that night. I remember Vicky's screams of pain, but she was so weak, they were hardly screams at all, as if she was under water. And sometimes, when the thunder cracked outside, you couldn't hear her at all. You could just see her mouth open in agony. I tried to help, but all I did was get in the way, so Mama Rosa shooed me out of the room and sent me back to bed.

"Vicky's doctor was at the hospital and couldn't come, but he sent a midwife instead. When the midwife got there, she sent Rosa on errands, heating water, getting more towels and sheets. I heard it all from my room, and I just cowered, afraid of the thunderstorm, afraid of Nick finding out about the child I had in my belly, afraid for Vicky. It was all too much, and I went into labor, too.

"At some point after that, the power went out, the phone went dead, and the rest of the night was total confusion, total hell. Rosa got candles, and tried to help me when I went into contractions, then would go to help the midwife when I was all right for a moment. It was terri-

fying, and lonely, and painful. Two women in labor was
more than Rosa and Brady and the midwife could handle,
so Brady sent Rosa out for help. She didn't find it in
time.''

Candice spoke haltingly, choking on the memories, and
I reached out to touch her hand. In a moment, she started
in again.

"Vicky gave birth to a little girl, but the baby was
stillborn. When Brady came in to tell me, he saw that I
was starting to have my baby, too, and he yelled for the
midwife. She came running and helped me deliver Glynnis. Brady held my hand through the whole thing, and just
cried. I made my decision then. I pulled him down to me
and told him if he had any feelings for me at all, he should
send the midwife home and switch the babies before Rosa
got back. He cried some more and said he couldn't, but I
swore that I would tell Nick everything when he returned
if Brady didn't do as I said. He realized I was right, realized that neither of us could take the chance. He did
what I told him.''

She took a deep breath. "Vicky didn't make it through
the night. She died before morning. That's what I've carried around all these years, what I've had to live with. Is
that what you came for?''

"What happened between you and Nick?''

"Things were never the same between us. Vietnam
changed him. Losing the baby did, too. When I wrote to
him, lied to him, that our baby had been stillborn, he was
crushed. He blamed me for losing the baby. When he
finally came home, he was moody and bitter for a long
time, and I realized that I'd made a mistake marrying him
in the first place. We got an annulment, and I left.''

"But you were in love with Brady. Why didn't you
stay, for Glynnis? How could you give her up?''

She laughed, a short bark that was harsh and bitter. "Brady didn't love me. At least he wasn't in love with me. I could see that. I'd known it all along, I think. He was still in love with Vicky, but she hadn't been able to satisfy him. I was there, a convenience for Brady. Don't misunderstand me. We used each other. We needed each other. But how could I stay? How could I keep living a lie? How could I do that to Nick? To myself? And I couldn't force Brady to feel more for me than he did.

"No, it was better to make a clean break. Glynnis was better off with Brady. He was able to give her things I never would have been able to. It broke my heart, but she was his child as much as mine, and I couldn't live with the guilt."

"And nobody found out?"

"Not that I know of. You're the first person I've ever told, Mr. Ward."

"Emerson, please," I murmured.

"You know, it feels good somehow to tell it, to share it finally with someone else. I've dreaded this day for years, afraid someone would find out. Now that someone has, I don't have to be afraid anymore. I trust you'll be discreet."

"Of course, but you ought to consider telling Glynnis. Now that Brady is gone, she could use a friend."

"Maybe someday. When we're both ready."

I thought for a minute. "You're sure no one knows about this?"

"Reasonably sure. If someone knew, I assume they would have come to see me long before this."

"Not even Rosa?"

"No, especially not Rosa. I think she might have killed me had she known. She never forgave me as it was. Besides, Rosa must be gone by now."

"You mean dead? She's still working at the studio as a cleaning lady."

"Oh, that couldn't be. She must be in her eighties by now."

"She looks pretty healthy to me." I paused. "Mrs. Carpenter, I'm sorry I put you through all this. I'm sorry you had to dig up painful memories, but I appreciate your truthfulness."

She sighed. "It had to come out sometime. But please, don't let this get back to my husband, I beg of you. I'll probably have to tell him, but I need to find my own way, my own time."

"I understand. I won't bother you again."

She nodded, then looked at the pictures on the table in front of her, reaching out to touch the photo of Glynnis. There was a look of sadness on her face, and longing, too.

"May I keep this?"

"Of course."

THIRTEEN

I THOUGHT ABOUT CANDICE'S story all the way home, and I had a lot of time to think. I got caught in the bumper-to-bumper crush of reverse commuters on the Edens and drove downtown at a snail's pace. It was a sad story, almost tragic, full of theatrical elements—unrequited love, bad luck, even death, with some wrath of God, sound, and lighting effects thrown in for good measure. I had no reason to disbelieve her. It explained the physical resemblance between Glynnis and a younger Candice. But there was a lot it didn't explain, and something about the whole thing bothered me.

It bothered me so much that when I turned off the Kennedy onto North Avenue, I stopped off at the bar at Bub City to mull it over with a beer. I even called Brandt to see if he was free for dinner. He said he'd jump into a cab and come right over. I reserved a table for us, and when he arrived we sat and ordered beer, a mess of steamed crabs, and red beans and rice. While we waited for the food, I told him the story. I told him everything, the Barnes family saga from start to finish. He listened silently, without interruption and with no sign of shock or surprise. The food came, but he let it sit untouched until I was finished. When I finally picked up a crab leg, he took it as a signal that I was done, and started in on his own plate. He took a bite, smiled with satisfaction, then looked at me seriously.

"So, what bothers you?"

"What bothers me," I said, savagely cracking a crab leg with a wooden dowel, "is that it's not enough. I understand how terrible it must have been for Candice Carpenter, how guilty she must have felt all these years, but it's not grounds for blackmail. It's old news. It happened a hell of a long time ago, and as unacceptable as it may seem to some, an illegitimate child just isn't all that shocking. Brady and Candice made a mistake. So what? I can understand it's not something either would want to go public with, but Candice divorced Nick anyway."

"It's still not something she would want people to know. It could complicate her life."

"Exactly. Though I can't imagine her husband wouldn't forgive her for something she did before they were married."

"So, who would benefit from the news getting out?"

"I don't know."

"What about Glynnis' trust? The one from her grandparents."

I thought for a moment. "I suppose if it could be proved she was illegitimate, and Brady didn't have adoption papers, she could be cut out of the inheritance. Ron would get it all." Brandt watched me think, and I finally shook my head. "It's not Ron's style. In that whole screwed up family, I'd say those two have the most affection for each other. Besides, why blackmail Brady? Why not just go public and take the issue to court? It doesn't make sense. Candice's story revealed a skeleton in the closet, but it's not the right one. There's something else going on."

"Are you going to tell her?"

"Glynnis? I don't know. I want to, but it's none of my business."

He nodded. "You've been spending a lot of time with her lately."

I flushed, though I shouldn't have been surprised he'd noticed. "I like her. She's really coming into her own, finding out who she is. It might mess up her head if I told her about Candice. That might be just a little too much for her to take right now. It's better to let Candice decide if she wants to be a part of Glynnis' life, I think."

Brandt nodded again. "I think you're right."

I DROPPED BRANDT OFF at his house after dinner, drove straight home, and parked the Alfa in the garage. The days were getting shorter, signaling the end of summer. It was just after eight and it was dark already. I'd forgotten to turn on any lights before I left, but there was enough light from the alley to make my way across the patio, and even though the back door was in shadow, I put the key in the lock from memory.

The dark house felt empty. I walked from room to room turning on lights, but even their brightness didn't dispel the shadows and the hollow feeling in my chest. Brady and I had not been so close that I mourned his loss the way I knew I would someday when Brandt was gone, or the way I had for Jessica. But Brady's death still left a big hole in my life. Even more, it was a reminder of how fleeting life is. I hadn't been a good enough friend to Brady. That was the shame. Life's too short not to take the time to get close to friends.

I paced the house, antsy and restless. I didn't want to be alone, so I locked up the house tightly, throwing all the deadbolts, then got the Alfa out of the garage.

The moon was near full again, rising above the treetops.

It was hard to believe it had been almost a month since Brady's phone call. The moon was dispassionate. It had seen a million Bradys come and go and didn't care a whit for my small problems. I drove up to Old Town and found a place to park less than a block away from Glynnis' house. She was surprised to see me.

"I didn't expect you," she said through the screen door. "We didn't have a date, did we?"

"I should have called first. I'm sorry to bother you so late."

"No, that's okay. Come in. I'm glad you came by." She opened the door for me. "I was just having a glass of wine. Do you want some?"

"A beer would be better, if you have one."

"Sure. You sit, and I'll be right back."

I did as she said, making myself comfortable on a couch in the living room. She was gone only a moment or two, coming back with a glass of beer. She put the beer on a table and sat next to me on the couch, tucking her feet up under her.

"You know, I've been thinking a lot about us," she said. "This past week has been an extraordinary adventure for me, Emerson. I want to thank you for that. I feel like I'm really living, for the first time in my life."

I started to reply, but she reached out and put a finger to my lips. Then she quickly leaned over and kissed me, pressing her weight into me. The gentle brush of her lips sent a current through my body, and I responded gently, cautiously. It was a soft kiss, sweet and tender, and when she broke it off, I thought it was just a simple thank-you. But her breath came a little faster, and she leaned into me again, pressing her lips on mine with more intent, more feeling, but with the same tenderness. She parted her lips ever so slightly and let the tip of her tongue touch me, and ran her fingers through my hair. Then she gently pulled away, sighed and put her face against my neck.

I held her close, not daring to breathe, not knowing what was going through her mind. It became evident moments later when she rose and took my hand in hers. I stood up, full of questions, but she put her fingers to my lips again and then led me through the house and up the spiral staircase to heaven.

She had made her decision, and knew what she wanted, so I let her take control. She led and I followed her example. We slowly undressed each other in the dim light of her bedroom, and I found myself in awe of a goddess, a schoolboy feeling I'd not had since losing my virginity to a woman ten years my senior. Glynnis was beautiful, and her body glowed in the moonlight filtering through the windows. I couldn't take my eyes off the perfection, the softly rounded curves, the flat belly of a twenty-year-old, the taut definition of her calf as she stood on tiptoes. I pulled her close and reveled in the silky feel of her naked skin, the warm weight of her breasts and thighs pressed tightly into me, stirring me.

She kissed me again, then led me to the bed. With small tuggings and gentle direction, she let me know what she wanted and where she wanted me. I moved in response to her wishes, occasionally initiating a touch, a soft stroking. She either responded with sounds of pleasure and movement, or guided me. My senses were heightened, and I became aware of every touch, interpreting her every move. I so wanted to please this exquisite creature that I suddenly realized I was no longer moving with her, but was somehow detached, watchful, careful not to disturb her rhythm, her timing, her desire.

I let her use me, joyously, because she deserved to know all of life's pleasures. But I felt sad, too, and guilty that I hadn't let myself become emotionally involved enough. I wanted to be in love with her, but I wasn't, yet. As much as I'd told myself otherwise, my ego was involved. So when she gasped and shuddered, wriggling in surprise at the intensity of the pleasure she was finally experiencing after all those years, I couldn't share it with her. I held her close for a long time, questioning my own motives in the dark, until I finally fell asleep.

She was gone when I woke up later. The room was still dark, and I slid out from under the sheet to go look for her. She was sitting on a stool in the kitchen wearing a white robe, barely illuminated by the blue glow of moonlight.

"Are you all right?"

"I'm very much all right," she murmured. "Thank you." She reached out to take my hand. "I just needed to think a little. Go back to bed. I'm okay, really."

I gave her hand a small squeeze and padded back up the spiral stairs to the bed. I was asleep in minutes.

When I opened my eyes again, sunlight was streaming through the bedroom windows. I lay unmoving, blinking, remembering where I was. My eyes searched the room, seeing it for the first time. It was cozy, comfortable, and very feminine. Very unlike the clean, masculine look of the kitchen where she worked. Glynnis stood naked in front of a full-length mirror, turning this way and that, holding her breasts in her hands, taking stock. I propped myself up on one elbow and watched her admiringly. She finally saw my reflection in the mirror and grinned.

"You like?" I nodded. "I never realized what I've got here. This really gets you steamed up, doesn't it?"

"It's prime stuff, Glynnis, every inch of it."

"I think I kind of like it. I never really saw my body that way before. I guess last night kind of changed that."

I smiled. "I'm glad."

She came over to the bed and sat on the edge, taking my hand. Her look sobered.

"We need to talk. I told you I've been thinking a lot about us lately. Last night was wonderful, incredible, just what I fantasized it would be, and I have to thank you for helping me just be me, for helping me open a door I shut tight a long time ago."

"But?" I didn't think I was going to like what was coming next.

She dropped her eyes for a minute, then looked at me and smiled. "Now that I've discovered what all the fuss is about, I can afford to be choosy. It's not that you weren't good, Emerson. You were *very* good." She licked her lips lasciviously, enjoying being naughty. "You had to be to cut through all the garbage that's been cluttering up my mind, preventing me from enjoying life. And I'll be forever grateful to you. You're a very nice person."

The dreaded word "nice." I was in for it now.

"The fact is that I *can't* spend my life being grateful to you. I've spent three-quarters of my life taking care of men—my brothers, my father, my husband. I don't need another man right now. I've only just started learning how to take care of myself. You've opened a wonderful world to me, but if I stay with you, then all I'll do is try to take care of you. All I'll be is your woman. I don't want that, and I don't think you want that. No, it's better that we break it off here, now. Let it be a wonderful memory, but please don't try to make me stay."

My stomach dropped, and I couldn't think, couldn't breathe for a moment, trying to digest her words. "Does the condemned man get one last meal?" I tried a small smile.

She laughed. "Breakfast? Sure. Whatever you'd like."

"Friends?" I raised my eyebrows.

"Friends," she nodded, leaning into me for a hug.

I MOPED FOR THE REST of the day, feeling sorry for myself.
I'd conquered, but lost; tasted paradise but hadn't been let
in the gates. True, I hadn't been in love with Glynnis. I'd
been infatuated. But I wanted to believe I could have
fallen in love with her, that she might have been the one.
My ego was bruised, as much from the fact that she was
right as from the rejection itself, and I nursed it with a
therapeutic dose of self-pity.

I dragged out collections, envelopes, of old photos and
shuffled through them, trying to recreate the past. I looked
at the faces of friends past and present, wallowing in sentiment. My mood turned maudlin wondering where they'd
all gone, wondering why I'd let go of so many friendships
as easily as Glynnis had let go of me. It was deliciously
self-indulgent for a while, but a thought bubbling around
in my subconscious finally broke free and put an end to
it.

Pictures, pictures, pictures. They stared me in the face,
reminding me of where I'd been, who I'd known. Most
of my life was chronicled in photographs. So was Brady's.
They were only fleeting snapshots in time, but everything
came back to pictures, photos. That was the key. It had
to be. I called Nell on a hunch.

"It's Emerson. Can you talk?"

"Well, yes."

"Can you do me a favor when you get a chance? Check
all your purchase orders for film around each time you've
done a shoot for the liquor company in the past few years.
Can you do that?"

"Of course. But what are you looking for?"

"I want to know how much film was being ordered for

those sessions. You may want to go back a ways to see if it's changed at all over the years.''

"It may take me a little while.''

"That's okay. Take your time." I paused. "How are you doing, anyway?''

"All right, I suppose. Business has fallen off some. People are a little unsure of our capability with Brady gone. Most of our clients came to us because of him. I guess some of them don't realize that Brady didn't really get involved in many shoots for the past few years.''

"What do you mean?''

"Oh, he helped do set-ups and lighting, and such. But Nick and Marty have done most of the actual photography lately. Brady sort of directed, made himself visible to clients on the set. Now Nick is no help. He's just gotten moodier and moodier lately. Marty's had to take up all the slack.''

"I see." I hadn't realized that. "But how are *you* doing?''

"Goodness, I'm fine. I just need a break from this place, Emerson. It's enough to drive anyone crazy.''

"What if I offered to take you away for a while?''

"Well? So, offer.''

"How about dinner? Tomorrow night?''

"That sounds wonderful.''

"Where would you like to go?''

"I trust you can decide that. Aren't you supposed to know something about food?''

I smiled at the phone. "I'm sure I'll think of something.''

NELL CALLED ME BACK about ten the next morning. She told me that film orders for the liquor shoots had been way over normal for some time. Not every session, and not the two most recent. I asked her to check the client or agency invoices to see if the extra film had been billed out, but she was way ahead of me. She said it hadn't. The studio had eaten the extra cost. I asked her to find out who ordered the film. She hadn't thought of that, but said she'd have an answer for me when I picked her up at her apartment for dinner.

It was time for another trip downtown. Dave Kliewer was helping a matronly woman when I entered the shop in the Mahler's Building. She was the type that couldn't stop talking. If she wasn't asking questions about the jewelry Kliewer was showing her, she was telling stories about her daughter and son-in-law. I waited patiently, pretending to browse the display cases. He glanced in my direction a couple of times, and I thought he seemed nervous. Finally, the woman completed her purchase and walked slowly out the door, talking over her shoulder all the way.

"Remember me?" I walked over to the counter.

"Of course," he murmured. His eyes dropped, then looked at me.

"There were a few things I didn't think to ask you last time I was here. I thought maybe you could help."

"If I can."

"If someone gave you excellent photographs of a gemstone, could you reproduce it from the photos?"

"I couldn't. I don't cut gemstones."

"Could a cutter reproduce stones from photos?" I rephrased the question, unable to keep the annoyance out of my voice.

"Well, it would take more than a photograph. A cutter would have to have precise measurements of the stone, and the photos would have to be clear enough to count the number of facets, see the angles…"

"But it could be done?"

"I suppose so."

He grew increasingly nervous with each question. He was hiding something.

"Who could do it? There must be someone here in town. Who is it?"

"Excellent cutters are rare. To find someone who could actually cut a zircon that would pass for the real thing just from a picture, you'd probably have to go to New York or Amsterdam."

He put on a brave face, but his eyes flicked from side to side, never quite meeting mine. I reached across the counter and gently but firmly grasped a fistful of shirt fabric just under his chin. His eyes widened, and now they looked at me.

"I don't think so. I think you know exactly who cut those stones. I have to tell you, I'm getting tired of this whole thing, and I'm in a really bad mood. I want the truth out of someone, and I'm starting with you. First, I'll trash your store. If that doesn't convince you, I'll start on you next. Maybe fingers, maybe faces, I haven't decided."

"No!" The voice came from the open office door behind the counter. "No violence!"

A small, old, white-haired man came through the door and peered at me intently. I slowly let go of Kliewer's shirt.

"You were Brady's friend?" the old man asked.

"Yes, and I promised him I'd find out who stole the jewels from his studio."

"A loyal friend." He nodded. "I cut the stones."

"Father!" Kliewer said sharply.

The old man waved his hand and gave him a withering look. "No, David. We've done nothing wrong. It's time for the truth." He turned back to me. "My name is Saul. Brady's father used to buy jewelry for his wife from me long ago. When Brady first came to me, I agreed to do him a favor because I'd always liked his father. His father brought me a lot of business."

"What do you mean when Brady first came to you?"

"It was some time ago—five or six years. I knew Brady, of course, met him with his father when he was a boy. And he came in occasionally, but I didn't see him for a long time until he came in with the diamond. Such a stone I've never seen. It was beautiful. Not too big, but exquisitely cut. The light played through it so wonderfully.

"Brady said he was having a little financial trouble, and told us he wanted to sell the diamond. He didn't really want to part with it, but he needed the money. Business was bad, and I guess he couldn't get a loan at the banks, or didn't have time to wait. He came to us because he knew that I did some cutting when I was younger, and said that he wanted a copy made before he let the stone go. I offered to buy it. It was too beautiful to let it go to someone who wouldn't appreciate it. And I agreed to cut a copy of the stone. It was a challenge to see if I could come anywhere close to that perfection. You understand? A challenge."

"Yes." I nodded.

He looked at me shrewdly, then his face softened, and he sighed. "I can see you've faced them, too. David did not agree with me." He nodded at his son, who stood quietly, a little chagrined. "I didn't know, of course, that the stone was from a collection. It was far more than we could afford, but I had to have it.

"It was perhaps a year before Brady came back. He wanted to buy the diamond back from me, and this time he brought photographs of two more stones. He presented me with another challenge, to see if I could duplicate them from the photographs. It was then I knew they were from a collection. He told me he wanted to surprise his wife with copies of the jewels. Who was I to argue? He bought back the original diamond for more than I paid him, and I couldn't turn down the challenge of cutting the new stones from the pictures he gave me. Did I do anything wrong? No, I did what I was trained to do, what I love to do.''

"Father," Kliewer said softly, "you gave him exactly what he needed to be able to steal the real jewels. That's called being an accessory."

I had to think. The whole idea of Brady stealing the collection was taking a while to sink in. It just didn't figure. Why have me look for a thief when he'd taken them all along? It didn't make sense, and then maybe it did. I turned to the old man.

"You say he bought the diamond back? And you cut the whole collection?"

"I don't know. I cut perhaps thirty stones, maybe less.''

"If Brady intended to steal all the jewels for profit, why buy back the diamond from you?"

They both looked at me with puzzled expressions. I left them there wondering.

FOURTEEN

I PICKED UP NELL AT 6:30. Her apartment was in a three-flat on Wrightwood, a comfortable looking frame Victorian. Nell was standing out front in a pretty flowered dress with short sleeves that poufed at the shoulders and lace trim around the yoke. She smiled and waved when she recognized me. I pulled up next to a car parked at the curb and hopped out to bound around the hood of the Alfa and open the door for her.

I'd had a hell of a time figuring out where to go for dinner. Some of the best food in town is cooked up within the confines of my own kitchen, but I thought it would be too forward to take her there. And I didn't want to take her someplace fancy because I didn't want to give her the impression that we were on a "date" date. I couldn't consider a date so soon after what had happened with Glynnis. It was almost like getting divorced, or being a widower. I was feeling just a tad vulnerable. So I drove up Halsted to a little Mexican place just south of Addison that has what I consider to be the best Mexican food in the city. I watched her look around the restaurant as we entered. She seemed to approve of my choice.

We ordered drinks—a strawberry margarita for her and Carta Blanca for me—and both dove into the chips and hot salsa as if we hadn't seen food for days. She laughed as a little bit of salsa spilled down her chin, and I grinned with her, feeling better than I had the last two days. She was a pretty, cheerful companion with whom I didn't feel the need to be anything but myself. When our drinks came, we clinked glasses in a silent toast to nothing in particular.

"Nick ordered all the film on those shoots you asked about," she said after sipping some of her drink through a straw.

"Not Brady?"

"No, it was Nick all right. All the purchase orders have to be initialed. Nick signed off on all of them."

I sat back and took a slow pull on my beer. It was hard to say if any of it made any sense, but I was beginning to get a pretty good idea of what was going on. I'd had a chance to think about it all day, ever since my visit to Kliewer's shop, and as confusing as it was, it had been a hell of a lot better than thinking about Glynnis.

"Why did you ask me to check on those film orders?"

Nell's face slowly came back into focus. If anyone deserved to know it was her.

"I asked because I had a hunch. I found out today my hunch was right. When Brady first told me fake jewels had been switched for the Winton collection, the collection had been in the studio only a week. Not enough time to make duplicates that would fool anybody. It struck me as odd at the time, but I didn't think about it again until recently."

A waiter came and hovered near the table, interrupting me. Since we were both starved, I paused to let Nell look over the menu one more time before ordering. The waiter wrote down our choices and left with a nod and a smile.

"Anyway," I continued, "it finally occurred to me that perhaps someone could cut fakes from photographs if the photos were good enough. You confirmed that extra film was ordered for photo sessions with the client. And I'll bet that it was only those shoots that involved the jewel collection. I leaned hard on the jeweler Brady said he knew. The guy's father admitted to cutting the fakes for Brady.''

''No.'' She looked at me dumbfounded. ''Brady?''

I smiled wryly. ''That's what I thought. I couldn't imagine why he would have asked me to find out who stole the jewels if it was him all along. I think he wanted me to find out something else, but he couldn't come out and say it.

''Brady made a few mistakes along the way. He wasn't as perfect as we all thought he was. He made a big one a few years back. My guess is that he found himself in a short-term cash squeeze that must have had him pretty desperate. If you think about it, you might even remember when it was, maybe some slow period, some downturn.''

I watched her think. ''Goodness, of course. I don't know why I didn't think of it before. Brady took Kitty skiing some time ago, and had an accident. He broke his leg and sprained his back. We had to cancel a number of jobs while he recuperated. I remember he was very concerned about payroll at the time, but we managed to squeak through.''

I nodded. ''Because he came up with cash. Instead of working with the bank and his creditors, I think he got stupid and took one diamond out of the collection, had a copy made, hocked the original, and put the fake back in with the collection. The client never noticed because the collection probably wasn't on loan during that time. There was no need to check.

''I think he intended to get the original back all along, and he did a year later. He went back to the jeweler who bought the diamond and paid him back with a profit. But somebody found out what he'd done and saw a way to scam some big money. Somebody blackmailed Brady into having copies made of the whole collection, so the originals could be stolen and fenced. I think Brady went along with only half the plan. He had the fakes made. He took measurements and series of perfect photos to give the cutter something to work with. But instead of fencing the originals, he paid the blackmailer out of his own pocket. Brady took the photos, but Nick ordered the extra film. I think Nick was putting the squeeze on Brady all that time.''

"But why? Why would Nick do that after all their years together?" Nell looked consternated, almost offended that what I suggested could have happened under her nose.

"I don't really know. Maybe he just got tired of being second banana. Brady never cut him in on the business, never made him a partner. Maybe he couldn't take it anymore.''

"You really think Nick was blackmailing Brady?"

"I can't figure it any other way.''

Nell was silent for a moment, and her face changed expressions rapidly from consternation to distaste to disbelief. She spoke slowly, haltingly. "But that…but that means…Nick probably killed Brady.''

"It sure looks that way. It would account for his moodiness recently, wouldn't it? A little guilt, maybe, starting to eat away at him?"

She shivered despite the heat of the salsa. "It's been getting worse and worse lately, too. He's like a crazy person now. One minute he's okay, and the next he's screaming and yelling at everyone. He's not helping us at all anymore. Clients don't want him on the set, the girls are out of their minds trying to figure out how to stay on his good side, and Marty's fed up with his tantrums.'' She paused and looked away for a moment. "I still can't believe it, Emerson. What are you going to do?"

"I don't know yet. I can't prove Nick did anything. And I'll need proof before I bring Lanahan in on this."

She looked at me questioningly, and I explained my on-again, off-again romance with Lt. John Lanahan of the Chicago Police.

"Let's not think about it now. I'm supposed to be taking you away from all that, remember?"

For a time, we did take ourselves away from it. The food came, and we immersed ourselves in the wonderful flavors. Nell had a chicken dish with mole sauce, and I had *carne asada* with *pico de gallo*. We traded bites of everything and conversation about everything except work. I enjoyed her company, and suddenly realized with some surprise how attractive she was. It had never really occurred to me before, but her face glowed in the light of the little candle on the table, and her smile was warm.

I drove her home after dinner with some reluctance. Even though I hadn't wanted a date, I'd enjoyed myself so much I didn't want the evening to end. And it had given me a chance to stop thinking about what I was going to do about Nick. I wasn't quite ready to face reality again. She must have felt the same.

"Would you like to come up?" she asked hesitantly as I pulled up to her door.

"A cup of coffee wouldn't hurt, if it isn't too much trouble." I was pleasantly surprised. "I think I had one too many beers."

I let her out and found a tight place at the curb to squeeze into, then joined her at the door. She led me up the stairs to the second floor apartment. It was sparse but homey, clean but messy, a comfortable place, and I was glad she didn't apologize for it. She made coffee and we sat in the living room and talked some more, about life, and hopes, and dreams. Finally, we seemed to run short of things to say, and I felt it was time to go. I stood up and mumbled something about it being late. She rose, too, standing between me and the door, and we looked at each other awkwardly.

"I better be going," I said. I wasn't sure what to do, what to say to close the evening.

Nell nodded, but as I started for the door, she stepped in front of me and rose up on tiptoes to kiss me lightly on the lips. Taken aback, I didn't move, so she did it again, with more insistence this time, and slowly I responded, returning the kiss. I don't know what stopped me—guilt? fear?—but suddenly I had to pull away. Something wasn't right.

"Where's Darlene?"

"She's spending the night with a friend." Nell cocked her head to look at me. "You've been spending a lot of time with Glynnis lately. Is that the problem?"

"Well, yes. And no. We aren't seeing each other anymore."

"She broke up with you? And you were starting to get serious about her?"

"I guess. It shouldn't bother me. We didn't have enough time together to really get serious." I looked into her eyes, trying to read what was going on there. "I guess what I'm wondering is, why me?"

Her face was thoughtful for a moment before she spoke.

"I've known you a long time, and since you've been spending so much time at the studio, I've seen what kind of person you are. I'm not the sort to make a fool of myself, Emerson, but even if you were still seeing Glynnis I think I would have done what I just did.

"You see, all the good ones are taken. They're either

married or gay, and what's left for the rest of us are nerds, narcissists, or men who are just too screwed up to have an inkling of what a woman wants or needs, or what a relationship as simple as friendship is all about.

"You're one of the great ones, Emerson, because you're sensitive, kind, and *single*. Don't go puffing out your chest—you're not perfect. Goodness, none of us are. But you're as close as I've seen to a real man in this day and age, and if I can't have all of you, or if I can only have you for one night, I'll take it. Because if I don't, I'll forever regret not having experienced you, for not taking a chance and letting myself love you if only a little, and even if you don't love me."

I didn't know what to say, and I felt a little more than foolish. I'd been so blinded by Glynnis' beauty I hadn't seen Nell right there in front of me all that time. And now that she was making me an offer, I somehow felt as if I didn't deserve it.

"Well, are you going to stand there all night looking stupid?"

"No, ma'am. I'm going to accept your kind offer and take advantage of you."

She smiled and moved in for another kiss.

Nell was small-breasted and hippy, not meaty enough to be Rubenesque, but comfortable, and our bodies fit together well. In the dim light of the bedroom she became a different person from the shy, efficient woman I knew. She wasn't at all hesitant or modest, and she took an earthy delight in lovemaking that made me feel as if we'd been lovers for years. She rode me with sensual abandon, taking me up a mountain with her, until finally, we fell off the edge of a cliff in an explosion of fiery sparks that drifted in free-fall. In the intense rush of feelings, a piece of me stood by and watched with the awe and amazement of a little boy—fireworks and bells...

Nell snuggled into me like a contented tabby. It felt good, felt right, and I couldn't help smiling.

I woke up sometime later with a sense of urgency, and looked at my watch. I'd dozed off for only a short time. It wasn't yet midnight, and I looked around the dark room wondering what had roused me. Nell lay next to me, her breath soft and regular against my chest, an arm draped over me. There were no other sounds other than the noise of passing cars filtering in from the street. I frowned.

It was Nick. He was becoming too unpredictable. If it was guilt eating away at him, then I didn't have anymore time. According to Nell, he was reaching a breaking point, and I would have to solve this thing once and for all before he went off the deep end. If Nick *was* behind all that had happened, he'd killed already, and I couldn't predict what he'd do if he went crazy. He might bolt, or he might kill again. It was time to look for proof.

I gently slid out from under Nell's arm, got out of bed and searched for my clothes in the dark. They were strewn all over the room, and it took me a while to find them all and put them on. I sat on the foot of the bed to put on my shoes, and Nell stirred sleepily.

"Where are you going?"

"To the studio. There must be something there that will tie Nick to all of this. Go back to sleep."

"Do you have to go? Let it wait until morning."

"It's better now when there's no one around. Don't worry, I'll be back in no time. Keep a spot warm for me, would you?"

"You'd better be back. I'm not done with you yet."

I smiled and walked around the bed to give her a kiss. "That's good news."

It was a beautiful night, cool and crisp, with a moon that was nearly full in a cloudless sky. Traffic was light as I headed downtown, and I found a parking spot right in front of the studio building. I took a couple deep breaths of clean air, tempted to turn around and head back to the warmth of Nell's bed, but steeled myself instead and walked in the building.

I let myself in the studio door with the key and punched in the alarm code, then made my way down the hall to Nick's office and found a light switch. Nick's office was next to Brady's, and though smaller, it, too, was tastefully furnished. I didn't know what I was looking for, but I was sure I'd know when I found it. I started with the desk and went through it drawer by drawer, looking at every scrap of paper. Nick was not as neat and orderly as Brady had been, and there was no rhyme or reason to what he'd chosen to keep.

I wasn't having much luck, so I put everything back the way I'd found it. I was about to start on the filing cabinets when I thought I heard a noise in the studio. I cocked my head to listen, then decided to check. I padded down the hall to the double doors and opened one a crack to poke my head through. The studio looked cavernous and spooky, dimly lit by emergency lighting. It was silent, and I shivered involuntarily. The dark shadows stretching into black infinity gave me the creeps, the same sort of feeling kids have about basements and attics.

I shrugged and went back down the hall to Nick's brightly lit office to continue my search. The file cabinets were worse than the desk, with jobs stuffed in folders and folders stuffed in drawers seemingly at random. I'd been at it for some time when I was sure I heard the low sound of a door closing. Standing stock still, I listened hard. Nothing, but I knew I wouldn't be happy until I checked, so I sighed and walked down to the reception area and took a look around. There was no sign of anyone, and I chastised myself for being so paranoid.

I trudged back toward the office, and just about had myself convinced my mind was playing tricks on me when a piercing wail from the depths of the studio sent my heart leaping into my throat. I pushed through the doors at a half-run and saw the shadowy figure of a woman standing at the edge of a photography bay halfway down.

"Rosa?" I called. "Is that you? What is it?"

"It's-a my baby!" she cried.

I trotted closer, my attention diverted to the crumpled shape on the floor just inside the bay. Sobbing sounds came through the hands up in front of Rosa's face, and she stepped back as I knelt down by the body. I could barely make out Nick's face in the dim light. I felt for a pulse. His skin was cold and clammy.

It was all wrong, all so terribly wrong. Why weren't the lights on? Why was Rosa in the studio so late? Why was Nick stone cold dead? The thoughts started hurtling through my brain, but the alarms sounded too late.

I started to turn to look for Rosa when the first blow landed on the back of my head, pitching me forward and turning my vision red. She'd used something hard, maybe a mop handle, and I rolled and tried to scramble away. She hit me again, this time in the forehead at the hairline over my left eye, and I felt blood pouring down my face before the world collapsed in on me and everything turned black.

MY CHEEK WAS PRESSED AGAINST a cold, hard floor. Some sort of mask pulled the hair and skin tight on the side of my face, making it hard to see. My head was pounding

and bright light from somewhere in front of me hurt my
eyes. I opened them slowly, squinting, trying to assess the
damage. I was lying in a congealed pool of my own blood
on the studio floor. A sticky half-dried coating of it
cracked in spots on my face. There was a light on in the
bay, but the rest of the space was hidden in darkness. My
hands were bound behind my back. I lay still and let my
fingers play on the restraints, trying to figure out what it
was. *Stay calm and think! You're not dead yet.* A belt,
probably my own.

I opened my eyes a little more. I heard the sounds of
feet shuffling on the floor and high-pitched grunts. I
turned my head. Rosa stood a few feet away in front of
a bulky canvas tarp, trying to hoist it up on a wheeled
dolly. I watched her for a minute, wondering why she
looked so strange.

"You look different," I mumbled. She was thinner than
I remembered, and she wore blue jeans and a blouse,
something no eighty-year-old would be caught dead in.

She turned to look at me. "Lucky you've got a hard
head. Maybe not so lucky, actually. Now I'll have to kill
you slowly."

I frowned. Something else besides the clothes... Her
accent was gone. I peered at her face. It was the same,
yet different, younger, but not young.

"You're not Rosa."

She snorted, a short bark of laugher. "She's been dead
for years."

"Then who...?" My head throbbed, and it hurt to
think.

"Maria." She shrugged. "It was all so easy. A little
makeup, a little padding in the clothes. People always said
I looked like my mother."

A light was slowly dawning. I looked at the tarp. "That's Nick, I presume? Why did you kill him?"

She sneered. "He had no ambition, no balls. He could have been great, better than the great Brady Barnes himself, but he pissed away his life. All this could have been his. I had to push him constantly, but he balked at every turn. He was scared shitless. He thought he had no talent. He thought he wouldn't be where he is without Brady."

"Hardly a reason to kill him."

"He was about to break, admit everything. Spineless, gutless worm. He was going to tell the police about me. He didn't realize how close we were."

"Tell them what?" That you were blackmailing Brady? That you killed him?"

"Brady got what he deserved," she said simply. "My brother was too stupid to realize what Barnes did to him, too stupid to see that Brady took advantage of him all these years. But I saw. I saw Brady's contempt for him. I was even in his house when he screwed my brother's wife, when he got her pregnant. Everybody forgot about little Maria, pretended I wasn't even there, but I saw everything, heard everything, and I waited all this time to get back at him for what he did to us."

Her voice grew loud and shrill, and her face turned red with anger. She suddenly stopped, and an icy hardness took over her features.

"Revenge was very sweet," she went on calmly. "When Mama Rosa died, I saw a chance to get close to Brady, find out his secrets. I swore Nick to secrecy and took over for her. No one paid much attention to her, so they didn't pay much attention to me. I came and cleaned the studio, and I found out things."

"Like Brady's mistake with the diamond?" I had to

keep her talking and give myself time to think. It was so hard. My head felt leaden and fuzzy.

"Yes, that was a gold mine. Blackmail seemed like such a wonderful way to exact full measure. I told Nick exactly what to do, and Brady gave him money just like clockwork. It was perfect."

"And Wroblewski? That was your idea, too?" My hands worked busily behind my back, straining against the leather strap, trying to loosen it. I tried not to wiggle, tried not to let her see what I was doing.

"I found the photos in Brady's file. When I saw the one with Acardo in it, I knew I was on to something. I figured what the hell, why not make a little extra money? We sent a copy to the judge, and he bit like a hungry dog. The bonus was that he thought Brady had sent it. When he tried to have Brady killed, I couldn't believe our luck. All I had to do was finish Brady off, and we were done with the whole thing. If the police poked around, we would have made sure they discovered the connection between Barnes and the judge, and all our problems would be solved.

"It was so easy to get into the hospital. No one pays any mind to old cleaning ladies. I just mopped my way into his room. After that it was pure pleasure. I stuck the bastard, slid it right in past his eyeball and watched him wriggle and gasp like a fish. It didn't take him more than a minute to die."

"What went wrong?"

She frowned, and her eyes flashed. "Nick got stupid again. When we realized that the judge had set up a hit on Brady, he thought he could get one last payoff from the judge. He went to see him in person, let him see who had been scamming him. The idiot didn't figure out that the judge would have had him killed as easily as he tried to do Brady. I had to kill the judge.

"And then there was you. You complicated things. You asked too many questions. Nick warned me you were poking around. The minute I saw you, I knew you were trouble."

Her face turned dark, and she actually began to shake with hatred and anger. Dread roiled in my gut as she walked to a table in the bay and picked something up, something long, thin...oh, Jesus, an ice pick. I pulled my hands apart, straining to break the bonds, or at least loosen them some more. She turned and smiled when she saw my fear. *Don't show it! Don't give her the satisfaction. Calm down and think!*

"The way I deal with trouble is to get rid of it," she said as she knelt down next to me.

I wiped my face clean of any expression, wiped my mind clean of the fear that threatened to take over. *Be as cold as she is.*

"I was very angry with you." Her voice seemed almost childlike now, and her eyes kind of glazed, as if she'd slipped into some other world. She gently pushed the point of the ice pick into the fabric of my shirt at the shoulder. I could feel it touch the skin, and I held still, not daring to breathe. Her eyes widened, and she suddenly shoved it into the muscle. It was like a shot at the doctor's office at first, just a prick, and I didn't even flinch. The real pain set in a moment later when the brain realized the pick was much larger than a syringe. I gritted my teeth.

"You'll never get away with it," I said calmly. "They'll find you here in the morning still trying to get our bodies out."

"You'd be surprised how strong I am," she purred. Her

nostrils flared as she plunged the ice pick into my upper arm again.

It was all I could do not to cry out. "Bitch!" I gasped.

"You disappoint me. Is that the best you can do?" She moved down a foot or so, and I craned my neck to see what she was up to. "I want to hear you scream a little. The others died so quickly."

This time she skewered the big muscle in my right thigh. It hurt, no doubt about it, but it wasn't intolerable. Until she twisted the ice pick, tearing the muscle, sending a flash of searing red pain to my brain. My leg jumped and quivered involuntarily, and I heard myself snort like a horse stung by a bee. Tears came to my eyes, blurring my vision.

"Ah, that's better." She put her face close to mine to see me grimace, and gently stroked away a tear with her hand. She was definitely over the edge, and I couldn't very well hang around and wait for her to slowly kill me.

The pain filled me with rage. I used all my strength to lunge at her, butting her in the face with my head. She fell back with a cry, both hands flying to her face. I rolled away from her, blood pouring from the reopened wound on my head. There was enough slack between my wrists to work both hands under my butt and slip them under my knees. I managed to bend my left leg with the knee far enough into my chest to slip my foot between my bound wrists, but I couldn't make the right leg work.

I heard Maria's scream of rage and knew I had no more time. I forced my brain to believe there was nothing wrong with my leg, forced it to move, forced the knee up under my chin and worked my wrists over the heel of my foot. I rolled over and pushed myself up onto my knees, and suddenly she swarmed over my back, screaming and tearing at my face with her fingernails like a witch from hell. I twisted and rolled over again to get her off my back, then staggered to my feet. Blood ran down my face into my eye, and I blinked, swiping it away with my sleeve, trying to see.

She came at me again, her face contorted into a mask of pure hatred, and I swung my bound hands from the hip, smashing her in the side of the head. The blow whirled her around, and she fell. I was beginning to feel weak, and I didn't know how long my leg would hold me up. I raised my wrists to my mouth and got the belt in my teeth, tearing at it to loosen it enough to free a hand.

Maria wasn't human. She couldn't have been. I'd barely gotten one hand free when she charged me again, this time with the ice pick glinting in her hand. Surprised, I managed to ward off the first stabbing thrust, and it was all I could do to lean in and grab her in a clinch. She squirmed in my grasp like a hellcat, kicking and hissing, stabbing me again and again in the back and shoulders with the ice pick. My leg gave out, and I fell forward, taking her to the floor with me, pinning her with my weight. She flailed and kicked, trying to squirm out from under me.

I felt consciousness ebbing away with each new hole she punched in me with the pick, and I knew she was going to win. Blood leaked out of the little holes like air out of a punctured tire, taking my strength with it. She hissed and spit in my face and got her hands up under my chest and pushed, rolling me off. She came with me and straddled me, screaming like a demon, raising her arm to deliver the killing blows with the ice pick. Desperately, I grabbed her wrist and held tight.

Madness had given her the strength of bigger men than me, and she slowly forced the ice pick down toward my face. Malevolence and hatred emanated from her like a cold, black shroud, enveloping me, blotting out the light, sucking the life out of me. The cancer had festered in her for so long that she'd become malignant to the touch, poisoning Nick, then Brady, now me. Her face blurred in my vision as I strained to hold on. Dimly, through the roar of blood in my ears, I thought I heard shouting voices and the sound of running feet, and suddenly there was an explosion that echoed off the walls of the hollow space. Maria's body jerked sideways and her arm went slack in my grip. Her eyes widened in shock, her lips grimaced, and she fell over.

The ceiling high overhead was spinning slowly, and blackness was closing in on me. Anxious faces popped into view, swimming in and out of focus, peering at me, mouthing questions I couldn't hear. I recognized the ruddy complexion of John Lanahan and forced a small smile.

"Jesus, Lieutenant, you took your sweet time getting here."

I saw him grin before my eyes closed of their own accord and the babbling voices faded away in the distance.

FIFTEEN

THE SUNNY SKY WAS a beautiful shade of blue, dotted with cottony cumulus clouds. The fall air was clean, fresh, and just warm enough for shirtsleeves. The smell of autumn leaves and hamburgers sizzling on a charcoal grill wafted on the small breeze, bringing back memories of childhood. The back yard of the big house in Wilmette was filled with happy, smiling people, the loud babble of conversation and laughter, and children's cries of delight as they raced in and out of the house.

It was a good old-fashioned suburban backyard barbecue on the kind of day that made me glad to be alive. The host, Bill Kaspar, stood next to a smoking grill with a spatula in his hand, peering over the shoulders of a bunch of guys huddled around a picnic table. A small portable television was tuned to the Bears game, and the guys alternately whooped and groaned depending on the outcome of each play. Normally genial and soft-spoken, Kaspar was emotionally intent when it came to sports, and he reacted as loudly as anyone else at the Bears' fortunes.

His wife Medwin carried bowls of salad and condiments to the table with the help of some of the other football widows. Their two children came bursting out of the house with some other kids at their heels, arguing over who was going to get to feed the two pet rabbits caged next to the house. Dustin was big and chunky for twelve, and his sister, Tyler, only a year-and-a-half younger, looked pretty and petite next to him. Despite the argument, it was obvious they had a lot of affection for each other. I had to smile. The two rabbits, Snowball and Amber—to whom I'd been formally introduced when I first arrived—were oblivious to it all.

Brandt had convinced me to come, saying it was time I got out into the world again. He and Medwin were friends from somewhere—she was on the board of the Wilmette library I learned later—and she'd asked him to come up with an open invitation to bring friends. Brandt had brought his latest steady, an attractive, vivacious lady named Cheryl. And he'd brought me. He came up to me now with a fresh beer and a smile.

"How are you doing, friend?"

"Enjoying myself immensely, thank you. You were right to drag me here. It's a beautiful day."

"So it is, but aren't they all?" He beamed at me.

They'd let me out of the hospital after a week. The cut over my eye was split skin and easy to stitch up. Most of the little holes Maria had punched in me hadn't been too deep and would heal on their own. But she'd torn an artery in my leg. Even if I'd managed to keep her from killing me, I would have bled to death if Nell hadn't convinced Lanahan to come looking for me. They'd had to lay open the thigh, sew up the artery and the worst of the muscle tear, leaving me with an ugly zippered gash on my leg. I'd hobbled out of the hospital on crutches, but had graduated to a cane as fast as I could.

I went to visit Kitty a few days after being released. She was happy to see that I was okay, and she listened intently when I told her everything that had happened. She didn't even register surprise or shock when she learned that Brady had masterminded the theft of the jewels.

"I don't suppose he thought he had a choice," she murmured thoughtfully. "He thought he was protecting us."

"What's wrong?" She seemed to be in a funk.

"I don't know, Emerson." She sighed. "I'm glad it's over, glad that Nick and Maria paid for what they did, though it's all pretty ghastly. But I still don't know what I'm going to do. My savings are just about to run out. Brady and Nick are dead, so the studio is in a shambles. The money's all gone, and only Nick and Maria know where. They're certainly not talking."

"Well..." I thought for a minute. "The money may turn up. The police will search Nick's apartment and get warrants for his bank accounts. If the money does turn up, I'm sure Art Ryan can file suit against Nick's estate for damages, so you'll recover some of what's there.

"As for the studio, Marty's a pretty damn good photographer, and Nell knows how to run the business. I'll bet with a little time the two of them can do a pretty good job of building back the business. Give them a chance. I think they'll do okay by you."

She looked at me hopefully. "Maybe you're right." Then her face fell again. "But that's not the worst of it. The insurance company won't pay the claim for the Winton collection, and Irv Steinmetz's company is suing the studio. Even if Nell and Marty can keep the studio going, the lawsuit will bury us. We can't possibly..."

The jewels. Of course. Her voice faded away as I lost myself in thought. Puppy, the joker. He hadn't fenced the jewels.

"Wait a minute, Kitty," I said as a glimmer of light dawned. "I have to make a phone call."

She looked at me curiously as I went into the den to get out a phone book. I looked up the insurance company's phone number and spent the next ten minutes making sure I had the right person on the line. With a lot of insistence and bluster, I got traded up to a senior vice president at the Great Midwestern Property and Casualty Company, a Mr. Caswell. I told him who I was and asked him why the company wasn't paying the claim on the Winton collection.

"We haven't finished our investigation yet," he said simply. "It's our understanding that it may still be possible to recover the jewels."

"Mr. Caswell, will your company pay a finder's fee to anyone who recovers the collection?"

"Well, we have our own investigators on staff..."

"I've met Mr. Butler," I said gruffly. "You didn't answer my question."

"We don't normally have to resort to that, but yes, we do have a policy of paying finder's fees for the recovery of stolen property." He said it reluctantly.

"Ten percent? Five percent?" I pressed him. Kitty listened to my side of the conversation with a quizzical expression.

"Five percent."

"That would be...?"

"A lot of money," he said wearily, "but worth it if we don't have to pay on the policy."

"Thank you, Mr. Caswell. I'll be in touch." I hung up and turned to Kitty. "We need some tools—crowbar, if you have one, and a hammer."

"What on earth is going on?"

I smiled. "Puppy had a strange sense of humor. Do you remember the saying he had framed on his desk in the studio?"

She frowned, then spoke hesitantly. "I think so."

"Come on, then. I think your problems may be over."

She took me down to the basement to get tools, then I led her upstairs, limping up one at a time, down the hall to the master bedroom, and into the big walk-in closet. I flipped on the lights and blinked against the bright glare. A spot shone on the photo of the woman's foot at the end of the closet, just as I remembered. I limped over and took the picture off the wall. There was a wall safe behind it.

"The road of life is littered underfoot with stones," Kitty murmured in awe.

"Ain't that something?" I grinned. "You didn't know this was here, did you?"

"No. How did you…?"

"Just a guess."

I started in on the wall with a hammer, breaking the wallboard around the safe, then pried it loose with the crowbar.

"Sorry about the wall," I said as I yanked the safe out. "You should be able to get someone in here to patch it."

The front of the safe was built so no one could get into it, but the back was flimsy steel that bent easily under the leverage of the crowbar. Inside was a blue velvet Crown Royal sack. I pulled it out, loosened the drawstrings, and poured a sparkly collection of incredibly brilliant gems into Kitty's cupped hands.

"YOU IN THERE?" Brandt nudged me on the shoulder.

"Hmm? Oh, sorry. Just thinking." I stared at the happy people in front of me and took a swallow of beer. I felt Brandt's eyes on me still. "You know how angry I've been with Puppy. The son of a bitch suckered me into this whole thing, and all he had to do was tell me the truth from the very beginning. I would have helped him find a way to deal with Nick. He could have admitted he made a mistake, but no."

"There's nothing you can do about it now," Brandt said gently. "Stop kicking yourself."

"I know, I know. I'll stop." I took another swig "Sitting here watching those kids makes me realize that I'm really angry with Brady for how he treated his family. I've never met a more fucked up bunch of people in my life. Maybe he couldn't help it. Puppy was Puppy. But, Jesus, he sure messed up his family." I shook my head.

"Look at those kids, Brandt." I waved my can of beer over at the children now crowded around the picnic table. "They're happy, content. Their parents spend time with them. They have a real sense of family."

"Yes, they do," he said quietly, nodding.

"It makes me realize I haven't talked to my brothers in a while," I mused.

"You should call them. They'd probably be glad to hear from you."

"I think I will. I've always thought of you as my family, you know. We all kind of drifted apart after my folks died, but I guess blood counts for something."

"Yes, it does."

I turned to look at him. "You're awfully agreeable today."

He grinned. "It's that kind of day."

I smiled and turned back to look at the kids. Medwin was making her way through the throng of people holding the arm of the most beautiful woman I'd ever seen. They came up to stand in front of us.

"What are you two up to?" Medwin asked with a smile.

"Nothing much," I said, hardly able to take my eyes

off the woman at her side. "Just remarking on what a beautiful family you have."

"Thank you," she exclaimed, blushing. "I think your friend here is pretty special, too." She patted the woman's arm.

"She saved my life, you know." I reached out to take Nell Reilly's hand. She flushed and sat down next to me.

"Then you ought to keep her around," Medwin said.

I put my arm around Nell and pulled her close. She rested her head on my shoulder and sighed contentedly.

"I think I will."

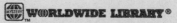

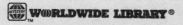

STEVE BREWER

dirty POOL

A BUBBA MABRY MYSTERY

Albuquerque P.I. Bubba Mabry's competition is William J. Pool, a Texas hotshot who asks Bubba if he wants some easy money. It's simple: drop off a large ransom payment to the kidnappers of a multimillionaire's son.

The money is picked up—by the young man himself, who quickly disappears. Now the rich father has a tantalizing new deal for Pool and Bubba: whoever finds his son first keeps the ransom money. *Nothing* will come between Bubba and $200,000—except murder.

"...pure, clean fun."
—*Albuquerque Journal*

Available July 2003 at your favorite retail outlet.

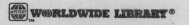

WSB462